THE BRASS KEY

THE BRASS KEY

I Can Never Use This Key To Get Back Home,
But I'll Forever Cherish It

Chris
To your reading
pleasure
Murray

Dorothy Murray

Library of Congress Control Number:		2021910597
ISBN:	Hardcover	978-1-6641-7605-8
	Softcover	978-1-6641-7604-1
	eBook	978-1-6641-7603-4

Print information available on the last page.

Rev. date: 06/08/2021

To order additional copies of this book, contact:
Xlibris
844-714-8691
www.Xlibris.com
Orders@Xlibris.com
829986

CONTENTS

Chapter 1

On the Spur of the Moment

It was the end of another cold winter that had kept me hibernating in front of the fireplace. It was quite a solitary existence indoor – not having much to do but read the daily newspaper, selected novels, and write my memoir. Life was gradually returning to some level of normalcy: Red hot coals no longer glowed in the fireplace: The long tweed and leather coats were retired for the winter season: Snow boots had been stacked in a safe place, to be retrieved once the snowflakes remind the folk that another winter has returned.

The northern hemisphere had gradually shaken off the effects of the long, cold winter. With the inclement weather finally subsiding, the spring weather was a swell. It was the season that extended an invitation to all living creatures, to emerge from their places of confinement and venture out into the warm outdoor atmosphere.

Chirping birds were once more heard and seen as they frolicked from tree to tree. They were certainly welcoming the new season of fresh flowers, new fruits and seeds for their hourly and daily consumption. Not to forget the arrival of a new season for mating and reproducing, and raising their young before the winter season returns.

Every tree and shrub, and all living creatures rose to greet the dawn of the new day. All waited to greet the slowly advancing sun as it made its ascent in the eastern horizon. It was a moment to cherish, after a chilling cold spell that had kept all living creatures in confinement – the earth-dwellers into their boroughs beneath the ground; others operating within the constraints set by the chilling cold climate.

On that clear, crisp spring morning in the month of May, the air was decently quiet in my suburban neighborhood. Folk who had been listed for their daily duties, were already on the pathways, and the freeways to their various work destinations.

It was with this frame of mind that I ventured out into the warm and inviting spring atmosphere. I breathed in the fresh morning air while basking in the warm glow of the sun. It had become my normal routine to rise with the sun and stroll around the immediate vicinity.

The earth had slowly ridden itself of the effects of the prior months of harsh cold weather of sleet, ice and snow. The snow had long melted, however, memories of the winter blizzards had still lingered in my mind. Hard, solid-rock soil gradually thawed under the warmth of the spring sun, giving rise to spring-time activities. With the emergence of spring, the seeds which lay asleep beneath the soil all winter long, had germinated. Tiny young buds gradually forced their way to the surface of the earth. The trees had long regained their foliage, and their variegated brilliant blossoms. The earth was once more adorned in its green, bright red, yellow and white colors.

I strolled leisurely along the quiet street, breathing in the fresh air, while absorbing the warmth of the early morning sunlight. I couldn't refrain from admiring the beautiful emerging spring blooms. They were a striking similarity to the foliage and blooms in my homeland. My mind had suddenly become inundated with a myriad of scenes from back home: The golden sun making its way across a blue and radiant sky – playing hide-and-seek behind patches of pure white cloud: The sound of the towering spring along the valley, and the joyful sounds of children splashing and wading in its bubbling streams: Birds of every species frolicking among the branches of surrounding trees, adding to the jubilant atmosphere of home.

The emerging new spring season brought back memories of my homeland – greening with lush vegetation, sustained by a warm and almost constant climactic condition.

The many intriguing memories of the days of my youth, triggered a sudden yearning to take a trip back to my homeland. My heart began to yearn for the joyful moments of bliss, at the place that was once my home – the place of my beginning.

It had been many long years since I left the shore of my homeland. More than fifty years prior, I bade goodbye to my loved ones and to my homeland, and landed on the vast continent of the U.K. My heart constantly ached by reason of the grief I carried, being detached from the place of my birth.

During my long absence, there'd been a constant yearning in my heart to return home. I had missed seeing my siblings, and my childhood friends I had left behind. While the memory of home continually plagued my mind, I had been living the good life on a distant shore, far from the shore of my homeland.

Leaving my homeland and arriving in the U.K was like a transition from death to life – death in my small village in Cavers Cove. I had carried the feeling that death had separated me from the land of my birth, and from my relations. At the time I had joined the exodus from my homeland, it was like being dead and arriving in paradise. As no one has ever returned from the grave, I had not returned to my homeland since departing from its shore.

The impulsive decision to take a trip back home had brought an abrupt end to my morning stroll. It was a heart-throbbing moment when I had promptly returned home, charged with the emotions of wanting to return to my homeland. As I commenced making travel plans, my mind became inundated with things to do and where to begin.

For one who hadn't flown in an aircraft for many years, I had quickly developed a phobia, which I had striven to overcome before the day of my departure.

Amidst a state of exhilaration and anxious fears, I was suddenly faced with uncertainties about going back to my childhood home. After more than fifty years of absence, what would I see upon my arrival? My parents had passed. An exodus of the village folk to towns and elsewhere, had gotten everyone on the move. My siblings had also joined the exodus, making their escape from village life and bad memories. Their whereabouts was unknown. At the time I left home, my brother Larry was left to manage the family estate. After fifty years, there was no certainty he would be home. I had doubts whether he was still alive.

Not knowing what I would encounter upon my arrival, I felt the urgency to make contact with someone, prior to making travel arrangements.

I had communicated with my uncle Harry while he lived in America. I knew he'd returned home after more than sixty years of absence. There was a certainty that he'd resumed permanent residence in my home village. Uncle Harry was equipped with a cellphone, with which he makes continuous contacts with his offspring he had left behind in his foreign homeland. I had also communicated with him since his arrival back home. He'd therefore remained my only contact.

There was an urgency to purchase an airline ticket, but I had been reluctant to book my flight – fearing that Uncle Harry may have left to visit his offspring in America. Amidst my fears and uncertainties, I decided to give him a call on his cellphone. Uncle Harry picked up on the first ring.

"Hello!" a loud voice answered. I immediately identified Uncle's high-pitched voice. I couldn't have mistaken his voice as anyone else's.

"Hello, Uncle Harry! This is your nephew, Jimmy." He'd remained poised to hear of some ominous news, but it was to the contrary. "Uncle, I've made plans to return home for a visit." Before ending my first sentence, Uncle expressed his delights and wishes to see me after a long absence from home.

"You're welcome to visit, Jim. You'll have to stay at my home. There are no other options," Uncle said in a rather exhilarating voice. Whatever message he'd tried to convey was not important at that point in time.

"I certainly will, Uncle Harry," I said. "I'll provide more details during my next telephone contact." At the end of that brief conversation, I felt confident that my trip was "A go."

The sharp vibrations I had subsequently felt from the telephone, still held in my hand, were likely the heart tremors of Uncle Harry.

The news of my visit had been, no doubt, exhilarating and beyond his wildest dreams. Whatever exhilarating feeling the news of my visit had brought into my uncle's heart was left only to one's imagination.

It was quite an impulsive preparation, when I began to sort through my outfits; selecting the ones that were appropriate for the trip. I had quickly recalled that village life back home was simple, and therefore didn't require much of anything.

Upon arriving home, I wish to recapture that feeling of waking up in the atmosphere of home. I was eager to retrace my foot-steps: to set my feet in the very places that had once brought pleasurable moments and happiness. As I was equipped with my village attire, I anticipated basking in the atmosphere of home, just as I had done during those cheerful and exhilarating days.

In a state of urgency, and with a feeling of anxiety, I drove up in front of the Travel Agency. My dreams of going back home had culminated in a genuine travel arrangement. Except for the purchase of train tickets for long-distance travels, I had not purchased an airline ticket since arriving in the U.K. My heart had become overwhelmed when I realized that, in a matter of two days, I would be embarking on the long journey back to my homeland – my ticket being a testament to that fact.

Chapter 2

A New World

Going back home was a constant dream gradually becoming reality. I had a heart-felt longing to return to the place that holds lasting memories and thrills of my childhood and adolescent years. My homeland was the place, where it was my birthright to remain and exist as an important branch of the family tree.

In my childhood years, I had maintained hopes and dreams of a bright village existence. I had striven to follow in the foot-steps of my parents, who'd established themselves as prominent and noble village folk. All prospects, however, ground to a halt when, still at the prime of their lives, my parents passed away – the family-tree uprooted, leaving the offspring to seek a livelihood elsewhere.

As young offspring, not having a foundation on which to build a future, my siblings and I had joined the exodus of the folk, who'd abandoned village life – leaving all prospects behind to seek a livelihood elsewhere. While my girl siblings sought a livelihood in the small town of Brighton, my young brother, Larry remained in the home to sort out his future. I had landed on the shore of the U.K, a distant foreign land where my uncle Brayson became my new beacon of hope.

Upon arriving in the U.K, my foreign homeland, I had made my best effort to adapt to the new culture. However, there was a constant yearning in my heart to return to the place of my birth. My mind had become bombarded with many frightening thoughts. The pangs and pains of separation from my homeland – the place I had known all my young life, had become excruciating. I had arrived in a strange land where everyone was a stranger. Not seeing my uncle Brayson for the many years since he'd migrated from my home village, he too was perceived as a stranger in my strange and new world.

Amidst my mounting grief and nostalgic moments, I had made a firm decision to go back home. I therefore approached Uncle Brayson with my firm decision.

"Uncle Brayson," I said, in earnest. My uncle stood to attention in the center of the hall, in front of the fireplace where he'd sat to keep warm. "I won't fit into this strange and new world. I must go back to my homeland. My heart yearns to return to my village, and my siblings I left behind." My uncle was in no way perturbed by my discouraging thoughts and wishes. In his eyes, I was perceived as a coward, who needed sound chastening.

"Jimmy, you're not a child anymore," he said. "You've grown into manhood. As a young man, you must begin to perceive and challenge the good life ahead of you. When you attain the age of manhood, you put away childish thoughts." Uncle Brayson continually scolded me during my moments of deep despair.

Amidst great fear and discontent, my uncle's words of encouragement had brought me through the turbulent moments that swayed my hopes like a boat on a tempestuous ocean. My heart had become torn between two worlds. Thoughts of the good life I had had back in my village continually prompted me to return home. Despite my uncle's words of encouragement, a compelling force had constantly pricked at my mind to go back home. Percolating within my mind, however, were the thoughts of being in a foreign land of countless opportunities. With my persuasive self-assurance, I felt that, by remaining in my foreign homeland, I could create small wonders, thus making my life worthwhile.

I quickly perceived the difficulties of fitting into a society where technology ruled, and skilled labour geared to man and machine.

I grew up in a village governed by a, man-and-his-tool-on-the-farm lifestyle. With my uncle's words of sound wisdom and encouragement, I quickly realized that, learning was what it would take to challenge my new world. With a firm determination to remain in my new world, I was ready to walk on water.

My thoughts immediately reflected on Grandfather Grovel's clever art of building his house on the crest of the low-lying hill. I further reflected on his fine wooden bench he'd so cleverly built around the trunk of the Red Top tree. It was his joy and pride observing travelers seated beneath the tree to have their well needed rest on his bench before continuing on their long journey.

My father had quickly acquired the technique of building, and had constructed his house adjacent to Grandfather's. The fine wooden bench Father had built beneath the cedar tree, had also been fashioned after my grandfather's bench he built around the trunk of the Red Top tree.

As a vein of the blood-line, I immediately sought the knowledge, and had quickly learned the art of technically designing and building structures. With my newly acquired skills, I quickly became absorbed into the culture of my new foreign society.

As I struggled through turbulent times, I had found true friendship and brotherly love in Uncle Brayson, who'd pledged to become my guiding light. With my newly acquired skills, I had quickly solidified my vow to remain in my foreign homeland. However, many negative thoughts had gotten the better part of me, until I finally broke through and achieved success in whatever I had willed to do. As I slowly adopted the culture of my foreign homeland, there was no need to worry about my yesterday, or the life ahead. While I enjoyed living in the comfort zone of my new environment, I hadn't struck it rich, but life had been comfortable.

Life in my foreign homeland took on momentum when I met my future wife, Loretta. After a short period of courtship, we'd solidified our endeavors to be married. On the day I walked the aisle with Loretta, Uncle Brayson's words struck my mind like a speeding bullet: "You can make it if you try, Jimmy." These were his encouraging words that had carried me through my most turbulent moments.

Throughout the most challenging child-rearing years, Loretta and I had raised three offspring: Jarreth, Amy and Mondette, in age order. I saw them grow up and attain their level of education, and the profession that was vital to their future. Loretta and I had proudly watched the offspring establish themselves in their foreign society.

Time had been swiftly passing, adding to the years of my life in a new world. My mind became preoccupied with thoughts of growing old. I had watched Uncle Brayson live his life to an old age, and had finally made his exit. I therefore had no reason to doubt that, that wouldn't also be my fate, and the fate of Loretta.

I had remained comfortably in the place I learned to accept as my foreign homeland. Loretta and I were preoccupied with nestling in the empty nest. As proud grandparents, we'd devoted valued time nurturing and entertaining the adorable grandchildren.

Each day, throughout the cold winter season, I counted my blessings sitting with Loretta in front of the fireplace. The warmth from the glowing coals had kept my body temperature at bay. And while I relied on the warmth from the glowing flames in the fireplace, I continually reminisced on life back home, where the warmth from a glowing fireplace was not the means of keeping warm during the winter months. A golden sunlight and the soothing warmth from its heavenly glow, is all that was needed to keep warm throughout the winter months. My homeland is the place where summer and winter offer a similar climatic condition – a warm brilliant sunlight and gentle breeze that cause the branches of the trees and the brilliant flowers to wave continually.

I had sacrificed the warm glow from a radiant sun in my homeland, to seek warmth and comfort in front of a glowing fire burning inside my foreign home. As I had perceived, it was a definite trade-off.

Many years prior, at the invitation of Uncle Brayson, I arrived in a strange world. During these many years, I had basked in the sunshine of my own perceived paradise. Memories of my past existence in a humble village back home, however, remained indelibly in my mind. As each day approached, the people, places and things, that had once contributed to my exuberant existence, continually played hide-and-seek with my imagination. The pursuit of a better life in my newly found foreign land had continually detracted my attention from the place of my childhood. My childhood home was the place of my beginning, where a life of hard work, and simple village living was once the guiding light that should have transitioned me into manhood.

Throughout my many years living in a foreign land, there had been a constant prick at my conscience to return home for a visit. I had remained reminiscent of the fact that the hearts of my siblings, other relations, and the folk who knew me, had been yearning to know my whereabouts – most of all, to see me after my long absence.

Why should I allow my conscience to dominate? I thought to myself. My uncle Brayson didn't return home to visit his family, or close associates he'd left behind. He wasn't the traveling type, and this had therefore justified the long absence from his homeland. Uncle Brayson had maintained frequent telephone contacts with Uncle Harry while he had resided in America. But no other relations Uncle Brayson had left in his homeland, knew his whereabouts. It was obviously much too late for him when he'd reached his milestone. The years had left him in a vegetative state, which resulted in him being placed in the confines of a home for those who're on the last leg of the journey to their final home. Uncle Brayson had no doubt departed this life with a feeling of guilt that he didn't return to see his relations he'd left behind in Coopers Village and elsewhere.

During the many years of absence from my homeland, life had been joyously comfortable. I had, however, become agonized by the feeling of nostalgia. Uncle Brayson wouldn't have imagined that, despite his kind words of encouragement, my heart had been constantly yearning to go back home. Loretta and the offspring had no feeling of attachment, or a yearning in their hearts to return to a humble far away village on a distant shore. They'd therefore shown no empathy to the yearning within my heart to return to the place of my origin.

The years had been coming and leaving at a rapid pace, taking the youth of the offspring in their firm grasp. From the confines of my quiet foreign home, Loretta and I counted our blessings – becoming grandparents of adorable grandchildren, and showering them with tender love and kisses.

Without warning, it struck me like a bolt of lightning, when Loretta took ill and had failed to recover. Modern medicines could not have restored her health, which deteriorated by the hour. No one had expected Loretta to depart this world at her tender age of sixty-five. Her passing had quickly plunged me into my deep valley of despair. I was forced to come to grips with the realization that she'd departed, permanently. With Loretta's passing, I was left alone, and in the home that had become my place of solitary confinement.

As I remained in my empty world, my mind became preoccupied with thoughts of returning to my homeland. I had for many years, borne the guilt of abandoning my homeland. I had, however, endeavored to someday, return on a pilgrimage while I still breathe the breath of life.

Chapter 3

Dreams Do Come True

It was a sunny, and most pleasant Tuesday morning in the month of May. I awoke at the crack of dawn to face the astounding reality that, in three hours I would be embarking on the most exciting journey back to my homeland. I had become haunted by thoughts and visions of my home, and those I had left behind many years prior. A state of joyous expectation had overwhelmed the very core of my being, and had prevented me from having a night of restful sleep.

Throughout the long night, I reminisced on my childhood home, the place to which my heart had been yearning to return. I reflected on the commencement of the exodus that had caused folk to abandon village life in search of a better way of life in the towns, and in foreign places.

As I anticipated a joyous arrival in my home village, my heart had been revving up with anxiety.

I hadn't seen my uncle Harry for many years, and had therefore lost my perception of his appearance. Nonetheless, I waited in joyous anticipation of my meeting with him. I prayed ardent prayers that I would see my siblings, and that they would all be alive and well. If their whereabouts will be known, I anticipate meeting their offspring. My younger sibling, Larry I imagine, has a wife and adorable offspring. These are my potential nieces and nephews I've never met.

After my long absence, I had developed a mind-set that I was about to embark on a journey back to my homeland. I therefore said my ardent prayers that it would be the brightest, hottest and driest day when I arrive home. An afternoon downpour would certainly put a damper on my endeavor to immediately survey the vicinity of my home village upon my arrival.

At the early dawn, I had stretched my limbs and muscles, and carried out my usual wake-up routine before getting out of bed. I was sadly reminded, however, that I had not slept during the long night, and therefore had no sleep from which to wake up. Not having to rise early like the working folk, I could have done with a few more moments of rest. But, in my state of overwhelming exhilaration, that certainly wasn't the time for slumber.

On a prickly rose twig beneath my window, a small brown bird perched and tweeted its usual morning melodies. Its melodies had been rather soothing after my sleepless night. Amidst sleeplessness and anxiety, however, that wasn't the moment to enjoy bird songs. I couldn't have devoted my limited time to things and events that weren't relevant at that moment in time. My entire being had become emotionally charged with thoughts about going back home, and preparing for my departure.

Within a few moments, I would be embarking on the long journey to my homeland. I therefore quickly shuffled myself out of bed and proceeded to absorb whatever time I had at my disposal to prepare for the journey.

Within minutes of putting the last item into my attaché case, the doorbell rang. The cab had arrived to take me to the airport. It arrived on perfect timing. For airport assignments, every minute is critical. An aircraft never waits for anyone, except the pilot whose job it is to take it off the ground.

I quickly rolled my luggage into the garage and toward the vehicle waiting at the entrance. The chauffeur politely opened the trunk of the cab and gently placed my luggage inside.

"Good morning, Sir!" I greeted the chauffeur as he opened the rear door of the cab.

"A very beautiful morning to you, Mr. MacLeary," the chauffeur responded. "Please, take your seat," he said, in a polite manner. I sat comfortably in the rear of the vehicle – my attaché case containing my passport and other travel accessories firmly pressed against my chest. The cab momentarily rolled out of the driveway and onto the street, where it commenced its journey to the airport – just a short distance on the freeway.

To put a damper on my anxiety, I reached for the morning newspaper that had been conveniently placed on the seat beside me. But I soon realized that my thought process was incapacitated, making it difficult to absorb the contents of the newspaper. As any professional gentleman would have done, I continued to leaf through the pages.

The cab had been making its way leisurely along the freeway that had been practically void of vehicular traffic. As I had perceived, each minute was like an hour. My patience had been wearing thin as I anticipated an early arrival at the airport. I had quickly developed the frame of mind that demanded promptness. My entire being had been revving up with high expectation to be on time and avoid missing my flight. Amidst tense moments of anxiety, the cab appeared to have been moving much too slowly. In adherence to the rules of the road, the chauffeur had been driving carefully along the freeway, but I was of the opinion that rules can be broken in urgent situations.

How could I prompt the chauffeur to move at a faster pace? He'd received my scheduled time to arrive at the airport and had therefore showed up promptly at my home to commence the short journey. I felt that there ought to be a way to get the cab moving a bit faster.

"Sir," I said, in a pleasant tone, "how much longer before we arrive?" I felt a sudden jolt of the vehicle before it regained momentum and proceeded along its path.

"I should be there within five minutes, Sir," the chauffeur said. "Are you late?" he asked.

"No, Sir. I'm not late," I said. I immediately noticed a pair of large, round eyes in the rear-view mirror of the cab.

"I'm going according to the schedule you've given me, Sir," the chauffeur said in an appeasing tone. "The next exit leads right into the airport." I felt that my display of anxiety may've been a cause for his raised eyebrows. I attempted a last-ditch effort to appease the, apparently annoyed chauffeur.

"Pardon me, Sir," I said. "As you can imagine, I'm going back home for the first time in more than fifty years. Anxiety has taken hold of me. I'm going back home to reconnect with my roots and to visit my childhood home after my long absence. I know I'll see my uncle Harry. I don't know the fate of my siblings I had left behind at the time of my departure. I don't know what I'll see of my home and my village when I arrive." I wondered whether my unsolicited explanation had justified my previous persistence that the chauffeur ignored the speed limit of the freeway – although he didn't bend to my will.

"I fully understand your anxiety, Sir," the chauffeur said – still displaying raised eyebrows and protruding eyes. He accelerated the vehicle a notch, as if he'd been sympathetic to my cause.

Minutes had elapsed when the cab took a right turn and gradually pulled up to the Departure entrance of the airport. I quickly alighted from the vehicle as the door slammed shut behind me. The chauffeur made his exit and promptly retrieved my luggage from the trunk of the vehicle. I quickly handed him my fare, plus a handsome gratuity. I politely thanked him for his service, while he nodded his appreciation of my use of his cab.

The chauffeur promptly returned to his vehicle and drove off, but not before bidding me, "Bon Voyage."

"Enjoy your visit, Sir," he said as the cab drove off. The chauffeur's well wishes had immediately set my mind and spirit in motion for my air flight, and the long journey ahead.

At the cab's departure, I rolled my luggage at a considerable speed along the smooth concrete surface of the airport terminal. My path to the check-in area was guided by a series of numbered lines. As I darted along the guided lines, my progress was impeded by a maze of partition belts. The hustle and bustle of passengers checking in for their various destinations had further hampered my progress.

I had finally made my way to the check-in agent, who stood poised to commence her interrogation session. Her litany of questions, amidst eye-piercing scrutiny of my documents had finally ended, when I was declared a bona fide traveler. My checked luggage had also survived the agent's close scrutiny before it was released on a conveyor belt that glided it to the aircraft. Like my piece of luggage gliding along the swift-moving conveyor belt, I wished I could have glided my way to the aircraft without further line-ups and interrogation. But the attendant had subsequently directed me to departure gate Number 99. I held my attaché case firmly as my electrified feet took me on a long path to departure gate 99. Upon arriving at the designated gate, I was overwhelmed by the large waiting crowd. I quickly perceived the long line-ups, and another delay in reaching the aircraft.

In the crowded waiting area, everyone sat in silence, and without a smile, as if in anticipation of an ominous event. In the far distance, I could see the airline attendants, waiting in still silence at gate 99 – the entrance to the aircraft. Folk who'd been seated, sat and gazed warily in the distance; whatever distance was within their immediate view. I had reluctantly joined the wary folk, but sat at the edge of my seat.

From my vantage point, I had a direct view of the marvellous airport runway. I admired the big jet planes soaring into the sky at minutes intervals. I had been privileged to have a close-up look at the modern aircrafts passing in my range of view. Each time an aircraft soared skyward, my heart pounded from fear and anxiety at the thought that, in a matter of minutes, I would be airborne. The thought of going home, however, had caused all my fears to subside. Whatever it took, I was on my way back home, and that was all that mattered at that moment in time.

It wasn't long before an announcement for boarding of flight 293 was made. I quickly joined the procession of anxious passengers making their way through Gate 99. Their travel documents had been once more, thoroughly scrutinized as each stepped quietly through Gate 99. I had promptly joined the long procession of passengers as they made their way along the path leading to the entrance of the aircraft. It was a giant step for me, when I set my foot into the fuselage of the aircraft. I had faced the difficult task of regaining my calm composure, and putting a damper on my anxiety before arriving home. To achieve these goals,

I must first overcome my fear of flying in a state-of-the-art modern aircraft.

A period of rushing and scurrying, amidst cries of "Excuse me," ensued as passengers searched for their assigned seat. It wasn't long before I escaped the rush and took my assigned seat in row 21-D. For the long flight ahead, I found the seating space more than adequate to accommodate my, slightly above-average length legs. Putting fear and panic aside, my mind had been set in motion to travel the sky – whatever it would take to reach my homeland.

The period of shuffling and restlessness had gradually subsided. Everyone had been finally seated in an atmosphere of wariness. An announcement, followed by a series of instructions appeared on television screens located in the ceiling of the aircraft. The announcement triggered a series of rhythmic clicking sounds. All had been adhering to the fastening of seat belt rules.

Amidst my anxious fears and tense moments, I carefully snapped my seat belt snugly around my waist, and made every effort to relax. I had been faced with a double whammy; being overwhelmed by the anxiety of returning home for the first time, and building up courage for an aircraft flight I hadn't taken for such a long time. And as I was about to fly in a wide-bodied, state-of-the-art aircraft, I may as well perceive that I was about to fly in an aircraft for the first time.

The length and width of the aircraft, and the unusually large number of passengers waiting in curious anxiety for take-off, had staggered my imagination. I was immediately overcome by a feeling my anxious heart could not accommodate. I had become overwhelmed as I sat in such a state-of-the-art aircraft, whose cross-section accommodated an unusually large number of seats. From my seating position, I couldn't have perceived the number of seats along the aircraft's entire length.

As the aircraft made preparations for take-off, my thoughts immediately reflected on the aircraft that had taken me from the shore of my homeland, more than fifty years prior. The aircraft back then appeared not much larger than a transport truck, equipped with wings, and propelled by windmills. As the small aircraft soared into the sky, its windmills spun like those my brother and I had once made from the branches and leaves of hillside trees. The home-made windmill was activated by the wind. As I ran full force against the wind, the windmill spun to a speed so that it appeared like the buzzing wings of the hummingbird. The small aircraft had flown on a six-hour, non-stop flight which seemed like a journey around the world. Many years later, and according to my airline ticket, the flight time back to my homeland would be approximately four hours.

My patience had climaxed at its saturation point as I remained buckled in my seat. There hadn't been a doubt that the patience of other passengers had also reached its peak, while they waited in silence for take-off. Another series of announcements was heard as images began to appear once more on the television screen. A polite and charming young lady appeared on the screen. One would think that her presence was meant to calm the anxious fears of the waiting passengers. She'd promptly commenced a series of demonstration of procedures in preparation for take-off.

During the process of rigid instructions of procedures and precautions, the aircraft commenced its slow movement backward. I felt the rhythmic pounding of my heart as great fear took hold of my being. The aircraft subsequently commenced a forward movement, putting the airport building farther into the distance behind. It advanced gradually along a path guided by thick white lines, before coming to the edge of what appeared to be its final runway. It was the runway on which I had seen large aircrafts take off and soar into the sky while I waited in the designated area of Gate 99. At that point, I knew it wouldn't be long before I was airborne, and on my way back to my homeland.

The aircraft slowly moved onto its final runway. Its rapid speed took on momentum as it continued along a guided path. For one who'd never flown in a modern aircraft, it was like a series of ignited atom bombs, when its engines began to roar under the early morning sky. In an instant it zoomed into the bright and almost cloudless sky. Unlike the aircraft that had taken me from the shore of my homeland, this was quite a smooth take-off, and a joyride to every thrill seeker.

The aircraft continued to soar skyward, reaching new heights as it ascended. My fear and panic had quickly given way to jubilance, and a feeling of renewed anxiety to be finally on my journey back home.

There was a sense of calm while the aircraft took to the sky. No one uttered a sound. The aircraft had finally reached its required height, and had settled in the sky. Sounds of giggles and laughter suddenly permeated the atmosphere. Whatever was the passengers' reason for their cheerfulness, I was on my way back home, and that was a lot for me to cheer about, amidst my quiet and anxious moments.

Chapter 4

The Life I Left Behind

The aircraft's continuous series of upward ascents ended with its wide wing-span resting on the airwaves. The mega aircraft had now settled in mid-air, and commenced gliding across the sky. In my anxious mind, this was modern-day ingenuity.

The aircraft was finally on route toward its scheduled destination – to my homeland. I was no way in my comfort zone – being involuntarily locked inside an aircraft zooming across the sky. However, I had remained in a reclining mode, my body resting against the seat, whose height extended behind my head. A soft and small cabin pillow, like the one I received during my first flight, could have certainly added more cosiness and comfort to my rest. Nonetheless, I quickly took advantage of the carefree moment to doze, while reminiscing on the exhilarating life I had had back home.

I had remained partially laid back in the comfort of my seat, hoping to slowly doze off and have a time of restful sleep. This, I felt, would be a prelude to a triumphant arrival in my homeland. However, after a long night of sleeplessness, sleep was still not welcome in a mind preoccupied with thoughts of going back home after many years of absence.

In a state of restlessness, my thoughts had become inundated with vivid memories of the home I had left behind more than fifty years prior. I immediately reflected on home and what life used to be before

I joined the exodus. My mind had also been preoccupied with thoughts of what home would be like when I arrived. I had vivid memory of my dainty home on the crest of the hill, and the wonderful life I had had with my siblings and other children of the neighborhood. My childhood home was the place where my parents had instilled in me, bright hopes of becoming a prominent village peasant.

The reality of returning to the place of my youth had set my thoughts and imagination in motion. I had vivid memory of the crystal-clear waters of the spring flowing along the valley. It wound its way along deep valleys and into its estuary – a wide river stretching across the plain. After a heavy downpour, the stones and pebbles beneath the surface of the spring were washed ivory clean. The jubilant sounds of children as well as grown-ups, could be heard as they frolicked in the bubbling streams of the spring. My siblings and I, along with the neighboring children, played in the crystal streams until the surface of our hands and feet were like wrinkled prunes. One could never imagine the jubilance a constant flow of crystal waters over stones and pebbles, offers to the soul of those who found solace frolicking in its continuous bubbling streams.

On rainy and windy days, the branches of the trees had often rocked and swayed against the force of the boisterous winds. In the night hours, strong winds howled against the window-panes, forcing the folk to securely tighten their shutters. Strong winds, accompanied by heavy rain-showers created harmonious sounds in the night atmosphere. The rain-showers brought on a spectacular display of large raindrops, hammering on the leaves of surrounding trees, and on the metal roof of the village houses. As the heavy night showers persisted, a deep slumber hovered over the folk until morning. A warm feeling of solace, and a sense of security had always nestled each heart as heavy rains pounded the village.

A humble white concrete house – its roof covered with metal sheets, rested on the crest of a low hill. The original house was regarded as my grandfather Grovel's masterpiece. He'd proudly designed and built the house as his family dwelling. As a close-knit family, my father had subsequently built his house adjacent to Grandfather's, creating a structure similar in shape, size and color.

Grandfather Grovel, had planted an elaborate flower garden, which added beauty and elegance to his dainty house resting on the crest of the hill. At the completion of his house, my father followed suit by expanding the flower garden. The extended garden had never ceased to portray a kaleidoscope of colors as the flowers bloomed. The garden displayed a rainbow of radiant flowers all season long. Scarcely a day went by that the garden hadn't displayed its fragrant flowers of every color, size and variety. There were flowers for every season and every occasion.

From the vantage point of the wooden bench beside the gate, the houses could be seen, nestled in the garden of radiant flowers. There'd always been a display of white, pink, yellow and red roses in a neatly arranged bouquet on the rails of the porches. Their aromatic fragrances permeated the air as the flowers swayed in the breeze that constantly fanned the atmosphere. My grandmother, Eavie, had often sat on the porch to admire the beauty of the garden as it displayed an abundance of radiant flowers. In the cool of the evening, after her work was done, she enjoyed the intriguing fragrances of the flowers as they were constantly fanned by the gentle breeze.

Back home, an oil lamp had always been placed on the oak vanity in each room, and on the large table in the hall. Oil lanterns were always hung in the kitchen and in the ceiling of the big hall. At the appearance of dusk, a lit candle was carried throughout the house to ignite a flame on each lamp. I, along with my siblings, had thoroughly cleaned the prior night's soot from the glass shade on the lamps. It was always a black and sticky chore, cleaning the soot from the lamp shades each morning, or during the hours after school. Throughout the night, the tiny glow on each lamp continuously flickered beneath the shade of the freshly cleaned lamps – until thick, black soot once more formed inside the shades.

The entire household had always felt solaced by the words, "Home Sweet Home," inscribed around the mid-section of the shade on each lamp. The thought of the home being toasted by those assuring words had brought added comfort to the entire household.

There was a deep-rooted belief in my home village that, whenever a lamp shade broke, it had a connotation of clearing bad luck from the home. Nonetheless, no one had ever deliberately broken a shade. It would have been too costly to break it for the sheer purpose of ridding the home of bad luck. Replacing a lamp shade meant foregoing the purchase of an essential household item.

For those in need of a closer look at objects during the night, the small glow from the lamp offered a faint view into each semi-dark room.

A lantern suspended from a tree branch by the side of the house, casts bright beams around the vicinity. Its bright glow allowed more time for outdoor evening events, and for my siblings and me to play under the early night sky.

While I remained partially reclined on my seat, the aircraft had maintained its required distance from the earth and had been gliding across the sky. As it continued on its path, my thought process had remained pre-occupied with people, places and my exhilarating life back home. A series of atmospheric disturbances caused the aircraft to shiver and shake. The unexpected tremors had quickly put a damper on my imagination. Fear and panic continually gripped my heart as I perceived the distance I was from the surface of the earth. Amidst the series of turbulence, I dozed in and out of consciousness, while anticipating a joyous arrival in my homeland.

The aircraft had been gliding at maximum speed across the sky, taking my imagination to new heights. I had vivid memory of the quiet winding road passing through my village, and the narrow road Grandfather Grovel had made, from the gateway to his house resting on the crest of the hill. On that narrow road, my siblings and I, along with neighboring children, tossed homemade Tops on smooth surfaces – curiously watching to see whose Top spun the longest, and the smoothest. I joined my siblings in the game of throwing marbles in circles charted on smooth surfaces of the narrow road. After stacking marbles inside the circle, there was a fierce competition to see who knocked out the most marbles. There hadn't been a trophy awarded, but the feeling of being declared a winner was just as rewarding.

Grandfather's narrow road was the place where my siblings and I sat on hot summer days. The radiant flowers were in continuous bloom along the pathway – contributing to the gaiety of the season. The village atmosphere had been constantly stirred by soothing summer breeze, while cheerful birds continually frolicked among the swaying branches of the surrounding trees. Their cheerful chirps had further contributed to the joyousness of the summer season.

My anxiety had begun to soar to new heights as I reminisced on the road that would take me up the little hill to my home. I imagined walking toward the gate of my home, and resting on the sturdy wooden bench around the root of the wide-spreading Red Top tree.

At the entrance of the gate, Grandfather Grovel had planted the tree he felt would provide shade from the constant sweltering heat of the sun. The tree bloomed perpetually throughout the greater part of the year. It had always beautified the gateway with a barrage of bright red flower petals it constantly cast to the ground. My grandfather had found it fitting to name the tree, "Red Top." The botanical name, and the species from which the tree originated, was not of significance to the family, and the passersby who admired its branches, beautifully crowned with bright red flower petals. Finding the botanical name for a tree, or plant, was not considered essential back then. "Red Top" was just the simple and fitting name for a tree that produced such adorable red flowers. In addition to its radiant red bloom, the tree grew in height, and spread its branches across a wide circumference around the gate. Its shade of protection provided much comfort to those who'd stopped to rest on Grandfather's wooden bench built around its root.

As added comfort to the travelers' rest, Grandfather Grovel built a wooden bench around the root of the Red Top tree. Scarcely a day went by that a traveler hadn't been seen seated on the bench beneath the tree. There were particularly long-distance travelers who'd stopped to take advantage of the cool shade. With the lack of local transportation, the folk were forced to complete their journey from the outskirts of the villages by walking long distances – hence, their need to stop for a rest on Grandfather's bench beneath the Red Top tree.

After travelers had had a well-needed rest from their tiring journey across villages, or from Brighton Town, they continued on their way.

As a place of recreation from the hilltop sanctuary, my entire household had often spent the evening hours seated on the bench beneath the Red Top tree. My siblings and I were joined by other children in the neighborhood – cheerfully gathering flower petals as they were showered onto the grassy ground beneath the tree. All children were certain to receive a treat from the folk who had stopped to rest beneath the Red Top tree.

My parents had always been delighted to greet and treat the travelers to a glass of cool water. After a brief conversation session, and some well-deserved rest, they continued on their journey.

Grandfather Grovel had greatly adored his children, and subsequently his grandchildren. He'd therefore prepared and maintained a wide field for them to play. While seated on a fallen tree trunk, he'd spent tireless moments at the end of each day, being entertained by his grandchildren. He'd always been delighted to watch them play in the wide grassy field, where they chased brightly colored butterflies and played games in the tall grass. In my grandfather's perception, a day without the presence of his grandchildren was like a day without brilliant sunshine. He'd no doubt felt the same about his offspring, while they were children.

On bright and sunny days, when the entire neighborhood was dry and inviting to the children's fun and games, my siblings and I played in the field. The gentle breeze rustled and swayed the grass in the field like waves in the ocean. From the fallen tree trunk, Grandfather had often spent thrilling moments admiring his grandchildren as they pretended to swim the ocean, while frolicking among the swaying grass in the field so consciously made for them.

As added excitement to the household's pleasures, Fancy, the prized and most playful dog, frolicked among the tall grass as she joined the game of hide-and-seek. Fancy's ears popped up like antennas as she skipped above the grass to participate in the games. She particularly enjoyed being chased in the field, and had as much fun as the children.

Fancy's white furry coat, and her long fluffy light-brown tail, made it easy for her to be spotted as she glided among the tall grass. With her long and skinny tongue, she'd often hunted and returned the ball, or any object tossed into the field for her to retrieve. It was a sad day when Fancy had died of old age. My father buried her on the north side of the field. After Fancy's passing, her friendly and playful bark was no longer heard in the field; nor was she present around the house as the fine watchdog she once was. After her passing, Father had never found another of Fancy's type to replace her.

At the end of his long day working in the field, from the comfort of his porch, Grandfather Grovel had often admired the hillside sceneries – the green foliage in their red, yellow and white bloom, waving in the breeze. Particularly on dry and sunny autumn days, the entire household had joined him on the porch to view the hillside in its autumn splendour. Grandfather Grovel admired the spreading tree branches as they were rocked and swayed by the soft, gentle autumn breeze. It was like hearing the melody of a fiddler's fiddle as the overlapping tree branches swayed and squeaked with every passing breeze. While the gentle breeze swayed the treetops, the birds flew leisurely along the hillside, making brief stops among the swaying branches. My grandfather had always been mesmerized by the enchanting melody of the birds in their hillside sanctuary. Their sweet melodies were often complemented by the constant hammering of the woodpecker on the trunk of a nearby tree. The quiet porch was a beguiling and restful place from which Grandfather enjoyed the hillside sceneries, and the wide grassy field on the plain.

In the hearts and minds of the entire household, the cedar tree served as a constant reminder of the joys of growing up. The tree remained indelibly in the minds of the entire household. It was planted by Grandfather Grovel at the time he'd built his house – long before I came into existence. Over the years, as the tree grew older, it provided pleasures for the entire household. Its strong branches held the sisal ropes from which I and my siblings swung in the cool shade.

Just like Grandfather Grovel's bench he'd built around the trunk of the Red Top tree, my father had built a log bench around the cedar tree's ever-widening trunk. Over time, the tree grew tall and gigantic, thus rendering its large branches unreachable. On hot summer days, the entire household sat beneath its branches to take in the cool and soothing breeze. The cool shade beneath the cedar tree became the venue for family entertainment. Uncle Herbert had always been delighted to entertain the household with his guitar. Most entertaining were his sunset visits to my parents' home, when the entire household danced beneath the branches of the cedar tree. The most thrilling moments were times when my grandfather Grovel and Grandmother Eavie stood to dance. My siblings and I had our moments when we danced to entertain the household.

My uncle Herbert had always been assured of an audience to listen to his songs – accompanied by lively music, and anxious feet waiting to dance in the cool shade beneath the cedar tree.

Over time, the cedar tree cast its seeds around Grandfather's property, producing a few offspring. The offspring gradually grew into large and tall trees. When my little brother Charley passed away, my grandfather had hewn down one of the small cedar trees to prepare board for his casket.

Over the years, the original cedar tree Grandfather Grovel had planted, outgrew its normal height and size, and was therefore much too tall to be so close to the houses. My grandfather maintained great fear that an overhanging branch could collapse, causing costly damage to the metal roof. He'd therefore consulted with my father to trim the branches that could potentially damage the houses, particularly the large kitchen over which they hung.

On a stormy day in the month of October, however, strong winds, accompanied by heavy rain, pounded the village, sending the cedar tree crashing to the ground. It landed by the side of the field, just yards from the chicken coop. The large branches of another cedar tree – an offspring of the first, over-hung the fallen tree trunk, casting a cool shade from the afternoon sun.

It was my grandfather's greatest delight to see the tree lying on the ground. Most of all, the fallen tree had not caused damage to the houses, or the kitchen that had become the most vulnerable target of its overhanging branches.

My grandfather had made the fallen tree trunk his sanctuary. It had become his place of attachment from which he admired the beauty of his most graceful house. From that vantage point, he also had an uninterrupted view of the hillside sceneries, his cultivated fields, and the field where his grandchildren played.

From the day the cedar tree fell, and for the rest of his life, my grandfather had found a sanctuary on the fallen tree trunk. It was his perception that, as he hadn't been able to enjoy the tree he'd planted, standing upright and flourishing, he would gain a continued benefit having the fallen tree trunk as a place of rest – and so he did until he passed away. And like a chip off the old block, after Grandfather Grovel passed away, my father had also made the fallen tree trunk his place of attachment.

As I reflected on my grandparents, and my parents, I was compelled to face the reality that, it has been more than fifty years since I had seen my three siblings. Whether they were alive, or they'd passed on, this had become anyone's guess. As the aircraft glided closer to my homeland, I was on my way back home, having many questions for which I hoped to find answers.

I had been sadly reminded that my grandparents had passed. They therefore wouldn't be home when I arrive. I had been mindful that my parents had also passed. Had my brother Charley not pass away, he would have been a grown man, and up in years. There had been growing uncertainties whether I would see any of my three siblings I had left behind at the time of my departure. Nonetheless, I anticipated a joyous arrival at the place that had once given me an exhilarating life and joyful pleasures.

During my childhood years, I had perceived life as a never-ending time of great family fun and laughter in a village that offered a pleasurable existence. But young Charley's passing had quickly changed my perception of life. His passing had caused me to perceive the joys and sorrows of human existence.

While in his toddler years, my brother Charley was admired as the only chubby child of the household. He never refused food and it certainly showed on him. Since he hadn't shown symptoms of any particular illness, my parents didn't see the necessity to take Charley to a doctor in the town. Unless one had become noticeably ill, the folk didn't see a necessity to visit a doctor. It was a common feeling among the village folk that, since all doctors worked in the towns, they were only for the town folk. As a result, there was a snake oil remedy for every illness in the village.

Charley had finally become noticeably ill and had therefore ceased from eating with his big appetite. My parents felt that, that wasn't a case to administer the snake oil remedy. They'd therefore sought Dr. Martin in Brighton Town. Mr. Renwick was immediately summoned to drive my brother to town. Everyone had expressed great concerns when Dr. Martin ordered that Charley be kept at the small hospital in town. Mother told my siblings and me that, because of a severe heart condition, Charley wouldn't return home any time soon.

Two years went by and Charley didn't show any sign of recovery. His condition had gotten progressively worse, while his size continued to increase. Just days before his seventh birthday, Charley had succumbed to his illness. As he was the last child Mother had borne, she'd become stricken by the loss of the son she'd held dear to her heart. She, however, continued to devote tender-loving care to her remaining offspring.

With my brother Charley's passing, and Grandfather Grovel and Grandmother Eavie moving up in age, the fabric of our close-knit family continued to unravel.

My grandparents were long-time residents of Coopers Village. Grovel MacLeary had married his childhood sweetheart, Eavie, while they were still in their teen years. As attested to by some folk of the village, the couple had never been seen engaging in any form of argument. The folk had often said they were a couple made in Heaven.

My grandmother's favorite pastime, when she ventured outdoor, was to pick cotton from the trees spread around the field. I had always admired the cotton trees when they commenced blooming in early spring. The blossoms gradually fell, exposing young cotton pods at the tip of each branch of the trees. Within a few weeks, the pods burst open, exposing a bundle of pure white fuzzy cotton.

Grandmother Eavie, and my mother, knew it was time to reap the cotton when the pods became dry and the pure white cotton exposed. My siblings and I hadn't grown to the height at which we could reach the branches of the cotton trees. We'd however, joined the fun, detaching the cotton from the seeds after they were picked and brought into a small room in the house.

The entire household had always been kept busy stuffing freshly picked cotton into new pillows, and replenishing those that had been flattened due to frequent use. There were large pillows for the adults and children, and small fluffy pillows for the toddlers. The village folk had always been self-sufficient in their need of certain basic items, such as pillows, and cushions for the hardwood chairs.

It was my grandmother Eavie's strong belief that her rightful place was in the home. She'd dutifully assumed the responsibilities of marriage. Grandmother Eavie was scarcely seen by many of the folk who knew her. She'd spent most of her days indoor, as she said my grandfather must be fed and looked after. She therefore felt it was her matrimonial duty to devote her time to his care. There hadn't been a doubt that Grandfather Grovel felt the same about his soulmate. On Saturdays, grandmother, Eavie habitually traveled to Brighton Town to purchase household goods. On Sundays, she'd made it a ritual to walk by Grandfather Grovel's side to the Stone Church.

Grandmother Eavie was rather short in stature. She'd always needed an extended arm to get items that had been stored out of her reach. Grandfather Grovel, and my parents, were often called to carry out that chore. Whenever my parents were unavailable to assist, my older and taller siblings offered their extra arm's length to perform the chore. My grandmother had always compensated her grandchildren with slices of the most delicious breads, and a handful of freshly baked cookies.

For a woman in her mid-seventies, my grandmother moved in brisk strides, and was quite alert as she performed her daily house chores. On Sunday mornings, on their way to the village church, Grandfather

Grovel had always been left breathless as he tried to keep up with his wife.

Despite her display of strength and vigour, Grandmother Eavie hadn't been in the best of health.

It was my greatest wish that my grandparents would be around throughout my young life. However, this hadn't been the case for Grandmother Eavie, who'd surprisingly become incapacitated.

My parents, who'd devoted their lives to caring for their elders, took on the added responsibilities to assist Grandmother Eavie. Whenever the weather was conducive to outdoor activities, my siblings and I had sat her down on the fallen tree trunk, where she soaked up the warm glow of the sun. It had been my parents' hope that their care and nurturing would have kept Grandmother alive for a long time. Their belief, however, had been to the contrary. It wasn't long before Grandmother Eavie had succumbed to the hard throes of a second stroke.

Grandmother's passing had left another rip in the fabric of a joyous and exhilarating family existence. My parents were left to encourage and boost Grandfather Grovel's wavering spirit – with the hope that he would be with the family for a long time. Their hope, however, had been gradually fading while they took on the responsibility of caring for him.

The weeks and months had turned into three years since Grandmother Eavie had passed. Grandfather Grovel had become despondent after his heart-breaking separation from his life-long love. Grandfather enjoyed the few years going it alone without Grandmother Eavie's presence, and her devoted care.

For a man in his mid-seventies, my grandfather was in the best of health and therefore saw no reason to throw in the towel. He did whatever he could on the farm, according to him, to maintain his health and stamina. As a widower, and one up in years, Grandfather Grovel out-did his senior peers with his sharp wits and sound wisdom.

My grandfather had welcomed the loving care showered on him by my parents. Their spirit of caring, however, was in no way a substitute for Grandmother Eavie's presence, and her care and nurturing. My grandfather's strong will and firm determination, and my parents' care and nurturing, had carried him through his moments of grief. My parents, however, had begun to raise fears and suspicions regarding my grandfather's health and well-being. He'd begun to display signs of poor health – in his actions as well as his demeanor.

My grandfather had often sat countless hours on the trunk of the fallen cedar tree. Life didn't seem to matter as each day came and left. His savory meals Mother placed on the table, had always gotten cold, and often left uneaten. Grandfather Grovel had been living a life of solitude as he remained at his place of attachment – on the trunk of the fallen cedar tree, and in the quietness of his house.

It was quite out of character for Grandfather Grovel to remain in bed long after sunrise. For many years, he'd followed a regimented rule of, "Early-to-bed, early-to-rise," but he'd been in violation of his rule. Grandfather Grovel's actions were sure signs of the imminent.

My parents began to have serious thoughts about Grandfather's well-being. He'd displayed obvious signs of illness, that had prompted them to side-step the snake oil remedy. They'd been giving Grandfather the assurance that everything would be ok. Despite their assurance, Mother didn't take his condition lightly and had sought Mr. Renwick's assistance to summon Dr. Martin in Brighton Town.

Dr. Martin didn't offer much hope to Grandfather Grovel when he diagnosed his ailing heart condition. And as life comes and goes, Grandfather Grovel had slowly succumbed to his diagnosed illness. Another thread had snapped in the fabric of a family so closely knitted and enjoying the comforts of life.

At the loss of his parents – first Grandmother Eavie, and not long thereafter, Grandfather Grovel, my father was left in a state of deep despair.

It was my perception that my grandfather had grieved the loss of Grandmother Eavie and as a result, had succumbed to the throes of a broken heart. At my young age, I had limited perception of the toll the swiftly passing years had taken on my grandparents' health and their well-being. I didn't perceive the significance of losing a member of the household, until the reality came knocking at my parents' door. The passing of my brother Charley, Grandmother Eavie, and subsequently,

Grandfather Grovel, had started an irreparable crack in the firm foundation of the MacLeary household. The brilliant sun that had, for many years, cast its glow and brightness atop the MacLeary hill, had been slowly going dim.

Life is a period of joyous living, growing old and transitioning to another world. At a stage of youthfulness and immaturity, I didn't perceive this truth. My grandparents who were instrumental in the young lives of their grandchildren, had quietly made their exit.

At Grandfather's departure, the hillside trees he'd once admired waving in the breeze, remained insignificant in the minds of those he left behind. The hillside birds that had often made their appearance within the range of my grandfather's view, had ceased to be noticed by anyone after he'd passed on. Grandfather's absence on the fallen tree trunk had lowered the curtain on the things and places of attraction that were once instrumental in his life.

At my grandfather's passing, Father was left to carry on the tradition of maintaining his own household, while taking care of Grandfather's house, as he'd promised to do. Father felt that he had a responsibility to perpetuate the house as a commemorative landmark, in memory of my grandparents.

My father, John MacLeary, was born and raised on the family estate. He was the third of three offspring, born to Grandfather Grovel and Grandmother Eavie. He'd met my mother, Mabel Goodwin in the village, as the Goodwin estate lay adjacent to the MacLeary's.

As the Goodwin's wealth gradually expanded, Grandfather Goodwin and his family acquired a new and vast estate, many villages away. My uncle Harry and his sibling, Mabel, were two of the Goodwin's offspring left behind to manage the first estate. Mabel had happily remained in Coopers Village to be close to her childhood sweet-heart, John MacLeary.

At a tender age of twenty, Mabel had become the beautiful June bride, when she and John tied the knot in the Stone Church. Grandfather Grovel had allotted my father, his portion of the vast estate on which he built his house. Until my grandparents and my brother Charley passed away, the extended MacLeary home had become a place of cheerfulness.

When Father built his house, adjacent to Grandfather Grovel's, he'd made a promise to maintain the up-keep of both houses – to preserve their original structure, as well as their elegantly painted white and dark-grey walls. My father had never reneged on his promise made to Grandfather Grovel. It had therefore become a tradition when, every Christmas season, Father worked hard to maintain the upkeep of the houses. His maintenance work was also completed in preparation for the excitement of the Christmas celebration, and the traditional family get-together.

My father's handy work was completed, but not without the full support of my mother, Mabel. Amidst her tender loving care, Mother was a true disciplinarian of the household. She was the joy of the household, and the one whose voice resonated from the floor to the ceiling. As her offspring grew up, she assigned certain house chores to the girls and outdoor chores to the boys. It was a mutual understanding that the chores she assigned to each offspring be duly executed. My father being in partnership with Mother and her disciplinary endeavors, had carefully sliced a long, thick belt from a yard of shoe leather he'd purchased in the town. The leather strap, my father said, was for the posterior.

Mother hung the hide strap on a nail behind the door in the big hall. And there it remained, should anyone forget to carry out the daily assigned duties; or "Gets out of hand," as she'd often said. At the commencement of each night, when the big door was shut, the strap remained visible to the eye of those who may have committed an infraction of the rules. The presence of the strap behind the door was the constant reminder to her offspring to carry out their duties, as assigned, and put their best behaviour on full display as much as they could.

My mother's pastime had always been her daily house chores, which she'd performed dutifully. Like my grandmother Eavie, Mother strongly believed that the vow of marriage meant a lifetime of devotion to house-work and raising her offspring. As my girl siblings, Eunice and Rita grew older, Mother had passed down her household skills to them. She was fully aware that the girls would someday, take the vow of marriage and make similar resolutions to serve in their household.

It had become one of Mother's assumed responsibilities to entertain the travelers, who'd stopped to rest on Grandfather Grovel's bench beneath the Red Top tree. As soon as the words, "Hello, Miss Mabel," were heard, Mother was on her way down the hillside, bringing a silver tray stacked with gold-rimmed crystal glasses. She carried a white goblet of cool water from the big urn she kept in a dark corner of the hall. The urn was my parents' means of maintaining cool water, since the words, "Electricity and refrigeration," were not a part of the village folk's vocabulary.

Mother promptly laid down her tray and began to pour cool water into each glass. A conversation ensued with the travelers, who were overcome by fatigue after they'd traveled unimaginable journeys. After a period of thirst quenching and much needed rest, the travelers continued on their journey.

The big appetite of my mother's entire household had always been compensated, when she'd served the most appetizing meals. Her wooden bread box resting on a shelf in the kitchen, had always been stacked with delicious breads and cookies she baked in the oven of the wood-burning stove. From oiled metal hooks in the ceiling of the kitchen were hung, smoked meats of a large variety. Never a day went by that the meat hooks weren't stacked with the most flavorfully cured meats; a smoked cow's tongue, thin slices of smoked beef, a smoked cow's tail, a leg of ham and a whole chicken Father so carefully prepared whenever he sacrificed a chicken for the day's meal.

Mother had always prepared finger-licking treats for the family. She knew how to compensate her household's big appetite with the foods and vegetables freshly harvested from the garden. Her foods couldn't have gotten more organic.

My mother was regarded by all as the mother of Coopers Village. Besides her role in preparing the Sunday communion in the Stone Church, she'd brought much joy and comfort to those who knew her. After her offspring grew past the age of fourteen, Mother presented herself at the home of sick elderly village peasants to provide her moral and spiritual support. With her tall and slim physique, she walked in quick strides, and had always stood ready to take on the day. Mother had always appeared to be a picture of health. Just a bit past the prime of her life, at age forty-seven, she'd sadly passed away. Father had involuntarily relinquished the joy of his life. He'd suddenly found himself in his empty world. At Mother's untimely passing, the MacCleary sanctuary on the hill lay quiet.

Time had passed, snatching another member of the MacLeary household in its firm grasp – and further rending the fabric of a tightly knitted family.

Amidst his cascading tears, my father attempted to solace his grieving offspring, who'd gathered around him. They'd hoped that he could provide answers for the many questions about Mother's passing.

"Dad, what if Mother's life could have been spared?" I asked Father amidst his overwhelming sobs.

"Jimmy, there was no way in which Dr. Martin could have saved Mabel's life. There were recommended therapies offered to her, but she'd been informed of their consequences. Mabel didn't accept the chemotherapy as she was made aware of the consequences. She also didn't wish to go through the gruelling bout with the loss of her beautiful head of hair, nor was she prepared for the many other tolls the therapy would have taken on her body. Mabel had her qualms whether the therapy offered to her would have saved her life," Father said, as his remaining offspring waited with hopes of obtaining answers for their many questions.

"Dad, Mother didn't wish to give the therapy a try to see if it would have worked," Rita said as she continually wiped the tears flowing down her cheeks.

"Too bad the cancer wasn't detected sooner. Mother would have had a fighting chance," Eunice said. But Father remained convinced that my mother had made the right decision to maintain her body in its original form to face her destiny, as she felt that her condition had deteriorated beyond the point of recovery.

"Mother didn't make an effort to prolong her life for the sake of us, her offspring. It's been a lonely life without her," my brother Larry said, amidst his frequent sobs.

"It was your mother's decision to refuse a therapy that had not assured her a promise of recovery," Father said as he attempted to solace his grieving offspring.

Mother's passing was like an atomic bomb exploding in the center of the MacLeary compound. It had destroyed what was once the family's sanctuary, so well structured and conducive to a thriving existence. I, along with my siblings, who'd been cemented to her, had made every effort to cope with the great loss. There'd been continuous sighs at the sight of Mother's empty room, and the realization that she'd no longer inhabited her space. Hope had become the only antidote for the grief brought about by Mother's passing.

The reality of my mother's untimely passing had struck the household like a speeding steel bullet. My father was overcome by the grief of her passing, and it showed up from day to day in his demeanor. As a result of his continuous tears, Father's eyes were never dry. He'd been left with more questions than he could have found answers. As he gradually faced the reality of Mother's passing, Father was left to nurture his adolescent and young adult offspring.

With the training Mother had passed down to her girl offspring, and Father's regimented rules laid down for the boys, the offspring had each played a role in keeping the fragile family structure intact.

The offspring's hope for survival with Father at the helm, however, had quickly faded. On a sunny day in spring, four years after Mother's passing, my father had been resting on the trunk of the fallen cedar tree – Grandfather Grovel's once favorite place of relaxation. Lately, Father had been spending unusually long hours on the fallen log. It was the assumption of his offspring that he'd particularly chosen the log to pass his solitary moments.

On that particular day, while Father lay on the log, I felt that he'd remained in the outdoors for much too long, and therefore went to investigate. Upon my arrival, in a faint voice, Father asked that Mr. Renwick be summoned as he hadn't been feeling well. Mr. Renwick arrived in the nick of time and drove off to Brighton as Father lay stretched out in the back seat of his vehicle. My brother Larry assisted, holding Father's head steadily as the vehicle traveled along the unpaved road on its way to Brighton Town. I was immediately concerned about my father's condition that had warranted his requested visit with Dr. Martin.

Upon Father's arrival in Brighton Town, he was promptly taken to Dr. Martin, who immediately began to browse through his medical record. Dr. Martin leafed through his tottered book, until he came to a stop at a specific page. He walked his fingers across the page with heightened curiosity. My brother Larry and I had passed the age of majority, and were therefore privileged to obtain Father's prognosis. Dr. Martin took a deep breath before he commenced reading from the page.

"Young men, your father's prognosis is not good. Earlier examination had revealed a heart condition," Dr. Martin said, as he continued to pass his fingers across the page in front of him. Father lay on the examination table in an adjacent room, incognizant of his prognosis being read to his children. I immediately realized that Father's condition was more critical than I had perceived.

Dr. Martin had promptly disappeared into a small storage room. He later returned with a pint bottle filled with a dark liquid, which he handed to me. There were hand-written instructions on a label attached to the bottle. Father was sent home with the doctor's order that he remain in bed for a while.

I had great confidence in Dr. Martin, and therefore felt that the bottle of herbal medicine would make Father well again. After returning my father to the automobile, he was on his way back home. I felt confident that he was given a new lease on life. The entire household had remained hopeful that Father would regain his good health and continue to nurture his young offspring.

I was unaware of Father's heart condition previously diagnosed by Dr. Martin. Father might not have disclosed his poor health to avoid adding to the mounting grief of his offspring. As his illness was revealed to his offspring, Father took all the necessary precautions – following Dr. Martin's order in his attempt at restoring good health.

My older siblings, Eunice and Rita, hadn't taken Father's diagnosis lightly. They were immediately reeling from fear and anticipation of an ensuing recurring event. They'd traveled that route before and hadn't ruled out the possibility of coming face to face with further grief. At that critical time in their lives, Father's offspring needed him more than they needed their daily meals. He was the only remaining main root of the crumbling family tree, and was therefore expected to take up the baton from where my grandparents, and my mother had left it. It was therefore of vital necessity that he took his required rest, and be nurtured back to some measure of health. As the single head of his household, my father had striven to carry on the daily tasks of maintaining his remnant family. His concerned offspring had willingly assumed their responsibilities in the household.

Two years had passed since my father's worsening heart condition. Since his first sign of having a serious illness, he'd made several visits to Dr. Martin. He'd also received further doses of the herbal medicine. But with a limited view of his interior, Dr. Martin could only assume that Father was on his way to recovery. Had he assumed that Father's health had been improving, his assumption would have been false. Just a bit shy of three years after Father's worsening condition, he'd succumbed to his illness. His offspring were cast, once more, into their deep valley of despair. The main root of the MacLeary family tree had crumbled, giving way to an avalanche.

Chapter 5

The Exodus

With my father's passing – the last kingpin of the family, the foundation of the MacLeary household had crumbled. Without a parent at the helm, my three siblings and I, were left to maintain the household. At that critical time, like sheep having no shepherd, a future livelihood on the estate appeared futile. I therefore began to focus attention on life elsewhere – with the assurance that I could have pioneered my own future.

While still a young adult, Uncle Harry had migrated to America, leaving the Goodwin estate in hired hands. At the time of his departure from Coopers Village, my uncle felt that he needed a change from a quiet village life. Shortly after Uncle Harry's migration, many households saw a gradual abandonment of village life by their offspring. Parents watched the decadence of the talents and skills they'd passed on to their young offspring, when the young folk commenced an exodus to towns and cities, and to foreign destinations. Deep-rooted village culture gradually gave way to a city lifestyle as the exodus continued. Uncle Harry's departure marked the beginning of a slow trend when the young folk had gradually followed suit.

The very fabric of the MacLeary's well-structured family, had further disintegrated when my siblings, Eunice and Rita, joined the exodus to Brighton Town. It was the beginning of an era that saw the abandonment of village life, and the once thriving culture instilled in the young folk by their parents.

And while my siblings tried to adjust to their town environment, my hopes had surpassed town life. I felt that, if my uncle Harry had successfully migrated to America while he was a young adult, there ought to be a way I could follow in his footsteps. I therefore set my focus on a new life on a distant foreign shore.

As the village folk interacted with town folk, they'd brought back books and magazines published in foreign countries. Such publications had widened their scope of knowledge of the fact that there was a bigger world than the village they knew.

From a book shelf in the hall, I selected a foreign magazine Eunice had purchased in Brighton Town. I commenced browsing the pages as a pastime – admiring far-away places and amazing structures, until a ray of hope suddenly shone across my mind: What if Uncle Brayson has an interest in a nephew joining him in his foreign country to which he'd migrated around the time of Uncle Harry's departure? This was an excellent idea worth challenging. My uncle Brayson could only say "No." I would then think of someone else. My uncle Harry was a possibility. I had Uncle Brayson's address he'd given to my parents at the time of his migration to the U.K. I remember Father giving me and my siblings a stack of papers to keep – in case we needed to know the whereabouts of relatives. I promptly searched among the papers and found Uncle Brayson's address intact. I immediately saw sparkles as my eyes glanced at his name and address written on a red, white and blue envelope.

With cautious expectation, I promptly wrote a letter to my uncle Brayson and mailed it at the village Mail House. I felt that there was no need to be cautious about Uncle Brayson's response. If his answer was "No," I had remained poised to submit my request to Uncle Harry.

A month had gone by before I dropped in at the Mail House. The postmaster handed me an envelope which I had gladly accepted. I was joyously delighted to see my name and address written on the envelope. Surprisingly, Uncle Brayson had responded to my letter. With eager curiosity, I opened the envelope and began to read its contents:

"My nephew, Jimmy! I'm delighted to learn of your interest in making a livelihood in the U.K. I'm therefore extending my warmest welcome to you. Kindly communicate by way of a telegram. In the meantime, I'll make preparations for your arrival. Signed: Brayson MacLeary."

Uncle Brayson's response was a big, "Yes." His generosity had paved the way for me to leave my homeland, and join the exodus of folk to a foreign country. This meant a transition from a humble village living to life on a big continent. It was my dream becoming reality.

With a cheerful heart, I had promptly returned home, where I pondered the reality of leaving Coopers Village – my childhood home. There hadn't been a shortage of kind words I could have sent in my response to Uncle Brayson's offer, but for a telegram that set a restraint on the number of words I was permitted to send. I had promptly returned to the village Mail House, armed with my telegram. After obtaining the much-needed guidance from the mail master, I sent off my response by way of a short telegram;

"Yes, Uncle Brayson. I will be coming to the U.K. Signed: Jimmy MacLeary."

Weeks after my uncle's affirmative response, and after a short period of further communication with him by way of telegrams, I had sorted out the intricacies of traveling to a foreign land. I had purchased an airline ticket with my portion of the funds Father had left in the Chest for my siblings and me. I had made all the necessary preparations to leave my home and village life behind. Meanwhile, my mind could not have perceived the foreign destination, and what life would be like when I arrive. I had perceived from the foreign magazines, that the U.K and all other foreign countries were unlike my village, or the other villages in my homeland of Cavers Cove. I had been waiting to see my uncle, Brayson after his long absence from his home in Coopers Village, but for the country and its people, my heart could not yearn for a place I had never seen.

While I made preparations for my departure, my siblings had come from Brighton Town to bid their sad farewell. It was my heart's wishes that I would live within close proximity to my siblings – in the village where we were destined to become adults and prominent village citizens. The passing of my parents, however, had forced their offspring to go separate ways, and distance apart, much earlier than they'd anticipated. My younger brother, Larry, the last offspring remaining in the home, was left to hold the family fort, while he planned his own future.

It was a bitter-sweet moment when, in the month of October, I sat in the front seat of Mr. Renwick's vehicle and watched Coopers Village and the home in which I grew up, slowly disappearing in the distance behind me. With a sorrowful heart, I was leaving the place of my birth, and my siblings behind. I watched my brother Larry's eyes constantly flooding with sad tears. Amidst hugs and kisses, I bade my aunt Edith, Uncle Gordon, and my cousin, Erwin a sad farewell. I was heading to the airport, where I would quickly vanish from the view of everyone who knew me; except my uncle Brayson who'd been anxiously awaiting my arrival.

The vehicle drove along the quiet road, as if it was part of a procession. As I made my farewell bow, like a caged tiger, I looked fiercely at every scene. I could hear the spring in the valley as its streams flowed over rocks and pebbles along its path. Under the warm midday sun, I listened to the hillside birds chirping their blissful melodies. I watched the leaves of the trees along the way as they were being rustled by the soothing autumn breeze. As the vehicle rolled along the narrow road, the gentle breeze rustled the leaves of the wayside trees, as though they were waving their sad farewell. I waved a hand to my close friends and neighbors, who'd stood by the roadway to bid their sad farewell.

My heart grieved as the vehicle took on momentum and gradually drifted away from Coopers Village, and farther away from my home. I glanced at the dainty village houses, sparsely spread out along the narrow winding road. The vehicle had finally left the village scenes and advanced onto the paved street leading into Brighton Town.

Upon my arrival at the airport, I was overcome by fear of getting close to an aircraft, and entering its interior for the first time. I was suddenly overcome by a feeling that I was about to be kidnapped by alien species from another world – the type my siblings and I read about in the books we borrowed from the village library.

I had promptly retrieved my luggage after bidding Mr. Renwick my sad goodbye. He'd slowly closed the door of his vehicle and drove off, leaving me in a state of panic as I watched the vehicle disappear in the distance.

As I walked cautiously toward the entrance of the airport, I could not hold back the tears flowing profusely from my eyes when I thought about leaving my home, and the place I had known all of my young life. Leaving home had meant, severing ties with my siblings, my other relations, and the friends and associates who were so conducive to my growing-up. But I took courage in the fact that, my absence from my village would be immediately followed by my presence in another world with my uncle Brayson.

The small check-in area at the airport had been overwhelmed with folk who were anxiously waiting to board an aircraft to their respective destination. I was promptly directed to a small office, where my travel documents were scrutinized, and my luggage checked in by a uniformed attendant.

As a way of finding an outlet for my revved-up emotion, I had hesitantly joined the group of anxious folk gazing toward the ceiling at the scheduled arrival and departure of the various aircrafts. While I sat in the waiting area, I felt as one in a trance, with no hope of waking or escaping. To get close to an aircraft for the very first time, and to actually enter its interior, was like being one of the members of the cast in a film show. The kind of film show the town folk watched in the movie theatre, and the occasional film show, shown in Coopers Villa schoolyard for village folk to watch.

Never in my wildest dream had I anticipated being close to an aircraft, or actually flying in one. Whenever an aircraft flew over Coopers Village, all eyes were quickly turned toward the sky. An aircraft flying overhead had provided a few moments of village entertainment.

The passengers had waited patiently for the boarding of their respective flight, when a gentleman, clad in a blue suit, beckoned my group of waiting passengers to follow his leading. With great courage, I had hesitantly joined the queue of anxious folk as they followed the path directed by the gentleman. A paved path led to a silver-painted aircraft waiting on a wide pavement at the rear of the building. The procession continued up a high set of stairs leading to the entrance of the aircraft. A pleasant female, also clad in blue uniform, stood at the door as she welcomed the anxious passengers aboard. It was like entering into a dream, when I walked through the narrow doorway and into the interior of the aircraft.

There was an air of suspense, amidst great anticipation of take-off. Not knowing what to expect, I sat motionless, waiting for what would transpire. A female stepped into the single aisle and commenced a series of demonstration of the dos and don'ts of flying. She was the female who'd greeted the passengers as they filed through the narrow doorway leading into the aircraft.

A moment of silence ensued among the anxious passengers. I had been anxiously waiting for what would transpire, when a series of revving sounds bellowed from the underbelly of the aircraft. The harmony of sounds became noticeably louder – as if a mighty thunderstorm had been looming on the outside. It was the type of rolling thunder that boomed across the sky during a heavy rainstorm in my village. When the aircraft commenced a slow shuffle backward, I knew it had been preparing for take-off. The aircraft began a slow movement forward, a sure sign that it would soon commence its flight. As the forward movement progressed, the booming sounds suddenly turned into a mighty roar. My heart pounded within my chest as I awaited the imminent.

The loud roaring sounds continued, until I felt a sense of weightlessness, followed by an upward thrust. Amidst fear and panic, I set my gaze toward the low ceiling of the aircraft as it continued an upward ascent.

I had regained a measure of composure before courageously taking a look through the tiny circular window beside my seat. I immediately noticed thick fluffy clouds like cotton-candy mountains, resting on a floor of cloud below the aircraft. If only my siblings and the entire village folk knew what lay beyond the clouds that hung above their heads. Above the clouds, as far as my eyes could see and my mind perceive, there was a rich blue sky that was void of any clouds. Whatever lay beyond the blue sky, and in the abyss of space, had been left only to one's imagination. During the night hours, the myriad of stars visible in the dark night sky, are not visible to the naked eye during the daytime. They gradually show up at the appearance of dusk. Only the night reveals what lay beyond the blue sky under a radiant sun. The moon always lingers, and often remains unnoticed under the sunlit sky, but shows up at the appearance of dusk, or whenever the night sneaks up on it.

Time had elapsed since the aircraft settled in the sky – on its way to my new world. It flew above a series of constant forming and un-forming clouds, allowing intermittent glimpses of land, or the ocean below. Putting fear aside, I was having the joyride of a lifetime, as I journeyed to my new and unknown world.

As the aircraft propelled across the sky, it was gradually advancing toward its destination. Meanwhile, the curtain had been slowly closing on the first chapter of my life, in the place I had known from birth. I felt that I was being taken into the dawn of my new day, and a new world.

The reality of leaving my village, and my homeland, had suddenly crept into my mind. I felt a sudden jolt across my chest as the pain of separation from my home gradually took hold of me. My heart was suddenly gripped by the urge to return home. I felt that I must say another goodbye to my siblings, and to Aunt Edith, Uncle Gordon, Erwin, and to my best friend Tim I had left behind. I felt that, if only I could return to say another goodbye, I would be prepared, emotionally, to face the new world into which I was slowly being engulfed. But as the windmill-propelled aircraft sped across the sky, I could hear the words echo clearly in my mind: "Too late. Too late!"

A sudden jolt, followed by a series of tremors, and a sense of weightlessness, aroused my awareness that I was seated in the comfort of a wide-bodied aircraft, gliding high above the earth – I was on my way back to my homeland for the first time in more than fifty years. I was immediately overcome by a feeling of joyous anticipation as the aircraft drew closer to my homeland. After more than fifty years absence, I pondered the state in which my home village would be in, and what I would see upon my arrival.

I was immediately immersed in a state of day-dreaming about my childhood days back home. With my head still resting against my seat, I had lapsed into a state of constantly interrupted thought process. Intriguing memories of my youth continued to crowd my mind as I reminisced on the life I had left behind, and the way life used to be back home.

I had vivid memory of the village church resting by the side of a hill, a short distance from my home. It was the place where folk gathered to worship, and to say farewell to a departed loved one; to observe a wedding ceremony, and most of all, to take in the excitement of Christmas events.

Just around the bend, before seeing my home, a stone bridge hung over the village creek. The creek had been constantly supplied with crystal waters flowing from the crest of the surrounding hills. It was the place where the children of the village played in the clear streams flowing over cleanly washed pebbles and stones along the creek.

In my village back home, it was a Saturday tradition, when the children of the neighborhood carried out their chores. They'd happily pruned the grass so that the yard was spanking clean, and ready for the evening's fun and games. The wide yard was the place where my siblings and I played a variety of sports under the brilliant evening sun.

Saturday and Sunday afternoons were fun-filled days for the entire household, as well as the neighborhood youngsters. Whenever the weather was dry, and the day bright and cheerful, Saturdays and Sundays were set aside for fun and games in the cleanly groomed yard. My grandparents, along with my parents, took their usual position on the log bench beneath the cedar tree, to take in the evening's fun and games. Youngsters of the close neighborhood teamed up for tournaments of baseball. The game continued until a team was declared the winner. While there hadn't been a trophy, being declared a winner was just as rewarding to the competitive youths. The boys subsequently played the sport of boxing, using their bare, hard fists. A gradual depletion of energy, coupled with sore knuckles, took them to the game of tossing Tops on smooth surfaces they'd prepared on the ground. The entire household had become absorbed in the game as they watched to see whose Top spun the longest, and the smoothest.

Meanwhile, the girls were engaged in the game of skipping, using long withes they cut from the field, or short ropes that were no longer needed to tie the animals. Other children of the neighborhood joined in the ring games, as many participants were needed to form a proper circle.

The sports-filled evening had often ended with a game of soft ball, in which both boys and girls had participated. As the name implies, the ball was made of cloth, stuffed tightly to create a round shape. During the spring season, a young round fruit was used as a substitute for the soft cloth ball.

As added fun and entertainment, both boys and girls enjoyed swinging from sisal ropes attached to a sturdy branch of the cedar tree. The ropes were made from strong twisted sisal threads obtained from sisal plants cultivated in the field.

The sports-filled evenings generally ended with a game of hide-and-seek under the early dusk. All games ended once darkness moved in. Whenever the new moon appeared, the games were often prolonged beneath a bright moon-lit sky. It was a thrill to hear children's laughter beneath the early night sky. When there was no moon, and the night became black, superstition, and a fear of the unseen, had forced the children indoor.

Sunday evenings had always been the grand finale for all week-end games. Sunday was the day when children made preparations for school on Monday. The Sunday afternoon activities were therefore kept to a minimum, and had often ended before the dusk approached.

While I reminisced on the days of my youth, my thought process was once more interrupted by an audible voice from the ceiling above. The brief announcement informed the anxious passengers that the aircraft was on course and would be landing as scheduled – in approximately two hours. The announcement stirred my emotions and sent shivers down my spine. My dream of arriving home had been gradually becoming reality. I was about to engage in my most adventurous event – I was going back home to the place of my childhood.

Chapter 6

Lensworth Adams

The aircraft had traveled over land and ocean since it ascended skyward. I had remained in my semi-conscious state of mind, oblivious of the time that had elapsed, and what had transpired.

With nothing else to occupy my time, I had been dozing in and out of consciousness, while awaiting my joyous arrival back home.

In whatever prior activities my seating companion had been engaged, I was oblivious of them. But he appeared to have been sound asleep from the moment the aircraft took to the sky. The announcement made by the pilot may have interrupted his sleep. A few slaps of his hands to his own ears were obvious signs of discomfort of sorts. His eyes had remained opened a fraction of an inch wider than their limits as he repeatedly cast quick glances from the ceiling to the floor of the aircraft.

"Pardon my interruption, Sir. Are you ok?" I asked. Not knowing whether he spoke my language, or he had his own mother tongue, I waited for a response.

"I'm quite ok," he said. "My name is, Lensworth Adams. May I know your name?" A few seconds of silence ensued before I responded;

"Most certainly. My name is Jim MacLeary." My companion remained silent for a moment, as if he needed to search his own thoughts for words. There were further signs of discomfort when he repeatedly shuffled himself in his seat. He habitually passed his hands over his cleanly shaven face, as if he'd been checking to determine how long his facial hair had grown since his last shave. Being the tall, slim-built fellow that he was, he could have done with more seating space for his noticeably long legs. The dark suit with white shirt Lensworth wore, suggested that he was unaware of the sizzling hot temperatures at his destination.

Not being able to catch a nap, or rest comfortably, a conversation was in my best interest. I had therefore sat poised to converse with my seating companion.

As if to compensate for his long period of silence, and whatever else may have triggered his silence, Lensworth had quickly sparked up a conversation;

"Jim, can you see the distant shore?" he asked, as he peered through a small circular window of the aircraft. "I can see land in the far distance ahead. Seems like we should be on the ground soon." Lensworth's noticeably dark eyes were partially closed, as if he'd been struggling to stay awake after his past two or more hours of slumber. From my window seat, I looked toward the horizon, but there hadn't been evidence of an early landing. The aircraft had still maintained its height of more than thirty thousand feet; according to the pilot's earlier announcement.

"Lensworth, I haven't seen a shoreline, or any trace of land in the far distance. According to the earlier announcement by the pilot, the aircraft will be on the ground in approximately two hours." As if he'd set a restraint on his own thoughts and movements, Lensworth sat still, while he kept his gaze toward the ceiling. A brief moment had elapsed before he continued to speak;

"Are you also a first-time visitor to Cavers Cove?" he asked. There was one less question to ask, and one less answer to give, when Lensworth revealed that he would be visiting Cavers Cove for the first time.

"Lensworth, you can say that I'm a visitor, but Cavers Cove is the land of my birth. I'm going back home for the very first time in the many years since leaving the shore of my homeland." Lensworth passed his right hand over his low-cut head of hair, as if he'd been searching for the relevant questions to ask. He'd quickly cleared his throat before proceeding with his fact-finding conversation.

"I heard that Cavers Cove is one of the most exquisite places one can ever visit. I therefore intend to spend a week there," he said, as he kept his focus toward the ceiling of the aircraft.

"Welcome to my homeland, Lensworth! You'll certainly enjoy every moment of your stay there," I said, with added assurance. There was a sudden reassuring look on his face as he nodded with a complacent smile.

"Jim, you must be quite happy to be going back home to the place of your origin," Lensworth said. With his right hand, he smoothed his low-cut hair before giving his head a gentle pat down. I immediately perceived that he was another creature of habits, or just overly conscious about his appearance.

"I'm excited to be going back home after my long period of absence," I said.

"Not only am I visiting Cavers Cove for the first time, I'm also flying for the very first time," Lensworth said, as he turned his face toward the ceiling. Lensworth's admission had immediately confirmed my suspicion that he'd shown obvious signs of fear and panic, hence, his justification for sleeping and maintaining his silence, since the aircraft took to the sky.

Lensworth appeared to have had a famine for words to speak, and when he spoke, he was uncertain whether he'd chosen the right words to conduct his conversation. I had therefore concluded that his mother tongue wasn't English – although his understanding of the language was above average. I had remained hopeful that Lensworth would voluntarily disclose his country of origin. With cautious expectation, I proceeded with my fact-finding conversation.

"Lensworth, there're many warm and exquisite places in the world. Why did you choose Cavers Cove as your vacation destination?" I asked. He'd remained hesitant before responding;

"You see, in my homeland, the residents are encouraged to travel to see the rest of the world – if they have the means of course. My parents have left me an inheritance. With my fortune, I wish to see the world before I move up in age."

As Lensworth spoke, there were questions raised, for which the answers hadn't been forthcoming. What of his siblings and his roots? For a man of around fifty, I perceived that his parents were in their late seventies. In light of the fortune left behind by his parents, I perceived that they'd passed, due to unexpected circumstances. Why was he traveling alone, and to a strange country? Lensworth had failed to address the issue of his reason for choosing Cavers Cover as his vacation destination. His garment didn't reflect that of one on a pleasure-seeking mission. There appeared to have been many mysteries surrounding my seating companion.

As Lensworth had spoken of his homeland, I felt that he would readily disclose his country of origin, and therefore attempted to delve into his personal affairs.

"Lensworth, what's your country of origin?" He'd sat in silence, and motionless before he finally spoke;

"I'm from a country on latitude with the U.K. My flight to Cavers Cove connects in the U.K," Lensworth said, but he'd still not disclosed his country of origin. I had therefore concluded that there's not much prying one can do to obtain the facts from a total stranger, who'd been bent on concealing his identity.

In the midst of my conversation with Lensworth, a voice was heard outlining instructions on making preparations for landing. With that long-awaited announcement, the conversation ended abruptly. The announcement immediately triggered a sudden stir. Passengers within my immediate view commenced a process of shifting and turning in every direction. Another announcement was made for seat belts to be fastened. A harmony of clicking sounds could be heard throughout the aircraft as the anxious passengers were in adherence to the orders announced. Amidst the clicking and snapping of metal buckles, Lensworth became suddenly silent. He'd begun to display further signs of anxiety as he focused his undivided attention toward the ceiling of the slowly descending aircraft. There hadn't been a doubt that he'd developed a genuine fear of flying.

Chapter 7

The Home-Coming

The gradual descent of the aircraft immediately created another atmosphere of silence among the wearisome passengers. Eager eyes peered through whatever circular window allowed an outside view. Everyone sat in anticipation of an exciting event of sorts. Whether it was meeting relatives and friends after long absences, or the anticipation of being once more on solid ground; a wave of anticipation lingered in the atmosphere as the aircraft cruised in silence toward its destination. While Lensworth maintained his total silence, with his face turned toward the ceiling of the aircraft, there hadn't been a doubt that he'd been anticipating a swift landing back on solid ground.

Whatever were the reasons for others' feeling of anxiety, my anxiety was going back home after many years of absence. Most of all, my heart yearned to see my siblings, and others I had left behind. I had remained in a state of great anticipation of seeing my uncle Harry. I knew he'd been waiting with the same anticipation after so many years of not seeing me.

The aircraft had been cruising in silence across a clear blue sky with patches of solid white clouds. Its wide wings continually tilted and turned, sending puffing sensations into my ears, and causing Lensworth to give a few more slaps to his ears.

I immediately sensed a feeling of being closer to my homeland, when the thick cotton-like pure white patches of cloud hung above and below the path of the aircraft. The thick white clouds reminded me of the days of my youth, when white cloud patches lined the sky under a blazing sun. I began to sense once more, the atmosphere of home – the cool breeze I had once enjoyed, seated beneath the branches of the tall cedar tree beside my home. I became nostalgic as memories of life in the home I once knew began to flood my mind. In a matter of a few minutes, I would be walking on the soil of my homeland. My anxious thoughts reflected on how beautiful life had been back home. The feeling of going back home had brought on an adrenalin rush and the ardent desire to reach my home village. I had been anticipating a joyous arrival at the place I had once called home.

The aircraft had been gradually making its descent, gliding quietly along the shoreline of my homeland. As Lensworth had prematurely announced, the shoreline and a beautiful landscape had finally come into view. The sea shore of my homeland was slowly unveiling before my observing eyes. The beautiful landscape – the sea with its waves listing toward a beautiful shoreline, could be seen and admired only from that aerial view from the aircraft. I had the added assurance that it wouldn't be long before I set my feet in the soil of my homeland.

The aircraft had finally escaped the patches of impeding intermittent white cloud. It gradually closed in on the runway, until I finally felt the long-anticipated touch of its wheels on the smooth surface of the ground. The sharp touch-down created a crescendo of revving, rushing, grinding sounds as its gears and engines screeched to a halt.

It was a perfect touch-down, amidst the cheers and laughter of anxious folk who were happy to arrive at their destination. And whatever other reasons the folk had for being cheerful, I was delighted to be back on the soil of my homeland after my long absence. It was like touching down in paradise, when every fibre of my being reached out to embrace the place of my birth.

The aircraft taxied slowly along the runway. I sat at the edge of my seat – as much as the restraining seat belt permitted. My patience had been revving up as I waited for the final announcement that would allow me to unbuckle and make a mad dash toward the exit. Further announcements, however, had quickly put a damper on my endeavors. An order was given for everyone to remain seated, with seat belts intact, until the aircraft arrived at its designated gate.

There was a period of stillness as everyone waited for that last announcement to unbuckle for exit. I was quite certain I could have made my mad dash ahead, and be first in line for that anticipated quick exit, and a triumphant walk on the soil of my homeland. However, I had become discouraged by the thought that my 21-D seating position meant that I had to wait in the queue formed by the passengers seated in the many rows ahead – another damper was quickly put on my endeavors. Amidst my anxious moments, I tried to remain calm and observe the stringent rules of buckling up and remaining in an upright position, while the aircraft taxied to its arriving gate.

The aircraft had finally come to a full stop, close to the rear of an unusually large building. It was the moment for which all had been waiting. The exit door of the aircraft was finally opened, bringing a sense of freedom to the passengers who'd been locked in for the duration of the flight. A final announcement was made, resulting in another series of clicking and snapping session. With all seat-belts quickly unlatched, a queue of passengers scrambled to obtain their overhead belongings while they stood in readiness to exit the aircraft. I happily joined the orderly stream of passengers down a long staircase leading from the aircraft.

The procession of relieved passengers continued along a path leading toward the large building. The overwhelming sights and sounds had quickly brought back vivid memories of my homeland. As the balmy breeze blew gently against my cheeks, with great enthusiasm, my entire being reached out to reacquaint with the sights and sounds of home. Each sound was like a, "Welcome-back-home," and a pleasant reminder of the day, more than fifty years prior, when I had left the shore of my homeland. The long procession to the building had given me the opportunity to walk on the solid ground of my homeland. The moment was further perceived as a red-carpet walk to the welcome, and the many pleasures awaiting my arrival in my home village.

The procession had finally come to a stop at the entrance of the large building, which housed the Immigration and Customs offices. The emotionally-charged arriving passengers streamed into the building, where they waited in air-conditioned comfort, while the officers commenced processing them as arriving visitors. In my heart, I had returned to my homeland and therefore felt that I shouldn't be perceived as a visitor.

There were folk from all walks of life, waiting to be cleared for entry into my homeland. I wondered whether they'd all been pleasure-seeking visitors, like Lensworth, or whether the majority were also returning to pay homage to their homeland. Among the muttering crowd, I heard languages and accents that had not been common to the natives' English language and dialect. I knew that Lensworth was a visitor, and a total stranger to the country, but for others, only the waiting officers could determine their motive for arriving in my homeland.

I had happily blended into the crowd of waiting folk in the large arrival area. The area had become overwhelmed with folk waiting for that moment when they would reveal their identity and state their reason for being in, for some, a strange country – Lensworth was no exception.

While the folk were being interrogated, individually, I took in the sights and sounds of the crowded arrival area. I was amazed at the airport and its state-of-the-art appearance. It wasn't like the small and partially dilapidated structure I had left behind at the time of my departure. The wide space and overwhelming modern offices were a far cry from the once small and partially dilapidated structure I had left behind. I immediately noticed the technological equipment in place to deal with modern travels, and the influx of folk as the aircrafts land and take off. The modern devices were also installed to deal with the intricate maintenance of the modern aircrafts lined up on the exterior of the building.

As my eyes circumvented the crowded space, my thoughts reflected on Lensworth, my seating companion. Amazingly, he was nowhere in my immediate view. Whether he'd advanced ahead of the crowd and had cleared immigration, or he was in the rear of the arrival area, he was nowhere in my immediate view.

The immigration officers were kept busy, processing the travel documents of innumerable arriving passengers. The frequent pounding of rubber stamps had become annoying to the hopeful folk who'd been waiting for a considerable period. My patience had been wearing thin, when my long-awaited turn finally came. A noticeably short and stern officer beckoned me to step forward. I walked anxiously to the interrogation booth – my passport and travel documents in hand. The officer said a polite, "Hello," before he commenced his interrogation session. I responded with my respectful, "Hello."

"Can I see your passport please?" the officer said. He sat sternly in his interview booth – his demeanor portraying his authoritative powers.

"Most certainly, Sir," I said, as I presented my passport – my other travel documents intact. The officer's glaring eyes suggested that he'd been expecting to obtain much more than my passport. His stern demeanor had suggested that he wanted to know much more than my reason for visiting his country. I was prepared to stand my ground and claim the land of my birth.

With his swift fingers, the officer repeatedly flipped and shuffled the pages of my passport. He then commenced pointing his pen across a few lines of my other travel documents before abruptly tossing the passport on the left side of his desk. With a piercing look in his eyes, he asked;

"Why are you here?" The atmosphere became rather tense as the officer waited in anxious anticipation of my response. A brief moment of silence ensued before I responded;

"I've returned to visit the place of my birth, Sir," I said to the interrogating officer. It wasn't hard to see and understand that I was on a return visit to my childhood home, but I perceived that the officer was bent on impeding my entry.

The interrogation session continued as the officer retrieved my passport he'd placed on his desk. He immediately commenced another round of shuffling and turning of the pages before he asked;

"And for how long will you be staying?" His inquiries appeared to have implied ensuing punitive measures if I should over-stay my time.

How could I over-stay my time in my own country? I thought to myself. I felt that I was being denied my birthright – to belong in the land of my birth. A moment of silence ensued before I politely responded;

"I'll be visiting for eight days, Sir." I waited for the officer's next series of questions.

"Where will you be staying?" he further asked. I had no doubt that, on the eighth day of my arrival, I would be promptly asked to return to my foreign homeland. With this thought in mind, I hesitantly provided my intended address – Uncle Harry's house in my village.

"I'll be staying in Coopers Village, the place of my birth," I said, as I stood poised for further interrogation. The officer waited with an intimidating look in his eyes.

When it appeared that his interrogation session had only just begun, the officer reached for his rubber stamp. He quickly raised his right hand and gave a fast and hard blow to a page of my passport. With that pounding blow from his rubber stamp, the officer's interrogation session had come to an abrupt end. He quickly closed the passport and shoved it across his desk. I promptly reached for my passport and reopened it to find a large blue seal that read, "Visitor," stamped in the center of a blank page. Within my mind, I had remained troubled by the word, "Visitor," stamped in my passport. But I had been overcome by a fit of anxiety, and the urgency to regain an entry into my homeland. I had therefore ignored the title.

A brief moment of silence ensued before the officer gave another eye-piercing look at the passport, then clutched firmly in my hand. It was no laughing matter when I noticed a rather frail smile on his face, and heard the words, "Welcome home," as they were forced from his lips. It was a long-delayed welcome, but I quickly nodded my acceptance of his welcome and rushed toward the luggage-claim area.

There's always a time of going around in circles, pulling and searching to find luggage in a crowded arrival area. This, for me, was such a time. I stopped along a slowly revolving conveyor belt to find my single piece of luggage. There'd been many pieces of luggage parading past the arriving passengers. With every piece of luggage seemingly the same make, style, size, and color, it was a difficult task finding my black piece of luggage among the many other similar pieces. Passengers had been removing luggage from the conveyor belt, and placing them in bundles on the floor, thus adding to the difficulty of finding a single piece. My search effort had become futile when a tall gentleman, dressed in brown uniform, and rolling a small cart, walked toward me with an inquiring look in his eyes.

"Mister!" he said, "What luggage do you have?" I had given a detailed description of my luggage, but soon realized that my description fitted most of the other pieces tumbling and turning around on the revolving conveyor belt, as well as those stacked on the floor.

"Sir," I said to the waiting gentleman, "I'm looking for a black piece of luggage with two wheels and a tall handle." The uniformed gentleman stood with a puzzled look on his face.

"Mister, there're too many similar pieces of luggage fitting that description. Did you attach your name to the luggage?" he asked.

"Yes, sir," I said, with certainty.

"What's your name, Mister?" the gentleman further inquired. He'd quickly commenced the tedious task scrutinizing each piece of luggage to find a tag with my name enclosed. A few minutes had elapsed when he came rolling my luggage forward. I had written my name inside the small leather tag on the handle of my luggage.

There was a traveling lesson to learn. In consideration of the mass production of identical luggage, I should have attached a specific tag that would have allowed me to readily identify my piece of luggage. I thanked the gentleman and handed him a folded pound note. He nodded his appreciation and promptly left the scene, pushing his luggage cart. I pulled my luggage into the immediate Customs waiting area, where I stood in one of a series of several long lines. I was immediately overcome by a fit of anxiety, hoping to gain clearance so I could escape to freedom to walk on the soil of my homeland.

Chapter 8

My Journey Home to Coopers Village

It was an overwhelming sight, when I had cleared my luggage through Customs, and ventured onto the street in front of the airport building. I immediately surveyed the vicinity that had been thronged with pedestrians, and lined with transport vehicles of varying shapes and sizes.

I remember the once narrow street passing through the small town. Vehicular traffic on the street were few and far between. On the day I stepped from Mr. Renwick's vehicle, I lifted my luggage as I walked toward the small airport building. More than fifty years later, the once narrow street has given way to multiple lanes, channeling through the town. The entire space in front of the airport building had been lined with taxi cabs, modern air-conditioned tour buses, and private vehicles of every make, size and color. All had been waiting with one motive – their operators vying for the handsome reward of the valuable dollars to be earned, transporting visitors and returnees to their various destinations.

The mid-afternoon sun glowed like an over-heated torch dangling over the town. Perspiration oozed from the face of folk hustling along the crowded street – many waiting to be transported to their destination. The folk appeared to have been at a point of indifference as they carried out their activities under the glow of the blazing sun, while the sun's heat took its toll on their well-being.

Each step I made, everything reached out in one way or another to welcome me home. The warm gentle breeze blowing against my cheeks, and the brilliant glow of the midday sun venting its fury on the unconcerned folk below, had quickly brought back memories of life in my homeland.

The constant hustle and bustle of arriving and departing passengers, created congestion in the immediate vicinity. Arriving folk lined the vicinity of the airport, seeking transportation to their various destinations. The process of private vehicles, taxi cabs and buses, loading and unloading passengers as they arrived at the airport, appeared to have been well organized, nonetheless.

As the anxious folk scurried in the vicinity, I stood as one without a sense of belonging. I was immediately overcome by a feeling of displacement and detachment, and therefore began to ponder which way to go, and how I would get to my home. Within my heart, however, I stood overjoyed at the reality, and the feeling of once more setting my feet in the soil of my homeland.

It wasn't long before a taxi pulled up beside me. An average-built, slim gentleman shuffled himself out of the vehicle and immediately opened the trunk.

"Sir," he said, "My name is Tomas Sanders. I'll be delighted to transport you to your destination. Where would you like to go?" Without giving any thought to the fare, or the distance to my home, I quickly stepped forward at the gentleman's invitation.

"I'm going to Coopers Village, Sir. It's a short distance from the outskirts of this town." The gentleman carefully placed my luggage in the trunk of the vehicle and politely opened the rear door.

"Take a seat, Sir!" he said. I promptly took my seat in the vehicle. It wasn't long before I felt a sudden cool and caressing breeze against my brow. I immediately realized that I was about to travel to my village in air-conditioned comfort.

The folk in my home village never had the luxury of air-conditioned comfort. The few cars, a single local bus, and the occasional transport truck that passed through, didn't afford air-conditioned interior. To keep cool under the blazing sun, drivers were fanned by the breeze created as their vehicle drove along dry and dusty winding roads – while their windows remained open. Village folk sought the soothing comfort of the breeze that passed in the shade of the spreading tree branches – along the narrow roadways, and from trees planted around their houses for that purpose. My grandfather's Red Top tree had always provided a cool shade for the travelers who'd stopped to seek shelter from the heat of the sun, while having a much-needed rest on the wooden bench around the trunk of the tree. The village houses maintained a cool atmosphere, from the breeze that constantly passed through their interior, while their windows and doors remained opened throughout the day.

I had remained alone in the air-conditioned comfort of the taxi for a considerably long period. Just as I began to ponder the absence of the chauffeur, he'd finally opened the door of the vehicle and taken his driving position – if only he knew the yearning in my heart to reach my destination.

"Where would you like to go, Sir?" the chauffeur asked, this time in a more beseeching manner. Should I repeat my destination for a second time? I asked myself. There was a constant yearning in my heart to see my home, my siblings, and the beautiful village I had left behind. My uncle Harry had been anxiously awaiting my arrival. It therefore didn't matter how many times I repeated my destination to the waiting chauffeur – whatever it would take to reach my village.

"Sir, I would like to get to Coopers Village," I said. "My village is a good distance west of here." I began to provide details of old concrete walls and mileposts leading into my village. The chauffeur, however, didn't seem to have an interest in my unsolicited directions. He'd quickly accelerated the vehicle – his head turning in every direction as he attempted to escape the congested airport traffic.

As the vehicle drove along the busy street of Brighton Town, I turned my head in every direction to reacquaint my eyes and ears with the sights and sounds of my homeland. At the time I had left my homeland, I could have counted the number of cars and medium-sized trucks and buses on the narrow street leading into the town. During my childhood and adolescent years, the town folk didn't have the term, "Congested traffic" in their vocabulary. During my childhood, I had the privilege of occasionally visiting the small town with my parents. They'd often spoken of the things and places in Brighton Town – the small hospital in the center of the town, and other places where village folk purchased items they couldn't otherwise obtain. The small hospital was where my little brother Charley was confined until he passed away. My parents had often spoken of the small building in which all of the doctors in town had their office. The doctors who held office in the town, had also maintained their permanent residence there. My parents had often said that, it was a small town with so few people and shops, that everyone knew everyone else by name.

The town my parents had spoken of many years prior, has changed drastically over the years. The small town through which I had passed at the time of my departure from the shore of my homeland, was a far cry from this big city. Its once small shops back then, which my parents said were family-operated businesses, have given way to large buildings, similar to those in my foreign homeland. There're large, modern department stores and boutiques displaying glowing neon lights under a brilliant sunlight. Folk walked aimlessly along the busy street – their eyes peering through store windows at elegantly displayed fancy garments, and shoes to die for.

In light of the over-crowded sidewalks, I immediately recalled the exodus of village folk to towns and cities. I perceived that Brighton Town may have been the destination of many of the folk, who'd flocked the town to entertain a new lifestyle. As I recalled, there hadn't been that many peasants in my home village, or in most other villages I knew. During my time, the villages had a decent number of peasants residing in houses scattered around the countryside. The small number of peasants in my village and in surrounding villages, however, couldn't have contributed to the overwhelming increase in the town's population.

As I traveled in the air-conditioned comfort of the taxi, I began to ask the many questions of where, when, how and why, for which there hadn't been immediate answers.

The congested vehicular traffic had drastically impeded the taxi's progress. The vehicle had been suddenly caught in a stop-and-go situation as it made its way along the congested street. In the midst of the congestion, and a yearning to reach my home, I thought that, if only cars could fly, my home would have been only minutes away. The progress of the taxi had been severely hampered by traffic moving slowly along the crowded street – as if all were adhering to a speed limit of zero miles per hour.

The taxi's progress had been impeded by a constant procession of slow-moving cars, large-sized transport trucks and buses of varying sizes and models. There were too many of everything – coupled with the sounds of aircrafts, landing and taking to the sky, the honking of horns along the crowded street, and pedestrians voices seeking transportation to their various destinations.

The street had become overwhelmed by pedestrians who'd fully developed the technique of skipping in and out of congested traffic. People and vehicular traffic had been vying for the small space, thus adding to more congestion everywhere.

Time had elapsed since the taxi became tied up in the long procession of vehicular traffic. The polite driver had maintained his silence, while his patience was being put to the test. I had become overwhelmed with the congestion that had been delaying the taxi's exit from the town. My tolerance had climaxed to its saturation point when I finally blurted out;

"How could this be? There're too many cars, buses, and even those heavy, wide-bodied trucks vying for the same roadway. And all appear to be in a hurry, but they're going nowhere." The chauffeur turned his head in either direction to check on the status of the traffic. He'd simply ignored my whining. Earlier efforts to move ahead of the traffic was quickly abandoned when all efforts became futile. The chauffeur therefore appeared quite care-free and nonchalant about the whole traffic situation. It had become obvious that he didn't understand the yearning in my heart to arrive home. I didn't explain my situation, and the urgency to reach my village. Nonetheless, my restlessness and agitation should have created a cause for his concern.

As if to give his assurance that I wasn't being ignored, after finally making a head-way in the congested town traffic, the chauffeur said;

"Enjoy your ride, Sir! I know just where you're going." With a great sense of relief, and in anticipation of the journey along the rough, winding road, I positioned myself comfortably on the fine leather seat. I felt that, only moments would unveil my home and the beautiful village I had left behind. As the taxi drove closer to my village, I had become nostalgic. Each minute seemed like an hour as the journey progressed.

It was smooth driving once the taxi escaped the congestion. I continually changed my seating position to have a better view of the places I once knew – incognizant of the fact that my restlessness had been kept under the close scrutiny of the chauffeur.

"Sir, are you in a rush?" he asked. I immediately noticed his enlarged eyes focused in the rear-view mirror of the vehicle.

"Yes. I'm anxious to see my home," I said. "I didn't anticipate the small town I once knew many years prior, to be so overwhelmed with automobiles and people. From where have these people and those numerous automobiles come?" I asked.

"From where haven't these people and automobiles come? This is the modern time. They call it the modern age," the chauffeur said. "Most people need an automobile to commute to town for work and business." He turned his head in both directions to check on the status of the traffic as the vehicle drove along the busy street.

Commute to work? I immediately lapsed into a mode of silence as I pondered the words spoken by the chauffeur. During my time in the village, the only resident who owned a Ford model automobile, drove to town whenever the need arose. He'd often ran errands to Brighton Town to buy the goods and services he couldn't have produced in the village. This resident had no work in the town that would require him to commute on a daily basis. No one else in my village had the means to own an automobile by which he would commute to town for work, or for any other reason.

The few folk of my village, as well as those in the neighboring villages, once relied on the single bus passing on the outskirts of the villages to reach the town. Folk had once commuted to the town where they sold their produce, and purchased commodities they couldn't have produced locally.

In my time, residents who'd abandoned village life, remained in the town to work and adjust to their new way of life. They didn't have the means – transportation or otherwise, to commute on a daily basis.

Who're these people needing automobiles to commute to work in Brighton Town? Before the exodus, work was generally on the farm. There were household duties and responsibilities village folk performed indoor as well as outdoors. Father and my grandfather Grovel, as well as other folk, tilled the soil and raised animals for a village subsistent living. Village folk traveled by the local bus to Brighton Town, whenever they needed certain items they couldn't have produced locally.

The school principal was accommodated in the small cottage built within close proximity to Coopers Villa School. There were other teachers who resided in neighboring houses so they wouldn't have to commute to work, when there were no means of commuting on a regular basis. They also didn't have the means to own an automobile.

During my school days, children whose parents had the means, attended boarding school in the town as there were no means of transportation that would have allowed them to commute on a daily basis.

During their adolescent and early adult years, folk had commenced an exodus to towns in order to escape village life. If the remaining village folk had acquired the means, and had become owners of automobiles, there wouldn't have been that many vehicles to have caused a traffic chaos in the town. Besides, Coopers Village, as well as, other local villages with their small remnant population, couldn't have overwhelmed the town's population and its vehicular traffic.

While I pondered the notion of a congested town and its commuters causing a traffic chaos, the taxi had finally escaped the vicinity of the town. It moved at a considerable speed along the countryside, where familiar places began to unveil in my exploring vision. The remote and quiet countryside, once sparsely populated with small houses, displayed rows of contemporary dwellings. Places I had once known became visible as the vehicle swerved around curves and onto the long winding road that would take me to my village. Like a child anxious to reach the zoo, my head swayed in every direction to get a better view of familiar places. There were places I thought I once knew, but I couldn't be certain, when they were over-grown by tall trees that created miniature forests.

The taxi was advancing at a much faster speed. In anticipation of tight curves and a rough country road, I pulled the seatbelt more snuggly around my body.

Green, red, and yellow foliage came into view and quickly faded in the distance behind as the taxi traveled along the winding country road. The vehicle had been making progress along the country road leading into Coopers Village. My heartbeat had become more pronounced against my chest as I anticipated a joyous arrival in my home village.

As the vehicle advanced, I quickly realized that dusty soil did not rise in the air behind it. Instead, I was greeted by a winding paved road. For a moment, it appeared that I had lapsed into a dream, but my mind had remained as sharp as the owl's. Familiar places continued to appear in my view and quickly gave way to another more familiar place. Scenes of places I once knew, quickly unfolded before disappearing in the distance behind the vehicle. I had been taking in each scene in silence as they passed in my exploring vision. However, I was immediately thrown into a state of emotional turmoil when the sign, "River Sports and Tourist Attractions," came into my view. I thought it was just my imagination, but soon realized that the scene was real.

"What have they done to my village?" I asked the chauffeur. "This small village is no place for tourists. Pardon me, Sir," I cleared my throat, "My name is Jimmy. You'd earlier introduced yourself, but may I ask your name?" The chauffeur slowed the vehicle before he responded.

"Most certainly! Tomas Sanders is my name, but you may call me, Tom," he said.

"Tom, I lived in this village throughout my childhood and adolescent life, but before this, "Modern Age" of which you'd earlier spoken. A strong wind of change has blown over my village, it appears." Tom shook his head – a confirmation of his understanding of my frustrations.

But he appeared quite complacent with the changes and the lifestyle, although he didn't reveal it.

"You're a foreigner, I presume," Tom said, in a polite manner. There hadn't been a doubt that he'd kept my accent under his close scrutiny.

"Yes, Tom," I said, "but this is my homeland. I was born in this village. My home is just a short distance from here. In my heart, this is still my village." Tom nodded, reaffirming his understanding of my detachment from my homeland.

"Entrepreneurs have found ways to lure tourists to the villages," Tom said. "The river bed is used for small boat, short canoe and kayak racing. Big buses like the one just passing on my left, take tourists to the villages for the daily river sports, also to visit the relics of ancient times." Tom continued to provide more of his intriguing details as I listened in discontent.

"Entrepreneurial enterprising: River sports: Ancient relics. I can't imagine the river passing on the edge of Coopers Village being occupied by boats, and canoes, and rafts – according to the signs I had just passed," I said, as Tom sat poised with more gruesome details about my village.

"I routinely organize tours for visitors to see famous places in the villages," Tom said.

Famous places in Coopers Village? I began to imagine the toll years of absence may have taken on my memory of things and places in my village. I didn't have an ounce of recollection of famous places during my time in the village.

"Tom, do you mean that old iron bridge over the river, and the cave into that hillside over-looking the spring in the valley?" I asked, as I waited to refresh my memory of the things and places of long ago.

"That's right," Tom said. "The cave's spring was excavated by entrepreneurs. Pathways were carefully constructed for better access into the cave. Tourists are now able to admire the crystal springs and the natural wonders inside. There are other places of attraction which tourists visit," Tom said. He spoke as one who was delighted to brief me on the changes in Coopers Village and other neighboring places.

"Tom, did you say the cave has been excavated?" I asked. "That cave was once a sacred place hidden from public view. Only the village folk knew of its existence." Tom held his silence, but listened nonetheless to my whining and expressed dissatisfaction with the changes.

Whether he was aware of it, Tom had been playing the role of my tour guide. His details of changes in my village had brought back vivid memory of places and things I once knew, although they weren't the most pleasant.

My faded memory continually lapsed back to the things that were, while Tom continued to entertain my thoughts with things of the present.

"There's nothing about a hole in a hillside for one to travel many miles to see," I said, with added assurance. "There's nothing there to capture one's imagination. That cave in the hillside is a place where the children of the village had once taken pleasure in visiting." Tom shook his head, his conformation of the cave being a place of attraction worth visiting.

"Jimmy, you'll never imagine the sights and sounds in a village that has been practically void of human existence. These are places which adventurers are anxious to visit. These places offer a golden opportunity to visitors, to observe some of the wonders of nature, and wonders of the world," Tom said, as he waited for a likely refutation of his claims.

"Tom, I must admit that the hillside cave was awfully scary, when the village folk listened from its entrance, to water towering beneath the rocks embedded inside." I felt that I may have provided Tom with information he needed in his effort to justify tourists traveling to the villages, particularly to the cave of Coopers Village. At that point, I became somewhat convinced that the hillside cave was a "Must see," and would have ignited one's curiosity. Nonetheless, my village was once a quiet and almost sacred place, where its peasants lived in harmony with the environment. The village has now been over-run by vehicular traffic – transporting visitors, who were charged with curiosity and an exploring mind. Not to ignore the inquisitive folk who've overwhelmed the village, destroying the once sacred and quiet countryside.

Amidst my expressed discontent with the changes in the village, Tom had failed to accept my points of view. It had become the issue of his adopted modern lifestyle, and my views and expectation of life as it once was in the homeland I had left behind.

"Jimmy, the modern world is wide open for everyone to explore the things and places written about in books," Tom said. "Tourists and the natives alike, travel to see many wonders of the world. And what better attraction, and place to see, than the cave's spring?" Tom continued his comments and justification for tourists visiting the village. His comments were meant as a solace to my grieving heart, but it was to the contrary. Nonetheless, while he spoke, I listened to his details with my ears perked up like those of a hunting fox.

"Tom, despite the disturbances in a place once held sacred by the quiet peasants, I'm delighted to know that Coopers Village, and my homeland in general, have made it into the books of the world." Tom nodded, but didn't resonate his thoughts. However, he'd eagerly waited to volunteer further details of things and places visited by tourists, who continually pay visits to my village.

As Tom provided more details of the changes in my village, my thoughts reflected on the elderly peasants I had left behind. They're resting in their graves while the villages are being over-run by tourists, and the prongs of modern technology. My thoughts further reflected on the peasants who're not so elderly, also those who're still young. They too might have become vulnerable to the technological change – as it affects their customary lifestyle.

It appeared Tom had provided convincing details in his justification of tourists visiting my village. He'd remained preoccupied with keeping his eyes on the road, but there hadn't been anyone else to whom I could air my concerns. I therefore continued to covet his audience, as long as he was willing to lend a listening ear, and continue to provide the information I desperately sought.

"Tom, my parents, as well as the elders of their time, would have rather seen things left the way they were," I said, in an interruptive manner.

"Why, Jimmy?" Tom asked. He appeared annoyed at my disapproval of the changes to the village, and the obvious interruption of century-old traditions. Tom had been no doubt, enjoying his life as an entrepreneur who owned a taxi – in addition to organizing tours as a result of the changes.

"The older folk are usually quite set in their ways," I assured Tom. "They're never ready to welcome changes, particularly where modern technology forces them to abandon their traditional way of life. Technology not only forces a change in century-old traditions; it restructures villages – as it has done to my village and its people. I couldn't imagine my grandparents, or my parents, opting for life in a village where the silence has been interrupted by frequent vehicular traffic." I continued to express concerns about the technological changes, and the effects on the lifestyles of the sacred folk. I thought about the village folk who may have involuntarily abandoned their normal way of life, and those who'd readily adopted the technological changes.

The taxi had traveled its distance along the long winding country road. There was a series of appearing and disappearing scenes, as the vehicle made its way closer to my village. I continued to turn and twist restlessly as familiar scenes came into view and quickly disappeared in the distance behind the vehicle. There were obvious signs of Tom's annoyance at my displayed anxiety, but he tried to remain the professional and informative chauffeur he'd portrayed himself to be.

Memories of home began to overwhelm my thought process. My mind reflected on the field where my siblings and I enjoyed days full of pleasures. I thought about the village spring, where the joyful sounds of gleeful children were once heard along the valley.

Sharp curves and quick turns of the vehicle had left me rolling on either side of the seat like one in a drunken stupor. The vehicle had been advancing at a much slower speed, but I was delighted that the slow speed allowed me a better view of places and things along the way. I had vivid memory of places I had once known, but they were shielded from view by the tall trees that formed miniature forests in the vicinity. There were familiar houses I couldn't see for the overgrown trees. It was anyone's guess whether they were still standing on their foundation. There were houses I thought I recognized, but I couldn't be certain as they appeared strikingly smaller than when I knew them. Whether other houses were still standing, I couldn't tell for the forests that obscured my view of the entire surrounding.

Whereas in times past, the folk had often walked long distances to reach their destination, there wasn't a pedestrian seen along the road leading into Coopers Village. Had I passed village folk along the way, I certainly wouldn't have identified them – particularly the younger folk.

As the taxi drove along the narrow road, Tom had reverted to precision driving to avoid veering into the path of automobiles that had been frequently zipping by on his left. There hadn't been a doubt that lifestyles had changed drastically in my village, and I presumed everywhere else in my homeland. I perceived that the village folk had adopted the lifestyle of traveling to Brighton Town, and across villages by way of automobiles, as opposed to the unimaginable journeys they'd once traveled by foot.

The vehicle made a sharp turn around a bend, and a familiar scene came into view. In a most exhilarating voice, I shouted; "This is Boton Hill!" The vehicle screeched to a halt. Its tires had no doubt, made their marks over the semi-rough paved road. What have I done to Tom? I asked myself. Is he in some dire straits?

"Is this the place? Are you home?" Tom asked, as he turned his head frantically to the left, and to the right. But there wasn't a house, or any form of structure to suggest that I had arrived home. While everything else had drastically changed, the passing years didn't take their toll on the hill that stood beside the road on the way to my home. There hadn't been a doubt in my mind that it was Boton Hill.

"We're not there yet. But once I see Boton Hill, it will be just a few more bends before I see my home on the hill." Tom remained silent as he gradually accelerated the vehicle. I quickly shuffled myself to the edge of my seat so I had a better view of familiar places on either side of the road. I couldn't afford a single wink in case I missed an astonishing scene.

The taxi had bent a few more curves when another familiar and overwhelming scene caught my attention. On impulse, I quickly shifted to my right, and toward the edge of my seat.

"Hold it!" I yelled. The vehicle screeched to a stop. I noticed Tom's enlarged eyes as they peered through the rear-view mirror of the taxi.

"Have I passed your home, Jimmy? Are we there now?" Tom asked. I managed to regain a measure of composure before my voice echoed through the open window.

"No! We're not there yet," I said, "but a Six-Mile post once stood where that modern house stands on your right – just in front of that sculptured wall. That sign post signaled that I was half a mile from my home, and six miles from Brighton Town. That sign post is no longer there. And that modern house standing half-way up the hill is not the type of houses the village folk build. I can't imagine the post being up-rooted to build a decorated wall. There ought to be government legislations in force that would prevent the removal of items such as, century-old legitimate signposts. That post was originally planted by a government body – long before my grandfather Grovel came into existence." Tom listened while giving his due respects to my discontent. My childish behaviour was by then, on full display.

"Jimmy, I can see that you've been absent from this village for a long time," Tom said. "There have been many changes, not only in this village, but everywhere else – including the changes you've seen in the town."

Tom's comments had gradually opened the eyes of my understanding of the fact that, my homeland had undergone technological and cultural changes. In Tom's words, "This is the new age." Evidence of change could be seen in the town and along the way leading to my village, and as Tom had said, everywhere else. Nonetheless, I continued to express my greatest dismay as I recalled the things and places that once were, but were no more. Those were things and places that had once played an important role during my childhood years.

The Six-Mile post was once a significant landmark of Coopers Village. To the village folk who'd walked certain distances to get to other villages, the sight of the Six-Mile post brought relief that they were soon to reach their destination. For the folk who had to walk long distances on their way from Brighton Town, the Six-Mile post was a signal that, another mile or so, they would be home.

To folk on their way to the Stone Church on the Hill, the Six-Mile post signaled that they had a mile or less to walk. To the general traveler, the knowledge of being so close to home offered some solace to their tired and aching feet. Children on their way to Coopers Villa School, knew that they had only another mile to walk when the Six-Mile post came into view. To the long-distance travelers, seeing the Six-Mile post meant that the Red Top tree was only a few bends ahead. They were sure to stop for a rest on my grandfather's wooden bench beneath the tree before continuing on to their destination.

As the taxi advanced closer toward my home, I began to develop a phobia of facing what lay ahead. A short distance from the place where the Six-Mile post once stood, another unpleasant scene unfolded. The village creek – the place that had once brought excitement to all children, lay in a state of decay and abandonment. That was a rather despicable state of a creek so close to my home. As the creek came into full view, I immediately lapsed into a state of deep despair.

"Tom," I said, as I tried desperately to hold back the tears flooding my eyes, "that creek on your right had once sparkled with crystal clear water. Children of the village once had their thrill, tossing bread crumbs into the creek and watching the tiny fish engage in a feeding frenzy. The small stones and pebbles that had once lined the bottom of the creek were always washed clean, particularly after a heavy downpour of summer rain. The colorful stones and pebbles were once collectible items of the children."

Tom was certainly no stranger to the village, or to its contaminated creek. By his own admission, he'd frequently organized tours to its amazing landmarks. I therefore continued to express discontent with the state of the village creek.

"Tom, that creek has been choked by plastic containers and milk carton boxes. I can also see the blue, yellow and white plastic bags along the sides of the creek."

Tom listened in silence while he kept his eyes on the narrow roadway for oncoming traffic. Nonetheless, I continued to covet his attention as I expressed my dissatisfaction with the appearance of the contaminated creek.

"Tom, during my time in this village, only town folk had to do with milk cartons and drinks bottles of many varieties, colors and sizes. My father had often told his household about street-side garbage bins, and large trash containers in Brighton Town. Big containers were placed in areas where town folk tossed their discarded wastes. The town's containers collected the discards of empty cans, boxes and bottles – big and small, and the volumes of trash produced by town folk." While I spoke, Tom had been closely scrutinizing the contaminated creek, but he'd failed to resonate his thoughts. "Tom, in my time, village folk didn't have anything instant. Nor did they have a million and one varieties of drinks in bottles to choke the creek with the discarded empties. There's no doubt that village folk have adopted a lifestyle of consuming products sold in containers. As evident everywhere, the discarded empty containers have choked the village creek." Tom nodded in agreement that the creek had been, in fact, contaminated.

"I fully understand your point of view, Jimmy. In these modern times, the village folk eat on the go. They consume ready-to-eat products, prepared and placed in disposable packages. Their empties and discards, if not properly disposed of, will end up in unacceptable places," Tom said. His reasoning had been well taken, but discarded empty cans, bottles and boxes by the sides of a village creek, was certainly not acceptable – although Tom may not have been directly responsible for such discards.

During my time at home, the folk never tossed their milk bottles in the creek, or along the roadway. The empty bottles were needed to store the next morning's freshly boiled milk from the cows, and from the milking goats. My parents had nothing to throw away – nothing that would have turned the village into a dumpster. Village folk who hadn't been able to raise animals, saved their milk bottles for the fresh milk they bought from local farmers, including my parents – if they had a surplus to sell. An empty bottle therefore was once a valued possession of village folk. Whenever a bottle broke, it was promptly replaced in the town, at a price that left a lighter weight on the pocket of the one who had to pay.

And while I remained in a state of utter despair, pondering the contaminated state of the creek, I began to imagine the state of other places in the village. The taxi had been gradually advancing closer to my home while Tom kept his eyes on the road, and his ears on constant alert for more of my unexpected and unpleasant surprises. Meanwhile, he'd remained attentive to my expressed discontent with the state of things, and had shown empathy where warranted.

The taxi approached the bridge over the village creek. I knew my home stood on the crest of the hill, just around the bend. With a cheerful heart, I kept my focus on the left side of the road as I waited to once more see the home I had left behind more than fifty years prior.

Chapter 9

Home at Last

It was my most ecstatic moment when the taxi drove over the old stone bridge and had bent the final curve. I breathed a sigh of relief at the realization that, in a few seconds, I would finally see my home after many years of absence.

My restlessness had prompted Tom to drive the vehicle at a much slower speed along the road. But he would certainly not be overwhelmed by my sudden reaction to scenes that may emerge. As the vehicle drove around the final bend, I waited in great anticipation of beholding the Red Top tree in its radiant bloom – with its branches spread over the gate. I had become overwhelmed when I blurted out with glee;

"Tom, this is it! I'm finally home." Amidst my expressed jubilation, Tom kept his eyes on the roadway while he waited to see my home in the vicinity. But my excitement had suddenly turned to despair. There wasn't a Red Top tree overhanging a solid wooden gate. Tall unfamiliar trees, branched out in every direction, making the vicinity more difficult to identify. I was therefore uncertain whether the vehicle had stopped at the right gate.

In a desperate effort to find my home, I identified parts of the dead trunk of the Red Top tree, strewn across the gateway. I knew it was the tree when I further identified two wooden posts standing at each side of the fallen tree trunk. The posts clearly marked the place that was once the entrance to my home on the crest of the hill. I further noticed Grandfather Grovel's wooden bench strewn around the trunk of the crumbled Red Top tree. In utter dismay, I yelled to Tom;

"Stop please. Stop! This is the place," I said, as tears flooded my eyes.

The vehicle came to a stop beside the tree trunk, lying across the entrance to my home on the crest of the hill. Tom had been suddenly stricken with silence – a state of silence that had spoken volumes. I felt alone, amidst my enthusiasm of finally returning home and not seeing a house resting on the crest of the hill. Tom turned his head in every direction to see a reason for my excitement.

"Tom, I'm finally home," I shouted, but not with much zest in my voice. I promptly opened the door of the vehicle and stepped out – breathing in the fresh air while I set my feet once more in the soil of home.

Tom exited the taxi, and with his surveying eyes, looked around the vicinity of the place I had claimed as my home. But he'd permitted me to reacquaint with the place I had once called home, and had been so excited to see.

I began to turn in every direction, as I reacquainted my eyes and ears with the sights and sounds of the place I had once called home. But there hadn't been much that I could see for the tall trees that formed a forest in my immediate view. I immediately anticipated Tom's barrage of questions for which I certainly wouldn't have found answers.

"Jimmy," Tom said, his head turning in every direction, "did you say this is your home?" His eyes surveyed the vicinity for the home I had been so excited to see. From my vantage point, there wasn't a structure that one could call a home.

I struggled to maintain a measure of composure, while breathing in the fresh air of home.

I was fully aware that Tom had held everything under his close scrutiny. Had he an ounce of patience remaining, it was certainly wearing thin.

I inspected the ruins of the once beautiful wooden gate Grandfather Grovel had built. Its decayed structure lay strewn around the entrance of the gateway, and beneath the fallen tree trunk. Years had ravaged what was once a beautiful setting of the entrance to my home on the hill.

"Tom!" I blurted in despair as I tried to restrain the tears flowing from my eyes. "This tree trunk is what remains of the tree the village folk had once adored. The tree that had once stood here was a landmark. It was always laden with brilliant red flowers from which it got its name, the Red Top tree. The beautiful wooden bench my grandfather had built around the trunk of the Red Top tree, also lay in rubble."

In my heart I felt that a fallen red top tree wasn't of interest to Tom. He saw an old and dilapidated gate, a crumbled wooden bench, and a fallen tree trunk strewn around the vicinity. There hadn't been items of beauty that anyone would have an interest in regarding the vicinity. There hadn't been landmarks that would appeal to Tom's tourists.

"Tom," I went on with my elaborated details, "this tree used to be laden with brilliant red flowers. Passers-by habitually stopped to rest in the cool shade its wide branches provided. They were thrilled to observe the black shiny bugs that seemed to find a sanctuary among the flower petals." I continued to express my grief at the loss of the place that was once a landmark. However, I quickly realized that Tom had no deep-rooted feeling of attachment to my ravaged home. Nor did he hold sentiments to a red top tree, and a wooden bench.

In a state of grief, I looked at the hollow posts standing at the entrance of the gate. They were parts of the remaining evidence that a structure had once stood there. Having no one else to whom I could express my grief, I had sought solace by further expressing my concerns to Tom.

"Tom! Under the Red Top tree, there was once a wooden gate guarding the entrance to my home on the top of this hill. The gate is no longer here, as you can see. Only these hollow posts remain as a reminder that a gate once stood here." Tom had maintained his silence while leaning against his vehicle.

I walked toward the place where the gate once stood and leaned against one of the rotted hollow posts. It was the post where, as a child, I had leaned and waited to get a first glimpse of my mother, or Father returning from Brighton Town. At the appearance of my parents, my siblings and I had always waited in anticipation of receiving delicious candy treats.

Amidst much dismay and overwhelming sadness, I commenced surveying the vicinity. My mind had become inundated with more thoughts than uttered words. Tom had been leaning against his vehicle while he guarded my luggage he'd placed beside the gateway. I had no doubt that there were deep thoughts he didn't express. Tom had been finally overcome by his greatest anxiety when he commenced resonating his thoughts.

"Jimmy," he said, with a measure of hesitancy. "For the many years I've traveled through this village, I have never seen a Red Top tree, or a house on the crest of this hill. It appears you've been absent from home for quite some time." I nodded in admission of his keen observations and assumption.

"Tom," I said, "this place was once my home. I grew up in a modest country house that once stood on the top of this hill. As you can see, there's nothing remaining but tall trees and thick bush. It has been more than fifty years since I left my village." I had become grief-stricken as I reflected on my childhood home.

"I fully understand your grief, Jimmy," Tom said. Tom had promptly reverted to silence while I stood to lament the loss of my home.

While Tom waited in silence, leaning against his taxi, I had slowly regained a measure of composure, and soon realized that, time for him was a valuable asset. As I poured out my grief, I thought about the town, and other folk who required his essential service. I therefore quickly opened my attaché case and paid my fare. I further handed him a decent tip. Tom nodded his thanks and quickly re-entered his taxi.

"It's been my pleasure traveling with you, Tom. I certainly appreciate your most elaborate details on the status of my village," I said as he sat poised to wave his goodbye.

"Jimmy, enjoy your visit with Uncle Harry! It's been my pleasure driving you home," he said, as the vehicle rolled along the road, on its way back to Brighton Town.

Moments of grief and solitude had suddenly gripped my heart as the taxi disappeared from view. I stood alone beside the dilapidated gate to face my dilemma. After my years of absence, I had returned and found no yellow ribbon that welcomed me home. There hadn't been family and friends who ran out to greet me with wide open arms and kisses – as they'd gathered to bid their goodbyes at the time of my departure. Memories of my parents and grandparents, my siblings, the neighboring children with whom I had once played in the wide yard of home, began to crowd my mind. Fancy, the family's friendly dog, would have been the first out to greet me with frolicking jumps and a wagging tail.

With a heart stricken by grief, and a feeling of solitude, I stood beside the dilapidated gate and looked at the crumbled wooden bench strewn beneath the trunk of the rotted Red Top tree. I stood alone in the place where I had once felt the joys of growing up – surrounded by family and friends. My home that was once exuberant with sounds of chirping birds, playing children, and the gleeful spirit of all its inhabitants, remained as rubble.

Tom had long left the scene. I set my gaze toward the crest of the hill and beheld the place where my home once stood. Knowing that a house no longer stood on the hill, the silence had become instantaneously unbearable. My modest childhood home on the hill had never been a quiet place. The hill that had once bustled with the day-to-day activities of my household, stood crowned with tall trees and shrubs. It stood void of the rainbow of radiant flowers that once adorned its crown. There hadn't been a structure, or form of a house visible in the vicinity. Tall trees had transformed the hill, making it appear as a miniature forest.

I held my face toward the crest of the hill, pondering whether I should venture up to its crest, or call it a day. While I charted out my next action, I suddenly recalled the old photograph of my home, taken by my uncle Brayson. He'd purchased a strange box in Brighton Town, and had brought it to my parents' home. He said the box was actually called a camera. Uncle Brayson had carefully concealed the box beneath large sheets of paper. I remember him saying; "Everyone look this way." He first positioned my mother and my father, then my grandparents, in front of the house before pressing a button on the camera. My siblings and I had become fearful of what might transpire. Nonetheless, we stood cautiously in front of the box, as my uncle had instructed. After the entire family had carefully posed in front of the camera, a series of clicking sounds were heard as my uncle pressed a certain button.

My uncle had subsequently taken the box to Brighton Town. Days later, he returned with pictures he said were taken by the camera. My father had been fascinated to see a picture of himself and his wife on paper. He'd become even more fascinated when he saw the picture of his house. Grandfather Grovel and my grandmother, Eavie, were mesmerized when my uncle presented them with a picture of themselves. At the sight of their picture on paper, my grandparents said that, the longer they lived, the more they learned about the world in which they had been living. Just before Father passed away, he'd given me the picture of the entire family standing in front of the house. I had taken the picture from the Chest and held it as my keep-sake.

I promptly reached for my wallet and pulled out the old photograph. I felt strongly that it would enhance my imagination as I faced the gruelling task of putting together the pieces of my home, which lay in rubble on the crest of the hill.

With the picture firmly clenched between my fingers, I entered the property through the rocky entrance where the gate once stood. My imagination had been quickly put to the task of retracing the path up the rugged hillside. The narrow road Grandfather Grovel had made leading to his house on the hill, had been sadly reclaimed by protruding rocks, stubborn shrubs and the roots of tall trees. The rough and rugged path had left me no surface on which to roll my luggage. I was therefore forced to carry it up the hillside.

Each step I took toward the crest of the hill, there was a sense of desertion and abandonment. It was my perception that everyone had vanished, leaving the place to dilapidation and decay. With my luggage carefully placed on my shoulder, I painstakingly walked to the crest of the hill. I carefully placed my luggage on a rock, while I stood firmly to inspect the rubble in the vicinity. My home could only be perceived through the eyes of my imagination and with the aid of the picture I held firmly in my hand.

I inspected the ruins of the house that was once the masterpiece, and the prized possession of my grandfather, Grovel and my father,

John. It was the place that had brought childhood pleasures and much meaning to my early existence. My home that had once proudly stood on the crest of the hill, lay ravaged like an abandoned and crumbled crab's shell. I perceived the end of an era, where life had abruptly ended for a people who'd once had a lively existence on the crest of the hill.

I soon came to grips with the reality that, my desperate attempt to reattach my body, mind and soul to my childhood and adolescence home, was not attainable. In my mind's eye, and from the photograph of my home, I saw the beautiful home that had once stood on the hill, but in reality, the house no longer existed. Only the still-photograph I held in my hand, and the remnants strewn around the vicinity, remained as a testament to my parents' and my grandparents' house – the place I had once called home.

I stood under the heat of the crisp evening sun; perspiration pouring profusely from my brow. There wasn't the sight or sound of another human in the vicinity. If there were birds sheltering among the branches of the surrounding trees, they didn't make their presence known by their usual chirps. If the birds chirped in the vicinity, there wasn't an audience to admire their melodious sounds.

The soft breeze continually fanned my wet and saggy cheeks. As I stood to inspect the ruins of my home, I reminisced on the joyful days when my siblings and I played in the open field. I reminisced on the days when I had taken frequent strolls through the beautiful grassy field with my siblings, and Fancy the playful dog. While I reminisced on my fun-filled days in the wide field of home, I could almost hear children's joyful voices in the field – now overgrown by tall trees and shrubs.

I reflected on the days of fun and games in the cleanly swept yard. My parents as well as my joyful grandparents, sat on the porch, where they were being fanned by the gently soothing breeze. They'd always happily cheered the children while they had their time of fun. I stood on top of the rubble to reminisce on the exhilarating days of my childhood, and the home that had brought joy and happiness to those within its walls. As I inspected the rubble strewn around the vicinity, I could almost hear the whisper of the gentle breeze saying, "There's no one home."

I had commenced the tedious task of inspecting the ruins of my home, while reminiscing on my days at the place that no longer existed. Only fragments of concrete, board and metal sheets remained to mark the place where the house had once stood. Most of its structure lay buried in the rubble beneath thick shrubs and the roots of tall trees.

New tears flooded my eyes as I gazed at the rubble of my crumbled home. I sadly reflected on the many pastime pleasures that were once featured within the walls of my family sanctuary.

With a heavy heart, I walked toward the crumbled foundation of my home. I placed my feet at the very spot where the porch had once stood. The porch – the place where the family's evening pleasures were once enjoyed, lay crumbled, with not a stone standing on another. I inspected the rusted rails of the porch as they lay strewn beneath tall shrubs and tangled withes. The venue for most household entertainment was on the very porch that lay crumbled beneath my feet.

My thoughts immediately reflected on the joyful moments the household had in the clear moonlight. Everyone gathered around my father while he took his favourite place on the bench placed in the center of the porch. My favourite spot was on the floor, beneath the brass lantern suspended by a brass chain attached to the ceiling. Everyone listened to Father as he reeled out miles of fables and fascinating stories. There were shrieks and laughter when he told the funniest stories. The older folk were just as amused and thrilled as the children, when Father sat on the porch to tell his stories and tall tales.

From the porch of my home, school songs and riddles, as well as fascinating stories, had often rung out across the clear moon-lit village. Songs sung by my siblings and I, had become moonlight serenades that entertained the neighboring folk.

There were series of never-ending rounds of songs – the girls sang soprano, while the boys carried the alto. The boys often took pleasure in blending their voices with the girls to sing soprano. Whatever was the chord, children's voices echoed in harmony across the moon-lit village. To the listening audience, singing under the early night sky had become live entertainment. This was the epitome of home and family life during my youth, and on the very porch that remained only as a memory.

Adjacent to the crumbled porch, I identified the very spot where the large family hall had once stood. I had quickly recalled the big door and the long hide strap Mother had always kept hanging on a nail. The hall was the place where my siblings and I had often gathered under the glow of the oil lamp resting on a table. The thick hardwood floor had often squeaked and crunched beneath the feet of anyone who'd dared to put too much weight on particular areas.

My thoughts reflected on the brightly painted white walls with not a single picture, or object suspending from them. The beautiful vase, stacked with the most brilliant flowers freshly cut from the garden, was sufficient to beautify the hall. I was quickly reminded of the cheerfulness, and that comforting feeling of home; particularly while the entire household gathered around the table in the hall for a time of fun and games.

As each night appeared, there was a sense of security, while my siblings and I remained locked indoor. I began to reminisce on the many riddles that had become the dominant entertainment of the night. At the chant of, "Riddle me this. Riddle me that. Guess me this riddle, and perhaps not," it was a signal to everyone that another riddle was forthcoming. The sibling with the most exciting riddle, was given the opportunity to speak first. After all guesses were verbally entered, each riddle was expounded only by the one who'd posed it. In the end, there were no correct interpretation of the riddles posed. Riddles went from the simple to the complex, and gradually became absurd. At that point, it was time to switch to a new item on the night's agenda.

My mind had become deluged with unfading memories of the home that remained in rubble on the ground beneath my feet. Though often times there'd been sadness, it was outweighed by the cheerfulness my heart had once felt. I was immediately dazed as I reminisced on my past pleasures in the place that had once offered a joyous existence. However, I was compelled to bid a sorrowful fare-well to my home as it lay buried beneath my feet.

I planted my feet on the crest of the hill, at the very spot where the family sanctuary once stood. There was nothing spectacular about the scenes in my immediate view, and beyond. There were relics, artefacts and what were considered family heirloom, broken and strewn across a wide area: a copper urn in which the family had once stored water from the valley spring: Chinaware Mother had stacked in her large cabinet: The Father Christmas vase placed on the table in the big hall. It was the brilliant bright red and ivory vase Mother had purchased in Brighton Town. I had vivid memory of the stout male figure with round, red cheeks. It had always borne a cheerful smile that caught the eyes of anyone who entered the house.

Whatever made it happy, all year round, the smiling figure remained in the big hall – bearing freshly cut flowers from the rose garden. At Christmas time, the vase was always stacked with bright yellow miniature sunflowers, which bloomed only during the Christmas season – as if to add cheerfulness to the heart of everyone during the festive season.

The household truly perceived the Father Christmas vase as a symbol of good luck; particularly when it was placed in the hall during the Christmas season – hence the vase got its name; "Father Christmas."

Besides adding cheerfulness to the Christmas season, the vase was regarded with much superstition. It was the family's strong belief that, if the vase was present in the home, it would bring good luck to those within. Hence, all year round, and particularly at Christmas time, my home was toasted with the presence of the Father Christmas vase, placed on the table in the center of the hall. No one had ever gotten lucky as a result of having the vase, but everyone had remained hopeful that good luck would have come some day. The hope of good luck had faded as the Father Christmas vase lay crumbled beside the porch. Until the vase lay crumbled in the rubble of my home, no one had made claims to good luck. No one had ever attested to any form of luck attributed to the presence of the vase in the home – so much for my family's false hope and a superstitious belief in the Father Christmas vase.

The chinaware, once the family's prized possession, were strewn around in broken pieces beneath the crumbled walls of the house. My mother had bought the chinaware in Brighton Town. Each trip to the town aroused her insatiable appetite for chinaware, and each trip added a set or two to her growing collection. Mother had always said that, each of her offspring would have a set of chinaware – once they're married and establish their own home. As a result, my siblings and I watched with keen interest, the chinaware stacked in a cabinet in one corner of the hall. Upon Mother's arrival from the town, she'd always brought additional china sets. My siblings and I scrutinized the new additions, and kept a keen eye on the new sets. As I inspected the broken chinaware strewn around the vicinity, I saw my Mother's hope for her offspring's home adorned with adorable chinaware, buried beneath the rubble.

Just steps from the crumbled family hall, I saw the spot where the kitchen had once stood. The partitioned kitchen, once attached to the rear of the conjoined houses, was only identifiable by its concrete foundation, and the corrugated wood-burning iron stoves resting on its crumbled pavement.

The kitchen was once the most sacred place in my home. It was the place where the household sat to enjoy Mother's hearty meals she'd prepared. Mother had regarded her most appetizing meals as a way of getting to the heart of those who consumed whatever she'd so consciously prepared. The crumbled kitchen brought back memories of the close attachment the family had to its small space, but great comfort.

There'd been pitch black nights when my siblings and I sat to read novels under the lantern suspended from the ceiling of the kitchen. The family had always been quite leery of unseen forces on the outside, particularly when the night was dark. As a result, many night-time activities were confined to the kitchen.

Tears flowed profusely down my cheeks as I stood beneath the glowing evening sun to inspect the ruins of my home – the place that had once been a fountain of life. It's the place that held unfading memories of a once vibrant family existence. In my exploring vision, my home lay as rusted sheets of metal scattered among crumbled concrete blocks and rotted wood.

Although both Grandfather Grovel's and my father's houses were built within many years of each other, both had suffered similar consequences – lying crumbled on their foundation. The houses lay crumbled with not a stone standing on the other. The porch where tall tales and fables once toasted the night sky, remained as crumbled concrete and pieces of metal rails. The kitchen where the family had once gathered for a common cause – to eat and maintain a sense of togetherness, lay only as a memory beneath piles of rubble.

The sun had been making its way toward the western horizon, but there was sufficient daylight time remaining to further inspect the vicinity. I therefore remained on the crest of the hill to reminisce on what was once my home, and the life I had enjoyed within its walls. Each relic strewn among the rubble, brought back memories of a once joyous existence. My village, once exuberant with the sounds of life of every living creature, stood silent and solitary after the departure of those who'd once made it their sanctuary.

Opposite the trunk of the fallen cedar tree, I saw the concrete foundation, and the rusted wires from the large meshed coop where the chickens once slept during the night. It was a regimented rule of my father that, both boys and girls were responsible for locking the chickens in the coop overnight. By locking the chickens in the coop, they would be safe from night predators. Those crafty rodents – oversized rats and wild cats, had often played havoc on the coop, making desperate attempts to snatch the young chicks while their mothers slept. It was often the girls' evening chores to collect the eggs and ensure that there was sufficient food for the chickens at the appearance of dusk. The girls made certain that the little creatures had their fill before they were locked into the coop. I reflected on the security the coop had once given to the active creatures that had made it their night sanctuary.

I had spent a considerable length of time surveying the rubble and grieving the loss of my home, and reminiscing on my past pleasures within its walls.

Evening clouds began to move briskly across the sky, expelling the golden glow of the sun. I watched the dark-grey, silver-lined cloud shielding the sun as it descended in the western horizon. Dusk had quickly moved in and shrouded the village. Darkness had begun to obscure my view, thus making it difficult to survey the remaining ruins.

It had been customary for the village folk to build their houses in approximate distance of each other – many on hillsides, and on the crest of low hills. The houses were accessible by a network of gravel roads and winding tracks criss-crossing valleys and hillsides. Some folk vying for the best view the village offered, built their houses on the crest of low hills, where they had a better view of the countryside. Folk who'd built their houses on the low-lands, saw the hilltop folk as being at the look-out-posts, where they had a first view of ensuing and ominous events – storms lurking over the horizons, or seasonable rainfalls that resulted in hillside avalanche.

Under the night sky, the houses could be spotted when the moon casts its glow on their shiny metal rooftops. On dark nights, however, the houses were identifiable by the glow of oil lamps visible through crevices of their wooden windows. On special nights, gas lanterns were often hung from the branches of trees, from which point they cast their beams across the entire frontage of the houses, thus making them more visible from a distance.

I stood and gazed in the distant places to see the houses whose lights had once beamed under the night sky, but from my vantage point, there were no houses visible. Had there been houses in the vicinity, they were most likely obscured by tall trees. However, under the night sky, the flame from their lantern would have revealed their location. As my eyes scoured the vicinity, I had quickly concluded that there were no houses. There was a sense of vanishment of, not only village houses, but an entire civilization.

The stars which had faded and vanished at the appearance of the dawn, began to peep from their usual spot in the universe. Bright stars began to appear, gradually brightening the early night sky. Whether the moon had been on its upward journey from the eastern horizon, I couldn't tell. I had no chart, or a calendar that showed the whereabouts of the moon in the universe from my vantage point. As I stood alone under the early dusk, my thoughts had become flooded with memories of the things that once were, but had simply vanished.

I walked a short distance from the spot where my home once stood, and placed my feet in the center of what was once the wide grassy yard. The yard, once carpeted by neatly groomed grass, could scarcely be identified for the thick shrubs and tall trees that re-occupied the area. I began to reminisce on the children's playground that had been reclaimed by the roots of tall trees, thick shrubs and protruding rocks. I stood at the very spot where, on pitch black nights, and under the watchful eye of my parents, I with my siblings, gazed into the galaxy to seek out constellations of the brightest stars. Whenever the moon was absent, the sky was lit by a myriad of bright twinkling stars.

Particularly on pitch black nights, and under a cloudless sky, my brother Larry had always been certain that he'd seen the stars of the Milky Way – the stars that were mentioned in the novels he'd borrowed from Coopers Villa library. Without a long-distance viewing device, it was unlikely that the stars of the Milky Way, and other known far-away groups of stars were visible to the naked eye. My brother Larry, nonetheless, was quite certain he'd seen such stars. Although on dark nights, my siblings and I attempted to count the numerous bright stars visible to the naked eye, we had no interest in their names. Our main interest was to be entertained by the spectacular view of numerous stars in the night sky, when the moon was absent.

There'd been dark nights when I joined my siblings on the porch to see stars darting across the sky. Fable had it that, whenever shooting stars dart across the night sky, this was ominous of the passing of someone in a village family. While this myth remained among the folk, there hadn't been a proven correlation between a shooting star and the passing of someone in a village household.

Darkness had swiftly blanketed the village, but I remained in still quietness to reminisce on my past existence at a place that stood bare and solitary.

I stood in awe and silence beneath the early night sky. I had tried to gaze in the distance, in whatever distance I could have seen, but I quickly realized that my view had been obscured by tall trees that replanted their root, even at the very spot where my home once stood.

The darkness had swiftly obscured my view of the vicinity, thus halting further survey of the ruins of my home. I reluctantly made my way toward the gate, lifting my luggage down the hillside. My heavy heart throbbed from disappointed hopes and expectations. I had returned to my childhood home I had left behind many years prior, only to find it buried in the rubble of years of abandonment. Its once joyful inhabitants had long left, leaving the structure, and a once joyous lifestyle to decadence and ruin. Amidst stumbles and falls, I stepped back onto the quiet road and commenced my short journey to Uncle Harry's house.

Chapter 10

Uncle Harry

From his house, just on the side of the adjoining hill, Uncle Harry had been anxiously awaiting my arrival. I had promised to arrive at his home before sunset, but the dusk had long settled over the village. What would he be thinking? Without a portable phone, I couldn't have confirmed my arrival on the soil of my homeland. It was my intent to walk on the soil of my home before seeing my uncle, hence, my tardy arrival at his house.

During the days of my childhood, visitors had often showed up unexpectedly. Whenever Grandfather and Grandmother Goodwin came to visit my parents, there were no fore-warnings. With no long-distance communication device, my grandparents had no way of alerting my parents of their intended visits. Likewise, when my parents traveled across the miles to Grandfather Goodwin's estates, they'd simply appeared at the gate, unannounced. Visitors' unexpected appearances had always brought pleasant surprises and good cheers to households.

I walked along the quiet road, carefully tugging my luggage – at times, rolling it on the semi-smooth surface. My eyes had been curiously surveying the immediate vicinity for whatever the darkness would have permitted in my exploring vision.

There hadn't been a sound, except the squeaks and cries of the small creatures resting in their night sanctuary. I had readily identified the squeaking sounds of the crickets. Though rarely ever seen, the tiny creatures' loud squeaks were always heard during the night hours. Their squeaking cries immediately brought back a feeling of being in the atmosphere of home.

Across the hill, opposite Uncle Harry's, I noticed another modern house displaying its brilliant lights. To my dismay, the Gainers' house that had once stood at that particular spot, was no longer there. In its place stood a contemporary house, whose structure appeared taller than any I had seen erected in Coopers Village. A reflection of blue flickering light, beamed continuously through the wide glass windows of the house. I could only conclude that the lights emanated from a television set within its walls.

As far as my ears could have picked up sounds, there were no children heard in the vicinity. Where are the children? I asked myself. The pre-dusk hours in Coopers Village, and other villages, had always teemed with the joyful sounds of playing children. But the pre-dusk lay quiet, except for the sounds of small creatures searching for a place to sleep. Whether there were children inside the house across from Uncle Harry's, I couldn't tell. If there were children inside, I could imagine them wading in the blue light of the television screen – interpreting the thousand and one words each picture painted.

Under the evening sky, the sounds of playing children were once heard all across the village. However, it had been one of the golden rules of the village households that, all children be indoor as soon as the dusk fell – except on moon-lit nights when the curfew was lifted to allow them an extra hour of play. After a shower of rain, and whenever there was no moon, the early dusk had become black. The darkness had always put a damper on the cheerful spirit of the playing children. At that point, their outdoor activities had promptly ceased as they sought refuge indoor to commence their night-time pleasures. A general fear of the unseen had further forced an early retreat indoor.

I gazed at the blue light beaming through the window of the house and felt that, the night air had been void of the sounds of children in the vicinity, as they may have been confined to the television set. I remember the little radio my father had bought in Brighton Town. It was a metal device encased in solid hard-board casing. The radio was powered by four "D" batteries. During those days, a radio was the only contact the village folk had with the airwaves. It was audible within the walls of the house, as well as without, for those who wished to be entertained by pleasant music, while they were engaged in outdoor activities. There were no pictures to captivate the children's attention, or confine them to a screen to spend countless hours indoor – staring at moving pictures beaming across a screen.

It was once a family tradition, when the household gathered around the radio after dusk. There were episodes of real-life situations, and pleasant music that provided sound family entertainment. On certain days, the most beautiful classical music and songs were transmitted through the radio from neighboring countries. As sound evening entertainment, my household spent the early hours of the night listening to the most entertaining music. It was the household's strong belief that Eunice, my eldest sibling would have someday, become a singing star. But, as she approached her early adult years, she'd gradually abandoned her hobby of singing the songs she'd heard over the radio.

The household's listening pleasure had always come to an end when the batteries died. At that point, the radio sat useless – until Father made it into Brighton Town to replace the depleted batteries.

With a heavy heart, I continued my slow strides under the dusk toward Uncle Harry's house.

Immediately around the bend, just a few steps from the road, Uncle's house came into view. Surprisingly, the structure had shed its antiquities. My uncle's house stood quite modern, and equipped with glaring light bulbs, which cast their bright beams around the vicinity.

I had tried to regain a measure of composure before meeting my uncle, and had therefore deliberately delayed my strides. It wasn't long before I had walked up a few steps and placed my luggage on the wide concrete landing. Moments had elapsed before I had finally built up the courage to tap softly on the door. I had waited a few moments under the glowing light bulb when the door swung open. A tall grey-haired gentleman appeared – the pupils of his eyes dilating as he stood speechless. There wasn't a doubt in my mind that he was Uncle Harry, the man I hadn't seen in many years. He'd still maintained his height and stature, but had lost that once muscular physique. My uncle hadn't lost his radiant smile, which was partly hidden beneath thick grey facial hair.

Uncle Harry stood speechless while he stared into the still night air – as if he'd been pondering what to do next. I took another close look beneath his thick facial hair and had the reassurance that the tall figure standing in the doorway was my uncle Harry. Beneath his thick facial hair, I could see his handsome features and the youthfulness of yester-years. The man who'd once boasted a fountain of youth, stood frail and solitary.

I had promptly brought an end to his moment of suspense and doubt, when I commenced my greeting;

"Hello, Uncle Harry!" I said with much enthusiasm. Uncle had remained hesitant for a while before he finally spoke;

"Is that you, Jim?" he said in a low, frail voice. Uncle appeared quite leery of strangers when he displayed signs of hesitancy to even say hello.

"Yes, Uncle Harry. This is your nephew, Jim." A bright glow quickly appeared on his face. A state of cheerfulness had quickly obscured his demeanor of doubt and suspicion. To gain added assurance, he looked down at my luggage resting on the step.

"Oh! Dear," Uncle Harry said, "It has been a long time. Come inside, Jim! It's getting dark." Uncle slowly swung the door open a bit wider, to accommodate my luggage. I promptly stepped inside the house – pulling my luggage behind.

Uncle Harry gently shut the door before taking slow strides toward the center of a large hall. With his long slender arm, he extended a firm handshake, and a heart-felt embrace. I reciprocated by giving my uncle a warm bear-hug. His eyes began to sparkle with delight.

"Take a seat, Jim," he said. Uncle directed me to the center of the hall, where a leather sofa stood. I had duly taken a seat on the sofa, as he'd instructed.

A bright glowing chandelier suspending from the ceiling, cast its beams in every area of the hall. As I sat in the comfort of the sofa, I felt pleasantly relieved to be finally seated comfortably, after many hours of travel, and particularly after a heartbreaking survey of my childhood home.

"Have a seat, Jim," Uncle said. It was a double welcome, and kind hospitality to a nephew he hadn't seen in many years. I was delighted to be welcomed by my uncle after arriving home and finding my home buried beneath rubble.

Uncle Harry walked across the hall to retrieve my luggage resting beside the door.

"I'll take your luggage, Jim," he said. Before I had the opportunity to assist, he rolled the luggage across the hall and entered an adjoining room. Uncle had subsequently emerged from the room and walked slowly back into the hall.

"I'm glad you made it, Jim," he said, as his eyes sparkled beneath the glowing chandelier.

"It's been long after dark and you didn't arrive. I said you may have changed your mind from coming home. But you're here now." Uncle spoke cheerfully, while he displayed a gleeful smile that had quickly obscured his solitary demeanor.

"Uncle, I arrived long before sunset. But I wanted to pay a special visit to my home I had left so long ago. My heart is stirred by the emptiness, and the still silence. Uncle, there has been such a sense of loss and quietness in the village." While I spoke, Uncle Harry moved at a slow pace, but with much vigour across the hall. For a man of eighty-three, he appeared to have been quite a picture of health. Physically, the years had taken their toll on him. His solitary life in the village had also shown up in his demeanor.

Uncle sat on a leather-cushioned wooden chair that stood opposite a window in his kitchen. He had a clear western view of the hillside, and the road passing just steps from the front door of his house. Close to the chair on which he sat, stood a small wooden antique table on which a cellphone rested. It was the cellphone by which I had made frequent contacts with him from my foreign homeland, and while he resided in America.

A cellphone in Coopers Village! I thought to myself. My parents may be rolling in their graves to be aware of a device that enabled my uncle to speak with his children in a foreign country, and to communicate with me in another foreign country, even though we hadn't seen each other for many years.

During my childhood years in the village, the longest distance from which one could have heard the sound of a voice was less than half a mile away – and only as the crow flies. And unless the voice was loud and high-pitched, it was difficult to hear the sound of a voice from a distance of a quarter mile away.

From my seating position on the sofa, I could see inside Uncle's kitchen that was equipped with every modern appliance a kitchen could accommodate. I admired his black refrigerator on the opposite side of the stove, and quick-cook devices – also in black, carefully positioned in the kitchen.

I sat amazed at Uncle's new home, equipped with modern electrical appliances, and a communication device. While he pondered his next activity, I engaged him in a conversation, I hoped, would bridge the gap between the present, and my last time actually seeing him. As the conversation ensued, Uncle Harry had promptly gotten out of his chair and commenced rallying around the stove resting beside an opposite window in the kitchen.

"Pardon me, Jim, but I must get you supper," he said. Uncle maintained his silence while he rallied around the stove in the kitchen.

During my time in the village, as a safeguard against a house fire, my family's kitchen was cautiously attached to the outside of the house. Although Uncle's kitchen was built within his house, he had no open fire that would create a hazardous situation. And while his kitchen was equipped with a modern electric stove with oven intact, my family's kitchen had a wood-burning stove – an instant fire hazard.

My parents didn't have anything instant during my time at home. There hadn't been an instant push of a button to ignite a fire for cooking. I remember the times my stomach growled, when my siblings and I waited for the morning breakfast. My parents first had to light the coals, or the firewood that had become wet or dampened by the previous day's rain showers. They waited for the flames to ignite on the firewood before the morning meals could be prepared. The remaining firewood were subsequently placed in the warm sunlight, so that they were dry and ready to be lit to prepare the evening meals.

While I reflected on the village folk's traditional way of preparing a meal, minutes had elapsed before Uncle emerged from the kitchen. He'd been carefully holding a tray as he walked to another area of the house.

"Come this way, Jim. Your supper is ready," Uncle said. I promptly rose from the sofa and walked into the adjacent hall – a large dining room. Uncle Harry had placed the tray in the center of a large table in the dining room. He'd taken his position at the table in readiness to serve the meal.

"That's rather kind and hospitable, Uncle." Without further ado, I dined on the appetizing meal Uncle Harry had prepared – steak and steamed rice with vegetables. I had duly expressed my thanks after enjoying the appetizing meal. It was a rather satisfying meal after my long day's journey.

At the end of the short dinner session, Uncle Harry returned to his chair, where he resumed his comfortable position. I promptly returned to the sofa and once more took my place beneath the glowing chandelier. My uncle's chair was on a 180-degree angle from the sofa on which I was seated. This seating arrangement had facilitated the night's conversation.

The night being still young, there was ample time to exchange news and views, and catch up on events, past and present. This gave Uncle the opportunity to fill a gap in his solitary existence, and he didn't hesitate to spark up a conversation.

"Jim, now that we're finally in each other's presence, how has life been in the U.K?" Uncle asked with eager curiosity. He gazed vehemently toward the floor as one in deep concentration. Uncle sat in great anticipation, and as one with an insatiable appetite to receive news from abroad. And while he waited in anticipation of receiving news, his eyes glowed under the bright florescent light beaming from the ceiling of the kitchen.

"Life has been good, Uncle Harry. As you're aware, my children have grown, and have established their own household. You're also aware that Loretta passed away. But I didn't marry another wife." Uncle repeatedly shuffled himself to be more comfortable in his chair.

"I was rather sad when I learned of Loretta's passing," he said. "I was further saddened when I learned that she hadn't been ill for very long. Had her condition been detected sooner, the medical practitioners would have likely found a cure for her illness," Uncle Harry said.

Uncle had remained silent as he anticipated receiving more details about life in my foreign homeland. But I had been waiting anxiously to hear his report of the life he'd been living since he returned home. I therefore commenced asking questions that would bring answers about my home village.

"How has life been since coming back home, Uncle Harry?" Uncle's face bore a faint smile as he sat poised to speak. There was a sudden change in his demeanor when he set his focus toward the window opposite where he sat.

"It's good to be back home, Jim," Uncle said. "I had a heart-felt longing to return to the place of my childhood, but unpleasant events have changed my outlook on life since coming back home." He tried to hold back the tears streaming down his cheeks and over his thick grey beard. "Things haven't been good, Jim. It's been a lonely life without Harriet." He set his gaze toward the closed glass window in the kitchen. Uncle wiped his face with a white handkerchief he pulled from his pocket. "I had returned home to give her a change of lifestyle, and a chance to improve her poor health, but as you're aware, she didn't stay very long. Her prognosis was that, it was much too late for her cancer surgery. Harriet, my dear wife…." Uncle's conversation came to an abrupt end as he quickly wiped the tears that had been constantly flooding his eyes.

"I buried her two summers ago," he said. "I laid her to rest by the side of the hill up there." He pointed toward the closed kitchen window. "You can see her resting place from where I'm seated." I had duly apologized for stirring my uncle's emotions as I watched him sob and dry the persistent tears flowing over his entire face.

"It's unfortunate that Aunt Harriet didn't survive to resume the village life she'd once lived," I said, in my attempt at consoling my uncle. It had become apparent that Harriet wasn't the best subject matter to discuss. My uncle's eyes had become pale and red from the tears that continually flowed over his cheeks. I might have touched a delicate chord of Uncle's already ravaged emotion by asking him about his life in the village. It appeared that every breath he took, and every word he spoke, he sobbed in grief at the loss of his beloved wife, Harriet.

Uncle Harry maintained his focus toward the window as the tears continued to flow down his cheeks. He was noticeably overwhelmed by memories of Harriet. My dwelling on the topic had, unfortunately, made matters worse. In Uncle's view, there were many other losses that were just as disturbing as the loss of Harriet.

Amidst his grief, Uncle Harry cleared his hoarse throat as he continued his briefing on life, and the state of the village since he'd returned home. What better setting for tales of events in the village, than under the early night sky. It was a pleasant reminder of the way life used to be during my childhood years. There were fun and games, and tall tales beneath the evening stars. My uncle had, no doubt, held lasting memories of his childhood and young adult days in the village. The present tall tales, however, weren't the type that appeased my uncle, who'd lost his wife, or me, who'd lost my wife, and my childhood home.

"Jim, some older folk, like your uncle Dalton, returned home last year," Uncle said. "But he soon discovered that things weren't the same as they once were. His home was un-inhabitable in its present state. In a state of despondency, Dalton returned to resume life in America, where he'd spent his past sixty years. He said that the sounds of the village had faded. The normal way of life no longer existed. His own relatives had left the village to seek a livelihood in the towns, and in foreign countries. Dalton took to the air and flew back to the lifestyle he'd adopted in his foreign homeland."

"Uncle, this isn't the most comforting bit of information." Uncle took a deep breath before he continued to fill me in on more details about the present state of the village.

"Also, other folk who'd once lived in the village, returned to find their houses dilapidated, and therefore couldn't accommodate their newly adopted lifestyles," Uncle said. "Jim, many returning folk had quickly turned around and left the village to start a new life in towns and elsewhere. They'd simply turned away from the ruined village that offered no prospects of a new beginning. My closest neighbor's house remains as a crumbled frame on its foundation. Gervan returned from America to find his house in total ruin. There wasn't a house remaining that could have allowed him to make a fresh start. He'd therefore left the village to reside in Brighton Town."

As I listened to Uncle's elaborate details, he'd had no shortage of words to describe the dilapidated state of Coopers Village. While on the subject of past village residents, I jogged his memory in an attempt to obtain details of folk whom I had left behind.

"Uncle Harry, I've not seen Mr. Renwick's house on the hill across the creek. His house appears to have been shaded by the cluster of trees in the vicinity. Have you seen him since returning to the village?" There was a period of silence as Uncle's eyes were focused toward the ceiling of the kitchen.

"Mr. Renwick? His house lies in rubble," Uncle said. "If you look carefully on the south side of the ruins of his home, you'll see a tombstone. That's Mr. Renwick's resting place."

"I'll pay a visit to the site during my survey of the key places I plan to see. Mr. Renwick was such a good neighbor. My parents had relied on the use of his automobile whenever there was an urgent need. Such a good man he was." As Uncle provided the much sought-after details on Mr. Renwick's whereabouts, my mind reflected on the loss of another humble village peasant.

The night had been fast advancing. I waited for any bit of information I could have obtained from Uncle Harry, who'd sat poised to provide more details about persons of interest, and the state in which he'd found the village upon his return home.

"Jim, this village isn't like the way it used to be," Uncle said. From my brief survey of the village's infrastructure, there was no telling that many things had changed drastically.

"Uncle Harry, why have the houses crumbled?" I asked, with heightened curiosity.

"Jim, the original village houses were poorly constructed by the former peasants. As a result, the years have taken their toll on them. The poorly constructed houses couldn't withstand the constant wind and rain. They'd therefore crumbled on their foundation – particularly those that were abandoned by the departing folk."

Based on Uncle's details on the nature of the infrastructure, I immediately perceived the frailty of the village houses, and their vulnerability to the elements – frequent strong winds and rain that had caused them to dilapidate over time. I perceived the frailty of my home that also remained in the rubble.

"And as you can imagine, Jim," Uncle Harry continued, "I returned home to find my old house in rubble. My home had crumbled on its foundation."

"Uncle, as I bent the curve, I immediately noticed your new home and its modern structure. It's quite a state-of-the-art building in this quiet village." As a gesture of his appreciation of my expressed delight in his modern home, Uncle gave a complacent smile.

"I'm glad you like my new home, Jim," Uncle said. He'd sat poised to receive praises for his new establishment.

"Uncle, my brother, Larry was left behind to maintain my parents' house, but it appears that he'd abandoned ship. Do you know the whereabouts of Larry?" Uncle set his focus toward the ceiling of the kitchen before responding.

"It appeared that Larry didn't have much time to preserve the house. According to your cousin Erwin, he'd left the village shortly after your departure to the U.K," Uncle said.

"Uncle, I must admit that, through my own negligence, I've lost contact with my brother Larry. I've also lost contact with my remaining siblings – Eunice and Rita, and am now left to ponder their whereabouts." Uncle raised his eyes toward the ceiling, as if he'd been seeking assistance from above, for his failing memory.

"When last I inquired, and based on the facts gathered, Larry had left the village to reside in Brighton Town," Uncle said. "He wanted to be close to his sibling, Rita. Since returning home, I've made many attempts at contacting him, but as I had informed you during our telephone conversation, I haven't been successful."

"It will certainly be a difficult task locating my siblings, but I remain confident that time will reveal their whereabouts," I said, feeling disappointed that Uncle hadn't obtained information about his nieces and nephew since returning home.

Uncle listened attentively to my expressed dilemma – my ruined home, and not being able to locate my siblings. However, he continued to express his grief at the state of the village, and his solitary life without Harriet.

"Jim, during the many years away from my homeland, time has passed, taking the older folk along. The younger village folk have escaped to towns and foreign places, resulting in strangers moving into the village to establish their new place of residence. The new folk have built modern houses, equipped with modern technological devices – a television set or two, and electrical appliances. Occupation of the villages by strangers brought about changes in lifestyles and in century-old traditions.

Uncle Harry was delighted to brief me on the state of the village, but there were many questions that had remained unanswered. Questions that had no doubt, lingered in his mind – the whereabouts of the children.

"Uncle Harry, Coopers Village is in a state of decay. As I can imagine, many of the older folk have passed on. I have not seen or heard the younger folk – the children in particular. Where are the children?" I asked, inquiringly.

"Jim, I returned home to find a quiet village, abandoned by the youth who'd always contributed to the joys and thrills of a once thriving village existence," Uncle said.

"Uncle, as I listened to the silence under the early night sky, I have concluded that there's an absence of children in the village. Have you seen the children, or heard of their whereabouts?" Uncle sat poised to relate the facts of the missing children, while I waited in great anticipation of receiving his details.

"Jim, you had passed through a congested town to get to this village," Uncle said with assurance. "The towns have become congested with young village folk, who'd joined the exodus to settle elsewhere. The young folk have no sense of attachment to a quiet village, and the low-keyed life it offers. They've flocked the town to live the fast-paced lifestyles, and bathe in the flickering neon lights sparkling under the night sky." Uncle's response brought the answer to one of the many questions I asked about the quiet village and an over-crowded town. "Jim, the young folk of the villages have flocked to the towns with hopes of realizing their dreams – having material possessions and basking in the glitz and glamour of town life," Uncle further stated. "While the young folk abandoned the villages, they've left the place to dilapidation. It was once an expectation that the offspring take up the beacon from where their elders left it. It was the young folk's responsibility to maintain the infrastructure of the villages – carrying on with what their elders had started centuries prior. The young folk, however, have abandoned their lifetime expectation of raising their offspring, tilling the soil and perpetuating their parents' estate. The younger folk have joined the exodus to towns and foreign destinations. They've also taken their offspring with them, thus leaving the village void of children."

Uncle Harry's reasoning had been well taken. While he spoke, it wasn't long before I realized that, he'd also held concerns about the absence of the children as well as the young adults from the village.

The night had been slowly progressing while Uncle continued to fill my insatiable appetite with more sad tales about the village. Uncle's emotions had been once more revved up as he continued to provide further details on the state of the village and the few remaining folk.

"As you can imagine, Jim," Uncle said, "the new residents who've moved into the village, have brought their automobiles with them. The village folk rarely meet them. They're often seen during the early morning, when they drive along the road on their way to Brighton Town, and during the evening hours when they return. As the vehicles drive along the road, their occupants occasionally wave a hand as a gesture of sending greetings."

As Uncle Harry spoke, I perceived his solitary life in a village that had been practically void of humankind. He seemed to have had very little contact with the few remaining village folk.

And while he related the incidents of new residents moving to the village, my uncle had just as well regard himself as a new resident. He'd returned after leaving his homeland for so many years.

"As you can imagine, Jim," Uncle went on with his elaborate details, "the new residents do not work the soil, or raise animals. Their foods, and all necessities are brought in from the town. They have no knowledge of the place, village life, and the fact that they've been treading on the graveyard of a village that was once alive with the sounds of a thriving civilization." While Uncle spoke, my ears were perked up like antennas as I waited for more details on the state of the village.

"Uncle, your information has given me a better insight into the present state of my village, my ravaged home, and the absolute silence everywhere. With the absence of the young offspring to till the soil and raise the animals, the village has been left abandoned, hence, its crumbled infrastructure."

It appeared that my uncle had ran out of steam, as he'd remained silent for a considerable length of time. He soon, however, regained momentum and continued to express whatever residue that had remained on his mind.

"On a different note, Jim, would you care to have a cup of tea?" Without an ounce of hesitation, I promptly accepted his kind hospitality.

"I'll be greatly delighted, Uncle. That's very kind of you." Uncle had been delighted to serve his guest. With painstaking effort, he rose to his feet and headed toward the kitchen counter, where a kettle stood glowing under the florescent light.

"Not to worry, Jim," Uncle said. "Feel right at home. You've been traveling all day."

It was a painful process as Uncle rose from his chair and walked toward the kettle. His steps were noticeably brisk, but his progress had been slowed by his, apparent, painful feet. He poured water from the kitchen faucet into the kettle and promptly plugged it into a set of sockets in the wall.

My uncle's modern house, equipped with electrical appliances, and particularly his indoor plumbing, had immediately sparked my curiosity. I therefore continued my impromptu interview for whatever additional information I could have gathered about his new village lifestyle.

"Uncle, I notice that your house is equipped with indoor plumbing and a ready source of water. From where do you obtain water?" It was an odd question to ask. However, I felt that, if Uncle had a modern home, equipped with a constant supply of water, there ought to have been a modern means of obtaining fresh water for his daily usage. He'd carefully ruffled his beard before smoothing it with the palm of his hands.

"The village has been equipped with a network of water pipes, which extract water from the spring at the crest of the hill," Uncle said. "Village folk who have the means, and afford to pay a charge, have water pipes installed in their homes. Those who have not the means, must go to the public pipes in local areas to obtain their water supply." Uncle's response was rather informative, as he provided details of the source of the water flowing from his kitchen faucet. I clearly saw the great divide between those who were well-to-do, and those who didn't have the means. Those who hadn't the means were most likely the older folk, and the few young folk who hadn't been fortunate to join the exodus.

In my time, village folk didn't have the luxury of indoor plumbing that channeled water inside their homes. Their only means of securing water was by fetching it in buckets from the spring in the valley. Uncle no doubt, recalled his days of fetching water from the spring. The youngsters, as well as the adults, made several trips into the valley, bucket-by-bucket, until a large container that was placed by the side of their house reached its capacity. During heavy rainstorms, water cascaded off the metal roof of the village houses. The folk collected and stored the fresh water in large containers for their daily washing needs.

As the night's conversation took on momentum, Uncle had promptly excused himself and walked toward the steaming kettle. Shortly thereafter, he emerged from the kitchen, holding a silver tray bearing a teapot, surrounded by cups and saucers. He rested the tray on the dining table and began to pour the tea he'd made. I was again, summoned to the dining table, where I joined Uncle for tea.

"Have some tea, Jim," Uncle said. I watched the steaming brown liquid flow from the long spout of a white teapot, having a line of solid gold around its rim. Uncle poured tea into a white cup lined with gold. He carefully put the cup into its gold-lined saucer and placed it on the table. Uncle subsequently poured his serving into a cup with a saucer of a similar description. To complement the serving of tea, Uncle opened a package of biscuits and placed them on a crystal dish he'd placed on the table. The night had been gradually advancing while the tea session continued beneath the bright glow of the chandelier suspending from the ceiling of the dining room. Uncle had quickly built up added vitality as he sipped tea from his gold-rimmed cup.

As the tea session progressed, Uncle Harry didn't seem to have a shortage of reports on the state of things in the village. Nor did I experience a tiring moment listening to his reports. Any bit of information was comforting to the soul of one who'd lost his childhood home. My uncle also found solace in relating the state of desertion and ruin in which he'd found the village upon his return home.

In the quiet night atmosphere, Uncle continued to provide more details on the current state of life in the village. Like a lecturer, with rapid blinks of his eyes, and his head turning in every direction, he continued to provide more elaborate details.

"Jim, there's not much remaining in the village for one to adore. There's nothing here that offers an incentive for one to remain. With no one to till the soil and raise the animals, the village has grown into a forest," Uncle said as his voice took on momentum. "There's not much to see when the entire village has been overgrown by tall trees. The cows and horses that had once grazed the hillsides are in extinction. The hillsides have been overgrown by trees and shrubs, which create impassable thoroughfares."

Uncle was brought to tears as he expressed disappointment with the state of his home village.

"Uncle, if I may interject. Around the time of my exodus from the village, I remember the village folk who'd owned several animals. Folk sold their animals to obtain the funds they needed for travels to foreign destinations. Some folk divested themselves of all the properties they possessed, in order that they could settle in the town." Uncle listened with keen interest. He'd been gaining an understanding of the lengths to which the folk went in order that they could leave village life behind.

"Jim, I remember my property where my animals once roamed while they grazed the wide grassy field, and the beautiful hillside. The caretaker had abandoned the property during my stay abroad. Whatever he did with the animals, remains anyone's guess. The property has been overgrown by trees, thick shrubs and protruding rocks, which hamper my most coveted stroll across the field." As Uncle spoke, I perceived further signs of his discontent with the present state of life in the village. I could have sensed his unexpressed regrets for returning to resume life in it.

"Uncle, things were never this way during my time, or in your time. The village folk had once worked hard to build and maintain a thriving community. And while they resided in close proximity to each other, there'd been constant interaction, and lasting friendships among them." Uncle nodded in agreement.

"You're absolutely right, Jim. This village was once a thriving habitat for all living creatures."

While Uncle spoke, I reflected on the Red Top tree and the folk who'd sat beneath the cool shade its branches had once offered.

"Uncle, the very Red Top tree that once stood beside the gate leading to my home, died with those who'd sought shelter beneath its branches," I said, as Uncle listened with keen intent. At my mention of the Red Top tree, he shuffled himself on his chair to be more comfortable. "The cool shade the tree had once provided, was a coveted place for passers-by. Folk traveling across the miles, had always sought shelter from the sweltering heat of the sun. They'd all sat on my grandfather's wooden bench to get some much-needed rest. My mother, Mabel, had always been delighted to quench the thirst of the traveling folk before they continued on their journey." I had jogged Uncle's memory of another aspect of life in the village, particularly the Red Top tree under which he'd once played as a youth.

"Jim, the modern folk, particularly the youth, know nothing about traveling long distances on foot. Nor do they see the need for a tree whose branches provide a cool shade from the sun. There're buses and cars that offer the few commuters of the village, easy access to towns, and to various other destinations across villages. There's therefore, no longer a need for the Red Top tree as a shelter from the sun." Uncle jolted my memory of the modern times that have rendered the past way of life obsolete.

Uncle's deep-set eyes revealed his state of loneliness as a result of the passing of Harriet. The physical disconnection from his offspring he'd left behind, had also taken further toll on his well-being.

I had developed a keen interest in Uncle's health and well-being, and felt that further investigation could shed some light on his village life. I also wondered about his security in a village where there's scarcely anyone in the vicinity.

"Uncle, I can perceive your many challenges living alone," I insinuated, while he maintained thoughts about the Red Top tree. He nodded in agreement, but didn't give resonance to his thoughts. Uncle habitually touched the glow-in-the-dark, green cellphone he'd taken from the small table and hung securely on a thick gold chain around his neck. The cellphone, it appeared, served as a constant reminder of his close connection to his offspring whom he'd left behind in America.

"My sister, Edith, although she often faced painful moments, drops by to pay her visit – whenever time does not permit me to drop by her house." As Uncle spoke, I could see new tears flooding his deep-set eyes. "My old friends from Brighton Town, drop by from time-to-time, to pay their homage," Uncle said.

"It's good to know that you have visitors who keep you entertained, Uncle."

"These are past students, fellow teachers and old-time friends who'd also joined the exodus from the village to places elsewhere," Uncle Harry said. "Each time they pay their visit, we converse incessantly about school days and what they'd accomplished after leaving Coopers Villa School. They talk about the professions they had during their working years. As well, they keep me informed of happenings in the town."

Uncle's demeanor had suddenly changed when he mentioned his past students. An occasional smile appeared on his pale face as he reflected on his profession as a once prominent teacher of Coopers Villa School.

As a teacher of Villa School, Uncle was regarded as a man of great stature. He was the tall, young gentleman, whom the village folk respectfully called, "Sir," and "Mr. Goodwin." I, along with my siblings, called him, "Uncle Harry," and "Uncle," when our unruly tongue had refused to co-operate by adding, "Harry."

Although Uncle had left home for such a long time, upon his return, he'd portrayed similar traits as he had during his days as a teacher. It was unfortunate that those who knew him had joined the exodus from the village to places elsewhere, and were therefore not around to give their due honor and respects upon his return home. As Uncle had stated, a few of his past students who'd taken up residence in the town, and who were aware of his return home, paid their visits to show due respects to a former teacher and a mentor.

Years of absence had taken their toll on Uncle's stature, as well as his lifestyle and well-being. His return home had left his heart torn between the lifestyle he'd left behind in his foreign homeland, and that which he'd once lived in his home village. Not being able to reattach to the old village lifestyle, and the pleasures he'd left at the time of his departure, Uncle built his new home on the foundation of his dilapidated house. At his new place of attachment, he established his imported foreign lifestyle. On the relics of his old home, he remained to reminisce on the village life he'd once lived, and the pleasures he had at the place to which he cannot make a reattachment. In his state of solitude, Uncle reminisced on his childhood home, buried beneath rubble. He sadly realized that he cannot make a reattachment to his home, and the joyous pleasures of his childhood.

While the night's conversation prolonged beneath the bright beams of the chandelier, Uncle had talked himself to exhaustion, and to the point where new information had become fewer and far between. The round brass clock suspending from a thick brass chain on the wall, had struck 2:00 am. By this time, Uncle had volunteered more answers than the questions I had asked. I was immediately reminded that older village folk habitually take advantage of every sleeping hour the night offers. My uncle was no exception. I therefore kept my inquiry to the bare minimum – at the same time, hoping that Uncle would excuse himself and retreat to his room.

While the night progressed, sleep was becoming a menace as Uncle's head continually drooped forward. Amidst the excitement of having his visitor, and sharing his views, his internal clock hadn't reminded him of his curfew. Uncle was finally overcome by slumber, when he unexpectedly rose slowly from his chair around the dining table. In preparation for his forward movement, it appeared that every joint cracked, while his bones snapped. As he made limping strides across the hall, Uncle's slow movements and his facial expression, were tell-tale signs of pain and discomfort.

Uncle continued his slow movement toward a door adjacent to the large hall. With some hesitancy, he opened the door and looked inside. While it remained open, he made a slight turn – as if he'd forgotten to take a bow.

"Jim! It's already long after dark. You must be tired. This is the guest room in which you'll stay." On that note, Uncle walked toward another door which he'd slowly opened. "Good night, Jim," he said.

"Good night, Uncle! Your kind hospitality is greatly appreciated. I'll go to rest momentarily." I watched as the door to Uncle's room close slowly behind him.

Uncle had directed me to the room in which he'd earlier taken my luggage. It was one of many rooms he reserved for his guests. He'd long retreated to his room, when I followed suit, entering my designated room to take that much-needed rest.

Upon entering the room, I commenced my close scrutiny of its contents. From my observation and close scrutiny, I first noticed the ceiling, made of solid concrete, and displaying an artistic finish. The interior of the two glass windows was painted light green to act as a shield from outside view, and from the glare of the sun and the bright glow of the moon during the night. The windows were adorned in fine embroidered curtains, displaying the sheer elegance of the room.

Further observation revealed a small night table beside the bed. On the table there was a lamp that had a shiny brass base, and a shade of pure white. The bed rails were made of a similar brass as the lamp. The brass fixtures and the remaining contents of the guestroom, were likely imported from Uncle Harry's foreign homeland.

During my childhood and early adolescent years, no one in my village afforded the luxury of brass fixtures and furnishings. The wooden furnishings were made by folk who possessed the skill of making furniture, using mostly fine mahogany wood grown in the local forests.

The room my uncle had set aside for me was quite hospitable to anyone who stayed in it. Uncle's entire house he built, at the very spot where his old house once stood, portrayed a slice of his foreign lifestyle he'd brought back home. By its very appearance – a big hall with an adjoining dining room, a state-of-the-art kitchen, my uncle's house was considered outlandish.

Uncle's house was built in the midst of an exquisitely surrounding landscape. Sadly, with inadequate upkeep, its beauty had become tarnished, and its view obscured by overhanging branches of oversized trees and thick bush, leaving my uncle to be like a forest dweller.

There hadn't been many hours remaining that would have afforded one a good night's sleep. However, I lay in bed to take advantage of some much-needed rest. My thoughts immediately reflected on the state of my home and the way life used to be in my village. I had wished that the much-coveted sleep would take hold of my being, but I was kept awake by the heart-breaking thoughts of my lost home, and the vanishment of those who'd once inhabited its space. A place that had once beamed with the pleasantries of my childhood life, lay buried beneath rubble – as if a strong whirlwind had passed through in the dead of night, taking all in its path.

It was a somber thought that I could no longer wake up in that atmosphere of home, and with that comforting feeling of belonging. The memories of home, and life as it used to be, remained lodged in the crevices of my mind. I didn't weigh the consequences of leaving the place of my birth to seek a better life in a foreign land. Upon returning home, I've been broadsided by the reality of not being able to reconnect with my past village life, and with those who'd contributed to a once joyous existence. As I lay in bed to ponder the loss of my home, sleep had slowly put a damper on the flurry of thoughts that had been flooding my mind.

Chapter 11

Breakfast With Uncle Harry

During my childhood days, the birds had never failed to chirp and sing their enchanting melodies at the slow emergence of the dawn. Their songs welcomed the rising sun, and beckoned in the dawn of another new day, when all their activities would commence. I had remained hesitant to rise out of bed while a single songbird sang sweet melodies from its perch on a twig beside my window.

It was my first day of waking up in the atmosphere of home – the place I once had the pride and joy of belonging. There was a comforting feeling as the sun casts its rays on the windows of my room, bringing back pleasant memories of my yesteryears. I perceived the glowing yellow sun casting its rays across the village – waking all creatures that had succumbed to slumber at the arrival of dusk. With a feeling of anxious fears, I waited to survey the ruins as the sun casts its light on the trees, rocks, and the rubble everywhere.

Just when the rising sun began to revive every living thing in the universe, I heard the sound of footsteps in the hall. Although he too had been deprived of adequate sleep, Uncle Harry didn't seem to have a reason to lie in bed. I reflected on the days of my youth, when no one overslept. It was an early-to-bed and an early-to-rise lifestyle then, and it seemed my uncle didn't break away from that tradition – even after his more than sixty years of absence. Although I had an almost sleepless night, I too felt the need to rise and greet the new day. My mind had been continually plagued by grim thoughts of what I would see when I further survey my crumbled home, and surrounding places.

The rising sun had expelled all traces of the early dawn. As the new day appeared, I had remained torn between, attempting to gain another hour of sleep, and rising to further survey the ruins of my home, but the latter prevailed.

The irresistible aroma of freshly made coffee, streaming from Uncle's kitchen, had entered my room through a fissure in the door. I lay wrestling with the promptings to rise out of bed, until I heard a soft tap at my door, then another. A voice was heard between each tap;

"Are you up, Jim? Hello, Jim!" It was the voice of Uncle Harry. I couldn't have ignored the persistent tapping at my door, and had therefore been forced to get out of bed.

"Yes, Uncle! I'll be out shortly," I said, as I slowly scrambled out of bed. With painstaking effort, I walked toward the bathroom. My curiosity had immediately sparked as I commenced a close scrutiny of the bathroom – equipped with the most modern amenities: A bathtub, equipped with a shower, and a sophisticated shower-head: A face basin made of pure ivory, or porcelain, or whatever was the material. There were over-head lighting fixtures which cast the brightest light – bright enough that the naked eye could see through the eye of the tiniest needle. This is sheer luxury, I thought to myself.

In my time, my parents didn't afford such amenities in their bathroom. Grandfather Grovel, built a bathroom on the south section of his house. When Father built his house, he'd added an extension to my grandfather's original bathroom. That was the place where the household took a shower – pouring a bucket of water to wash the soap suds from their bodies. The folk of the villages didn't have the luxury of indoor plumbing, and indoor amenities. Nor had they knowledge of such amenities. To ensure that his house was equipped with all the necessary amenities, my grandfather had built an outhouse, a good distance from the back-side of his house. At the time my father had built his house, adjacent to Grandfather's, he'd added a second compartment to the outhouse to accommodate the extended family. With two large outhouse compartments, the entire family always found some release when the need arose – there were no line-ups.

While my uncle waited patiently in the hall, I took advantage of a refreshing lukewarm shower, which had greatly enhanced my strength. I had quickly changed into my village attire – equipping myself to further inspect the ruins of my home. Whatever other unpleasant surprises the new day of exploration would reveal, I waited anxiously, and with great anticipation of facing them.

I opened the door of my guestroom and stepped into the hall, where I found Uncle Harry standing as one who'd been awaiting an upcoming event. It seemed the years hadn't put a damper on his stamina.

"Good morning, Uncle," I said. "It's still early in the morning, but you've been up and around." The smile on his face had left me with the guilty feeling of having overslept. My uncle was in high spirit, and stood as one ready to start the new day.

"Good morning, Jim," Uncle said, "I've prepared your breakfast." He made slow strides across the hall and entered the kitchen. "The coffee is getting cold. Will you come and join me for breakfast?" It was uncharacteristic of Uncle to be in the kitchen preparing his own meals, and also preparing a meal for me, his guest. Technology, and modern kitchen appliances had greatly enhanced his cooking capabilities.

"I'll be delighted to join you for breakfast, Uncle!" I walked across the hall and entered the dining room that had been permeated with an aroma of the finest breakfast menu. Uncle had prepared bacon and eggs, and crisp toasts that continued to pop up in his toaster. The overpowering aroma of the freshly made coffee had brought back memories of Mother Mabel's freshly cooked coffee from her kitchen.

Uncle directed me to his dining table of solid wood, surrounded by six wooden chairs with black leather seat. It was the table at which I had sat for supper, and subsequently tea, the night prior. I joined him at the table to enjoy the most appetizing breakfast he'd prepared at the crack of dawn. It was my perception that my uncle was elated to have the company of someone he hadn't seen for such a long time. As the breakfast session progressed, there was a pleasant glow on his face – a testament to his state of contentment in the company of his guest.

From my vantage point in the dining room, I had a full view of Uncle's large kitchen which stood in the front section of the house, and faced the road below. The entire frontage of the kitchen was surrounded by glass panels, through which he observed the flying creatures and rodents scampering across the hillside. He had a front-row-seat to vehicular traffic, and passers-by on the road passing through Coopers Village. While Uncle took in the sceneries from the windows of his kitchen, he may have enjoyed a chat with whoever had some time to spare.

As my eyes surveyed Uncle's kitchen, I noticed a modern coffee-making machine resting on the granite countertop. It was still percolating from the freshly brewed coffee he'd placed on the table. The modern kitchen and its appliances brought back memories of my parents' wood-burning iron stove, on which there was always a large enamel pot containing the most aromatic and delicious coffee. My parents wouldn't have traded their old way of cooking a perfect pot of coffee – not for an electrically operated machine that instantly percolates steaming coffee. My parents were in no rush to catch an aircraft, or leave for work before the clock struck seven.

In my childhood years, my parents didn't prepare instant meals. Nor did they instantly press a button to have fire in the kitchen. Father first had to light the coals he stacked in the wood-burning stove. The coals and the fire logs were often dampened by the frequent rainfalls. It therefore took a much longer time for the fire to ignite. When the glow had finally spread over the coals, it was time to commence preparing the morning, or evening meal. Nonetheless, my parents would have been quite comfortable with their wood stove, and their old way of cooking – particularly, a perfect pot of coffee.

And while I admired Uncle's kitchen, equipped with an electric stove and other appliances, my parents would have been quite leery of pressing electric buttons to obtain instant fire. Uncle Harry hadn't been in a rush to go anywhere, but for the lifestyle he'd adopted and imported from his foreign homeland, he couldn't have changed to his traditional village lifestyle, even if he'd tried.

Breakfast was in progress around the fine dining table. Uncle ate with a healthy appetite from the serving he'd generously placed on his plate. The manner in which he'd set his gaze, from the ceiling to the floor, was an indication that he was in the right mind-set to continue the prior night's conversation. My insatiable appetite had been yearning for more details about the ravaged village. I therefore didn't hesitate to continue the conversation session around the breakfast table.

Like my parents' home, Uncle Harry's original house had also succumbed to the effects of abandonment and dilapidation, hence, the modern replacement. I was eager to discover Uncle's reason for settling back into a quiet and abandoned village. Like the other returning folk, he could have also taken up residence in the town, or return to America. I therefore commenced another of my fact-finding sessions with him.

"Uncle, you appear to be quite complacent being in your modern home, also being back in the village. What has life been really like since coming back home?" As evident in Uncle's changed demeanor, his return to the village was not one of his best subjects for discussion. This was not the best position in which to put one already in a state of deep despair. But I perceived that Uncle had built up the courage to face his dilemma. Uncle had gradually emptied his mouth from a bite he'd taken from his toast before he spoke;

"I've not thought much about life in the village, Jim. Things didn't go the way I had planned them at the time I made the decision to return home." For a moment Uncle's eyes circumvented the dining room before he continued to speak. "Things would have been much better had Harriet survived, but I have to do the best I can to carry on here without her." I knew I had touched another tender spot of Uncle's fragile emotion. However, in my quest for further details about his health and wellbeing, I continued the conversation session.

"This has been a quiet village with not much neighborhood activities; and scarcely anyone seen, or heard in the vicinity," I said, as I watched the tears welling up in his eyes. "In what past-time activities are you engaged, Uncle?" He'd become silent for a moment, as if the word, "Pastime" had sounded foreign to him.

"Most mornings after the dew on the ground dissipates, I take short strolls in the immediate vicinity. While on my strolls, I pay frequent visits to Edith," Uncle said. "And on bright and sunny afternoons, I stroll along the road, as far as my legs will take me. I often drop in on my best friend who resides a short distance along the road – when she's unable to visit me."

Uncle's cheeks were aglow as he mentioned paying a visit to his best friend along the way.

"My brother, Samuel who resides on a distant estate, pays his occasional visit, whenever his offspring takes him on errands." Uncle appeared to have had no shortage of places where he'd been privileged to visit, also friends and associates with whom he'd been in contact. "I've been privileged to have my close associates in Brighton Town, take me on trips, where I have the opportunity to see changes and attend private events." Uncle went on with his apparent long list of places he visited, and recreational opportunities he had. "And those newspapers and magazines are sent by my children in America." He pointed to the large stack of magazines and newspapers in the rack beside his chair in the kitchen. "My friend who resides a short distance down the road, brings me the local newspapers from Brighton Town, whenever she goes shopping. Jim, I must keep abreast of news and views in America as well as in my homeland, and therefore read the magazines and newspapers on a regular basis." From that bit of information, I obtained the answer to my question about the origin of the large stack of magazines and newspapers on the rack beside my uncle's chair.

While I sat with Uncle Harry around the breakfast table, there hadn't been a dull moment listening to his long list of pastime activities. Uncle had had no shortage of information about his life in the village since he'd returned home. He therefore continued to provide more details, hoping to further address my concerns about his well-being.

"And as I was saying, Jim," Uncle continued, "I have frequent visits from my children in America. Also, from past friends and relations residing in Brighton Town." As Uncle spoke, I had the assurance that he was quite comfortable living in his modern home, also adjusting to the foreign lifestyle he'd imported into the village. He appeared quite comfortable with the close connections he'd maintained with his children in America. And also looked forward to the frequent visits made by his associates from Brighton Town, and elsewhere.

Although he appeared comfortable, Uncle's life wasn't a bed of roses. As he spoke, he continually took deep breaths as one trying to hold back an over-powering sob. I could have sensed that, within his heart, he wasn't in a state of happiness, despite his assurance that things had been going well. It was consoling, however, to be aware that, despite the distance between them, my uncle's offspring had been giving him their tender loving care.

The morning was quickly advancing. I had become eager to survey the rubble of my home. With a heavy heart, I waited in great anticipation of taking a tour of the vicinity.

Chapter 12

Beneath the Ruins

With the breakfast session ending, there was that, "What now," look on Uncle's face. I could have imagined his ardent desire to explore the outdoors. As the rising sun cast its beams around the village, I felt the urgency to further explore the rubble strewn around the vicinity. I had promptly excused myself from the breakfast table and headed back to my room, where I equipped myself with the most comfortable pair of village shoes.

To compensate my once childhood and adolescent addiction to the outdoors, I stepped out into the morning air to explore the immediate vicinity. Every weed, shrub and flower contributed to the myriad of intriguing fragrances in the air. I had a short survey of the vicinity, while breathing in the fresh and inviting fragrances. The overwhelming fresh air, and the aromatic fragrances, were just as they'd been during my childhood years.

As my entire being reached out to take in the fresh air, I felt it was an ideal opportunity to extend an invitation to Uncle Harry to explore the immediate vicinity. I therefore returned to the house, where I found him scurrying in the kitchen – washing and restacking the utensils. His activities were abruptly halted as I entered the kitchen.

"Uncle, you'd earlier mentioned your pastime of taking habitual walks around the village. Would you like to take a quick stroll around the vicinity?" Uncle was quite elated, and therefore gladly took me up on the offer.

"Jim, I would certainly like to go on a stroll, since I'll have you as my guide," he said. With his heavy feet, Uncle trudged toward a room adjacent to his kitchen. Minutes had elapsed before he emerged, his cheeks glowing with a broad smile. Uncle had returned from the room, equipped in his outdoor shoes, and a sturdy walking cane in hand. He stood by the exit door, ready to challenge the outdoors.

I quickly opened the exit door and walked onto the roadway – Uncle following closely. I was on my way to revisit the ruins of my home, and to give my uncle an opportunity to survey his property. Uncle walked in bold strides as he anxiously waited to survey what had once been his wide grassy field, and the farm he hadn't accessed for many years.

Uncle's slow movement had slowed my progress, but with the many daylight hours ahead, there was ample time to explore the vicinity. Thick shrubs and protruding rocks hampered his ability to survey his property. The land Uncle had once proudly cultivated, and on which he'd kept herds of domesticated animals, lay as wasteland with limited accessibility. As the journey progressed, with my assistance, he ventured into the unreachable areas he'd not seen since returning home. And for the umpteenth time, Uncle gazed at the resting place of Harriet.

While the day was still new, I returned to further inspect the ruins of my home. I walked slowly up the rugged hillside to ensure that Uncle had a safely guided walk. As I walked up to the crest of the hill, memories of the pleasures I had once enjoyed, began to flood my mind as more disturbing scenes came into view. My heart had become overwhelmed as I approached the crest of the hill – the spot where my home once stood. I walked toward the foundation of my ravaged home and reminisced on my life of pleasures and the sorrows that lay buried beneath my feet.

As I walked slowly toward my crumbled home, I reflected on the older men who'd once tilled the soil, and the fact that they lay buried beneath the very soil they'd once tilled. Those were the folk who'd greatly contributed to the good life, and to the joyful existence in a once thriving village.

My eyes surveyed the entire surrounding. Each item strewn around the vicinity had brought back vivid memories of the place I had once cherished as my childhood home. Everything lay as rubble, with relics strewn around as evidence of an earlier existence of life.

I glanced toward the distant hill to see the house of my best friend, Tim. As my eyes surveyed the vicinity, I noticed that Tim's house was no longer standing. His parents may have been in their quiet resting place. But Tim should have been in the prime of his life. I perceived that he may have very well joined the exodus to seek life in the town, or elsewhere – leaving his house to crumble.

As my mind wandered around the vicinity, I could almost hear the laughter of playing children, and the sounds of a village that had once beamed with joy and happiness on a bright sun-lit day.

I stepped away from the spot where my home once stood, and walked toward the area where the grassy field once waved in the breeze. A short distance from the edge of the field, I saw the fallen trunk of the cedar tree. It was once my grandfather's, and subsequently, my father's favourite place of attachment. Over the years, the tree trunk decayed and became part of the fertile soil beneath its under-belly. It was barely visible for the withes and tall shrubs that over-grew its entire length and height.

The cedar tree that had once spread its branches over the fallen tree trunk was no longer there. At the time of his passing, that was the tree the family had hewn down to make board for my father's casket. The remaining cedar trees stood around the property – tall and gigantic. That's the way Grandfather Grovel would have liked to see the off-spring of the original tree he'd planted many years prior. The cedar trees had brought back lasting memories of my pleasurable life at home.

As my tour progressed, and while Uncle showed his willingness to follow, I dropped in on my parents whose resting place lay by the north side of the once, grassy field. Uncle Harry had been following with added curiosity. He'd been slipping and stumbling each step he took, but had fully trusted my strong arms and support.

Tears streamed down my cheeks as I reflected on the joyful days with my parents at the helm. Many years had elapsed since they were laid to rest, but I stood in silence, and with a grieving heart as I inspected the site. A miniature forest of trees, shrubs, and tangled withes shrouded the area, making it difficult to identify the spot. It was an overwhelming feeling to cope with the loss of my home, and to see the resting place of my parents, and my grandparents, also my brother Charley. In my moment of grief and sadness, I asked myself; "Why can't humankind live forever and rid the heart of the many moments of grief and sadness?"

Uncle Harry had been quietly inspecting the resting place of my parents. It was his first time seeing the place where they were laid to rest.

"See the stones on your right, Uncle? That's Mother's resting place. And that's Father's resting place on the left." Uncle Harry held firmly to his walking cane as he gazed with much curiosity, at my parents' resting place.

"Jim, I remember when news came to me that Sister Mabel had passed away. As you may recall, not long thereafter, both of my parents had also passed," Uncle said. Uncle Harry bowed his head in silence, giving due respects to those who'd passed on.

"Uncle, Mother didn't have an opportunity to say a proper goodbye. It was such a devastating moment for the family. Father wasn't ill for very long when too had passed away," I reminded Uncle Harry as he kept his gaze at the resting place of my parents.

"I later learned that your father had passed away not long thereafter," Uncle said. "Jim, I'm privileged to finally see the resting place of your parents, and your grandparents, particularly my sister Mabel," Uncle said while he carefully scrutinized the vicinity.

I stood with a saddened heart as I reminisced on the joys and happiness my parents, and my grandparents had once brought to my young life, and to the lives of my siblings. I tried to hold back the tears as I inspected my family's quiet resting place. Uncle made an audible sigh as he stood, holding firmly to his walking cane.

On the right side of my mother's and father's resting place, I saw the resting place of Grandmother Eavie. The stones were in total disarray – since she'd passed long before Grandfather Grovel. Her resting place had become more vulnerable to the elements – frequent rainstorms, and the feet of roaming animals. Resting quietly on the left side of

Grandmother Eavie's, was Grandfather Grovel's resting place – the stones still somewhat intact.

While my eyes surveyed the vicinity, I tried to recall the place where my little brother, Charley was laid to rest. As I recalled, Mother's resting place was closest to my brother Charley's. But there were no stones intact to identify the exact spot where he was laid to rest.

And while I grieved the passing of my parents, and my grandparents, and my brother Charley, Uncle Harry made audible sighs as he turned his focus toward the adjoining hill.

"Jim, from where we stand, Harriet's resting place is also visible." Uncle pointed toward the side of the hill, where we'd earlier visited Harriet's resting place.

"Uncle, I can clearly see her resting place from where I'm standing." I assisted my uncle to stand more firmly so he had a better view of Harriet's resting place beneath the branches of a small Red Top tree. It was rather solacing to see a Red Top tree in bloom. That tree was no doubt, an offspring of the original Red Top tree.

Uncle's thoughts were focused away from my dilemma and directed toward his own. He'd tried to hide the tears flowing down his cheeks, but finally took a handkerchief from his pocket and wiped the flowing tears. While my uncle paid his due respects to those who'd passed on, my eyes were fastened on the Red Top tree overhanging Harriet's resting place.

"Uncle, I can see Harriet resting beneath a Red Top tree. That's wonderful," I said, as I set my gaze toward Harriet's resting-place. Uncle clung firmly to his walking cane to get a better footing before he spoke;

"Yes!" he said, "I had promised to give her a cool resting place, and had therefore kept my promise." The tears continued to flow down his cheeks.

I had given Uncle another opportunity to visit Harriet's place of rest. It was also a golden opportunity to have his first view of the resting place of my parents, as well as my grandparents, and my brother, Charley.

While I continued to survey the vicinity of my ravaged home, I gazed at my parents' resting place on my left, and Harriet's resting place on my right – on the side of the adjacent hill. With the passing of my parents, my grandparents, and my brother Charley, also Uncle's parents and his beloved Harriet, I began to perceive the finality of death. The very home, so consciously created by my parents – the place I grew up in during my tender years, lay deserted and silent as death itself. The village atmosphere, once exuberant with sounds of playing children, chirping birds and a gleeful spirit, died with the very ones who'd once contributed to its joyful existence.

I further reflected on the fallen trunk of the Red Top tree as it lay dried and rotted in front of the gateway. The dead tree lay as a memorial to a place that had once offered a cool shade, and rest to the tired feet of those who'd once sought shelter beneath its spreading branches.

No one remained to relate the sad tales of the tree's demise – whether it had been stricken by a bolt of lightning, or collapsed by reason of old age. Only the tree, and those who may have been present at the time, hold the mystery surrounding its demise. Just as the dead lay in silence, the village also lay silent. The entire village remained in a state of decay, with parts of its surrounding claimed by the prongs of new technology and a modern way of life.

While I surveyed the ruins in the vicinity, the morning had swiftly drifted away. Uncle had begun to show obvious signs of fatigue. His unusually long walk across the hillside terrain, coupled with impediments in his feet, had contributed to his discomfort. His sudden change in demeanor was a sure sign of fatigue. At this point, I knew it was time to head back to his house.

"Uncle Harry, the sun has been swiftly rising overhead. I believe it's time we return home," I said, as he stood holding firmly to his walking cane, while still scrutinizing the rubble strewn around the vicinity. A radiant glow appeared on my uncle's face as he stepped cautiously down the rugged hillside, clutching his walking cane, and relying on my added support.

As I descended the hill, amidst his great grief, Uncle had been enduring excruciating pains, resulting from his aching joints and muscles. Beneath the warm glow of the morning sun, I arrived at his house, where he'd promptly returned to his chair in the kitchen.

Uncle Harry was in no mood to speak as he sat slumped in his chair. The long morning stroll had taken its toll on his joints and muscles.

I had made every effort to avoid disrupting Uncle's relaxation while I planned my next activity for the day. Nonetheless, I felt I must alert him to my scheduled visit with Aunt Edith.

"Uncle! It remains a surprise that Aunt Edith's house has withstood the test of time. After so many years, her house has remained on its foundation." Uncle quickly shuffled himself in his chair as he looked toward the exit door.

"It is indeed a surprise," he said. "Edith's house is in disrepair, but it has remained standing, while most other houses have crumbled. Edith has been in poor health, particularly since her husband, Gordon passed away."

"I'll not return home before checking in on Aunt Edith," I assured Uncle. "While you take your rest, I'll drop by to pay her a visit." I promptly excused myself and stepped onto the road leading to my aunt's house. There was no telling the eagerness in my uncle's heart to join me on the trip, but I felt that he'd had his share of outdoor activities for the day.

Chapter 13

A Voice From My Childhood

I had commenced my journey in slow strides along the narrow road leading to Aunt Edith's house. My conscience had been slowly eroding from the conviction of, not maintaining a line of communication with her since leaving Coopers Village. There had been a compelling desire to pay that long-overdue visit to my aunt, who'd contributed greatly to my young life.

Aunt Edith's house stood at the side of a low hill, in close proximity to Uncle Harry's. Each stride had been taking me closer to her house. Just as I approach the stone bridge, my aunt's house became visible on the left side of the hill.

I made a brief stop on the bridge to reminisce on the days of my youth, when the creek passing beneath was a favorite place where children played. I reminisced on the days when I, along with my siblings, and other children of the neighborhood, attempted to catch the tiny fish as they continually swished around in the creek. As I played in the crystal-clear waters of the creek with my siblings, I collected pebbles that had been cleanly washed by the flowing streams. After a heavy shower of rain, when the creek overflowed its banks, tiny fish were often washed onto the grass. With whatever vessels there were at our disposal, my siblings and I, along with other children, scooped up the tiny creatures and returned them to the creek. The ones that weren't so lucky, were washed away among shrubs and thick grass, where they'd become a day's meal to flying creatures and rodents.

As I looked down at the stagnant creek, I was sadly reminded of the day prior, when I had noticed the disturbing condition in which it lay. It was an overwhelming sight of a place that had once offered joyous pleasures to my young life, and to the lives of all children of the village. While the stone bridge maintained its humble appearance over the creek, the sight below appeared disgustingly gruesome. The stagnant creek had been choked by thick green moss and bubbling dark froth – and discards tossed along its path.

The origins of the discards had become more revealing as I walked across the bridge. They were modern product containers that had their origins in the towns. Such refuse and discards were identified as products from the lifestyles of town folk who made frequent visits to the village. I further concluded that the few folk who hadn't joined the exodus, made frequent visits to the towns, bringing back with them, instant food products in modern packages.

A closer scrutiny of the discarded items revealed, empty milk carton boxes that remained afloat on the surface of the murky creek, and on its banks.

During my childhood, the folk of the village stored fresh milk in pots and glass bottles. To accommodate a modern fast-paced lifestyle, milk bottles have been replaced by waxed carton boxes, similar to the ones used in the towns and cities of my foreign homeland. Milk ready to be consumed, is packaged in hard, waxed carton boxes and plastic bottles – like the ones on the banks, and in the center of the creek. The empty discards surrounding the creek, and those floating on its murky surface, appeared to be the discards of frequent visitors to the village.

I immediately reflected on the days of my youth, when my parents, and other village folk, didn't have instant milk in carton boxes. Whenever my father, and Grandfather Grovel milked the cows, and their milking goats, the milk was promptly boiled and stored in glass bottles – until it was ready for use. I, along with my siblings, had often waited by the wood-burning stove to sound an alarm when the milk in the pot showed signs of boiling over. At the first sighting of bubbles on the surface of the milk, I had promptly sounded the alarm for my parents, or an older sibling to remove the pot from the fire. To neglect my duty, or give a late warning meant that half the milk in the pot had boiled over its rim and into the fire. As Mother had often said, "It's an awful waste having the cows produce milk and seeing it boil over into the fire."

While I observed the despicable appearance of the creek, I immediately perceived that, Coopers Village portrayed the trademarks of modern technology – instant products, mass consumption, and the discards that follow. The traditional lifestyle the older village folk had once embraced, has been infringed upon by modern customs and habits.

Interaction of the folk remaining in the village, with those who'd joined the exodus to towns and cities, had drastically altered what was once a village tradition. The folk remaining in the village, adopted the new lifestyle of relying on quick meals, and a town-lifestyle of eating on-the-run – consuming their foods from disposable containers and fancy packages, and tossing the discards along the village roadway, and into the creek.

In a state of disbelief, I continued my journey across the bridge and toward Aunt Edith's house.

Like Uncle Harry's, Aunt Edith's house stood only a few steps from the road below, and within close proximity to the stone bridge. It was once a decent village home, surrounded by a vast field of lush vegetation, and a wide yard space where my aunt's children had once played.

Although in a dilapidated state, the structure of Aunt Edith's house had remained intact – as Uncle Harry had confirmed. Protruding rocks, stubborn shrubs, and tall trees however, had returned to reclaim the once beautiful yard space, and my aunt's vast field of lush vegetation. They were the very rocks and shrubs Uncle Gordon had mowed over to prepare his yard at the time he'd built his house.

Aunt Edith's wide yard was once covered with variegated shades of green grass. Her husband, Gordon, had often paid my brother Larry and me a few coins to groom the grass after the cows had grazed on the new growths. Larry and I got to work with the newly sharpened knives given to us by Uncle Gordon. Within a short time, we did the finishing touches to restore the sheer beauty of the yard. As added compensation, my brother and I were treated to bread and biscuits freshly baked in Aunt's kitchen.

I had vivid memory of the days my siblings and I played sports with Aunt Edith's children in the cleanly groomed yard. As the games progressed, my aunt and Uncle Gordon had taken in every sport under the evening sun.

I proceeded slowly toward Aunt Edith's house – stopping momentarily to reminisce on life as it once was at her home, and in the vicinity. There wasn't much that I could see of the places where I had once had joyful childhood pleasures. There hadn't been much I could see for the tall trees that formed a miniature forest, obscuring my overall view of the vicinity.

In a state of despondency, and without further hesitation, I entered through the gate leading to Aunt Edith's house. I tapped softly at the front door.

"Aunt Edith! This is your nephew, Jimmy." Not wanting to sound overwhelming, I called her name once more. There was a slight shuffling sound behind the solid wooden door, followed by a feeble voice;

"Hello! Did you say, Jimmy?" The voice sounded as one in a state of delayed ecstasy.

"Yes, Aunt Edith. I'm Jimmy." I waited in front of the closed door.

A minute or two had elapsed before the heavy door finally swung open. A tall frail figure appeared in the doorway. Though the years had taken their toll on her original beauty and charm, I had immediately identified my aunt Edith by her habitual bashful smile. She stood clothed in a brown dress extending mid-way between her knees and her ankles. Her feet appeared to have been gasping for fresh air, as they were clad in thick semi-white socks and a pair of high-cut black shoes.

Aunt Edith's long frail hands clung firmly to a metal walker – as if her entire body depended on its support. She stood like a tall permanent statue in the open doorway. Her cheeks glowed from the thrills of my unannounced appearance.

"Hello, Aunt Edith!" I said in a most gleeful voice. She stood silent as one in a state of delirium.

"Hello, Jimmy! My long-lost nephew. Harry had told me you were coming home," she said in a most exhilarating voice. While she stood in the center of the doorway, Aunt Edith clung firmly to the walker – as if it had been her only means of upright support.

"So good to see you, Aunt Edith," I said, after extending a warm embrace. I had made every effort to show remorse for not communicating with her during my long absence. My gesture of remorse, however, had been overshadowed by her joyous delight at my presence.

"Come inside, Jimmy! Please come in," she said. She held firmly to the walker, while her long frail left hand reached for the door knob. As I entered the house, the heavy door slammed shut behind me.

With great effort, my aunt rolled her walker forward. She crawled slowly toward a wooden chair on which a red fabric cushion was placed. Her frail trembling body fell lifelessly on the chair. Aunt Edith sat still for a moment, as if she needed to catch up on her breathing.

I walked toward my aunt and placed a beautiful package in her hands. A glow suddenly appeared on her face as she reached for the package. With heightened curiosity, she slowly opened the package to reveal, among other items, the most comfortable pair of slippers. Aunt Edith was reassured that I had kept her in my thoughts.

"That's very nice of you, Jimmy," she said. Her face glowed with a brilliant smile. She'd carefully placed the package on a small table beside her chair.

"I knew you would have liked that particular gift, Aunt Edith." She reached for the package and took another look at the remaining contents with an even more cheerful smile.

"Jimmy, they're adorable," Aunt Edith said. "You knew I fancied every pair of slippers in the display windows during my days traveling to Brighton Town," she said as she returned the package to the table.

"It's been many years, Aunt, but I've been thoughtful of you and the things you fancy the most." She repeatedly scrutinized the slippers she'd placed on top of the package. There was a sudden glow, and a cheerful smile on her face.

"Have a seat, Jimmy! You must be a bit tired, after walking under the heat of the sun." She pointed toward a wooden bench resting in one corner of the hall.

Aunt Edith sat comfortably on her chair, while she looked repeatedly at the package resting on the table. I couldn't have ignored her repeated gaze toward an open window opposite where she sat. There appeared to have been a place of attraction that captured her attention, and kept her gaze at bay.

While Aunt Edith focused her attention toward the open window, my eyes were focused in the center of the hall, where there was a table, surrounded by four chairs. I immediately began to reacquaint with a place that held lasting memories of the days of my youth. It was the place where families had once gathered to savor Aunt's delightful meals. Amidst the devastated village, and my grief at the disappearance of my home, it was a delight to see and touch objects and artefacts from my childhood.

As each moment passed, my aunt had remained overwhelmed by her unexpected visitor. At times, she'd sat speechless, and when she spoke, it was often a repeat of the words she'd previously spoken.

"Jimmy, it's so nice that you've come home for a visit," Aunt Edith said. "I've always wondered where you were. I was delighted to see my brother, Harry, when he returned home." She sat and stared toward the kitchen with that habitual bashful smile on her face. The sight of Aunt's kitchen, particularly the wood-burning stove, brought back memories of the good times I once had at her home. Aunt's kitchen had never ceased to be permeated by the aroma of spicy meats and the tasty bakes she'd often made.

I turned my eyes toward the table with its four chairs. The sight of the table immediately brought back memories of life in the village, and life as it once was in my aunt's home.

"Aunt, it's so nice to see your table with its four chairs still intact. They certainly hold lasting sentiments of my childhood," I said, as I jogged her memory of the days of old. "I remember at Christmas time, and on special occasions, when all the families got together. Your table had always been spread with the finest meals for everyone." She looked at the table, surrounded by its four chairs.

"Those were the good old days, Jimmy. I'll never forget those exciting days," my aunt said. "The table and its four chairs were made by Gordon at the time we were married. That was Gordon's masterpiece from his long-time occupation of making furniture for the local residents." She looked at the table as one holding deep regrets, and having a longing to re-establish her presence in the place she'd once enjoyed the most. A sudden change in Aunt Edith's demeanor implied that, the old table and its chairs were not the best subjects to discuss, nor was she happy to be taken down memory lane to her days of vigor and vivacity. My aunt had become grief-stricken at a subject matter that had brought back unpleasant memories – her deceased husband, Gordon, and living at a place that remained void of the once exhilarating sounds of a thriving human existence.

With painstaking effort, my aunt rose to her feet, holding firmly to her walker. She rolled the walker close to the table and carefully sat on one of the hardwood chairs. Aunt appeared complacent as she sat around the table containing her daily necessities.

"I don't get around very much anymore, Jimmy," she said. "My son, Erwin helps me to get around, but he's always working in the field – reaping the crops and attending to the few animals." I quickly perceived how fortunate my aunt had been to have had a son who didn't join the exodus to seek a livelihood in the town, or migrate to a foreign country. "Jimmy," Aunt said, "I can no longer prepare my meals in the kitchen. Since Gordon passed away, I'm privileged to have Erwin prepare my meals."

With trembling hands, she reached across the table and took two cups from a silver tray. "Jimmy, would you care to have tea?"

"I'll certainly join you for tea, Aunt Edith. It's rather kind of you." I watched her place each of the cups on a gold-rimmed saucer she'd also taken from the silver tray. From a large enamel thermos resting in the center of the table, Aunt slowly poured tea into the cups. She opened a beautiful package and placed biscuits into a crystal dish which she placed on the table. I was immediately overwhelmed at the sight of the cups and their gold-rimmed saucers. It was the same set of cups and saucers in which my aunt had always served tea at Christmas time, and all other times she'd entertained guests. As I held the cup, it brought back memories of the life I once knew, and the joyful times I once had, being entertained in Aunt Edith's home.

The brilliant golden sun was slowly advancing toward the mid-sky. As the day progressed, I sipped tea and enjoyed tasty biscuits with Aunt Edith, while she briefed me on the state of things in the village. I was quite eager to hear her reports that brought back memories of home, and life as it once was in my village.

"Aunt Edith, there was a time when folk, young and old, abandoned village life to reside in the towns and cities. Some folk had left to reside in foreign countries, but you chose to remain here. Why didn't you join the exodus and migrate with your family?" My aunt replaced her cup into its saucer and sat upright as one preparing to give an astounding speech.

"Jimmy, I didn't like the idea of abandoning village life to live in the town. Gordon liked the village life, and so did I. We'd therefore chosen to remain here to enjoy the good life." A pleasant glow appeared on her face as she spoke. "My older son, Edward, joined the exodus to America, where he still resides. He likes the foreign lifestyle, but brings his family to pay a visit from time-to-time. My daughter, Beatrice, had moved to Brighton Town with her husband and the children." My aunt stopped to take a sip from her cup before she continued to speak.

"My younger son, Erwin, didn't like town life. He'd therefore chosen to remain here," Aunt Edith said. As she mentioned her son, Erwin, the sudden glow that appeared on her face had spoken volumes.

"Aunt, it was good that Erwin didn't join the exodus from the village to places elsewhere. The village is where his heart is, and he appears to be comfortable with farm life." She listened with keen interest. It was also her belief that Erwin preferred village life.

"Erwin followed in his father's footsteps, and therefore worked on the farm to maintain his family," Aunt Edith said. "Erwin's children have grown up, but his wife, Clarice, passed away a short while ago."

Aunt Edith held her face in the palm of her hands as she tried to hold back tears flooding her eyes.

Amidst her grief, my aunt continued to brief me on events I so much wanted to know. She'd taken a few more sips from her cup before continuing from where she'd left off speaking.

"Gordon passed away a few years back," she said. "You can see his resting place on the west side of the house." She pointed toward the window opposite her wooden chair, from where it seemed, she had an uninterrupted view of her husband's resting place.

"Aunt, I was quiet saddened by Uncle Harry's report on Uncle Gordon's passing," I said. My aunt remained silent as she tried to regain a measure of composure. She tried to hold back new tears that had been flooding her eyes. It wasn't my intent to cause further grief to Aunt Edith's already fragile emotion. I had quickly realized that, Gordon wasn't the best subject on which to dwell, and had therefore promptly changed the subject.

I looked up at the ceiling of the hall and noticed Aunt Edith's oil lantern, still suspended by a metal chain. It was the same lantern Uncle Harry had once used for outdoor lighting, whenever he had twilight parties and needed more light. I immediately began to reflect on the days of family fun, and village gatherings under the bright glow of the oil lanterns.

"Aunt Edith, I'm delighted to see your oil lantern still intact. It has brought back vivid memory of the times during special events, when the lantern sent its beams across a wide perimeter beneath the night sky." She turned slightly to acknowledge the presence of the lantern in the ceiling.

"Jimmy, I'm happy to have kept my oil lantern, also my oil lamps," Aunt said. "In a village where a few of the remaining folk have opted for the new technology, I've held on to the deep-rooted village traditions."

"It appears that the new technology could have benefited you and Uncle Gordon," I insinuated. Aunt Edith had quickly gestured her disapproval of my suggestion that she should have opted for the new technology.

"I'm quite comfortable holding on to tradition," she said. "Erwin maintains a constant supply of firewood and coal to keep my stove burning. He has maintained a constant supply of oil for the lamps and the lanterns. Adopting the new technology often comes with a price," Aunt Edith said. While she spoke, there wasn't a doubt that she had her qualms about adopting the technology.

Aunt Edit was among the few village folk who didn't trade their wood-burning stove for electrical appliances. She also didn't trade her lanterns and oil lamps for light bulbs. As I looked at my aunt's old radio resting on a small table in a corner of the hall, I immediately perceived that she, along with other folk, would have benefited from electric power to keep their radio playing – instead of depletable batteries. As the debate for, and against electricity continued, I perceived that the older folk, as well as the young folk who remained after the exodus, do not have the means to afford electricity and the appliances it demands.

Aunt Edith was fully aware of the benefits, the price attached, and the consequences of the old and young folk adopting the new technology: The monthly usage charges, and the big price paid by some folk who'd had their home destroyed by fire.

As she spoke, I perceived another downfall in equipping the old village houses with electric wires. The absence of proper fire extinguishing equipment, had hampered the folk's ability to put out a house fire, whenever one occurred. A house fire, triggered by electricity, required much more than a few buckets of water to extinguish the flames. These consequences, as related by Aunt Edith, had further reaffirmed her belief that she'd made the right decision to retain her traditional village lifestyle. She'd become leery of adopting technological devices that are foreign to her, and other older folk.

In contrast, Uncle Harry who'd migrated to his foreign homeland, upon returning home – more than sixty years later, he'd readily adopted the new technology. Uncle had gladly blended his foreign technology he'd imported into the village, with that which already existed.

It was the end of a rather lengthy tea session with Aunt Edith. I felt that she would rather devote her thoughts and the limited energy she stored to carry on with her usual daily activities. My thoughts reflected on Uncle Harry who'd been pondering my long absence. I had therefore ended the long conversation with Aunt Edith, but not before assuring her that I would return to pay another visit.

Aunt Edith rolled her walker across the hall, where she painstakingly slumped back onto her chair. For one of eighty-one, she'd amazingly retained her muscular structure. And although the years had left indelible wrinkles, her face had remained a symbol of beauty. I had reluctantly excused myself and exited the house. As I made my exit through the front door, I watched new tears flowing down her cheeks.

With careful steps, I made my way down the rugged path leading from Aunt Edith's house. The sun had passed its mid-point in the sky as I walked leisurely along the road leading to Uncle's house.

Aunt Edith's reports, and the very settings in her home, had brought back memories of life in my home village. Tears flooded my eyes as her details, and the relics in her home, jolted my memory of the joyous times of my childhood.

Aunt Edith did not join the exodus from the village. She'd therefore witnessed the gradual abandonment, and deterioration of the place that had once teemed with life and century-old traditions. She'd witnessed the exodus of young folk to towns and foreign destinations, and the new technology that effected the drastic changes in the lifestyles of village folk. Despite the technological changes, Aunt Edith remained devoted to her lifestyle of customs and traditions. A wood-burning stove continued to be her only known, and acceptable way of preparing a meal. Despite the availability of electricity and electric light bulbs, she held on to her oil lamps and lanterns – not adopting the new technological substitutes. The oil lamps continued to be the means by which she viewed objects during the night. Aunt Edith relied on the light of the sun by day and the brilliance of the moon, and her oil lamps and lanterns by night.

Like Uncle Harry, Aunt Edith had an uninterrupted view of Gordon's resting place. In their homes, they positioned themselves at a place from which they gazed continually at their deceased spouse's resting place – as if they'd still maintained matrimonial ties. Aunt Edith's repeated gaze in the direction of Gordon's resting place had left me to conclude that she had hopes for the imminent – to be some day, resting beside him. Likewise, it appears, Uncle Harry maintained his hopes of some day, resting by the side of Harriet.

In a state of sadness, I reflected on my aunt and uncle, whom time and circumstances had left in a precarious situation: Uncle Harry, partially incapacitated by reason of old age and severe pains: Aunt Edith, afflicted by reason of old age, coupled with debilitating pains that severely restricted her mobility. My aunt and uncle remained in the village to ponder their fate in a place where time seemed to have left them in the shadows. I perceived that each passing day, week, month and year, they've been waiting in unwavering hope that time would finally take them in its grasp, leaving behind, the place where they'd once had the pride and joy of belonging.

Chapter 14

The Spring Along The Valley

The sun had been making its way toward the western horizon, when I arrived at Uncle's house.

A visit to the spring in the valley was next on my itinerary. I felt strongly that Uncle Harry would be in no shape to go on another tour for the day, and therefore excused myself from the lunch session – not to his greatest delight.

I promptly stepped back onto the roadway and commenced my journey on the south side of Uncle's house, where I had faint memory of the narrow path leading into the valley.

My heart danced with glee as I headed toward the spring. It was like traveling down memory lane, as I reminisced on the wonderful days of my childhood. I anticipated seeing another landmark – the spring where my siblings and I, and children of the neighborhood once frolicked in its bubbling waters.

It was once a daily routine for my siblings and me to fetch water from the spring in the early morning, and if the weather permitted, during the evening hours. A constant fear of the arrival of darkness, prompted everyone in the village to make the necessary trips to the spring before dusk fell.

From the porch of my home, my siblings and I had often listened to the sounds of the spring. The crystal streams flowing over pebbles, stones and rocks, created a harmonious sound along the valley, particularly on nights when the village was drenched by a heavy downpour. The sound of the bubbling spring had always kept the children awake throughout the night. Children anxiously waited for the morning when they would frolic in the enticing waters of the spring. They watched the spring in spate as excessive water flooded its path along the valley. My siblings and I had happily joined children of the neighborhood for thrilling moments, frolicking in the bubbling streams. It was more than a miracle that no child or adult had ever drowned in the spring, or in the treacherous river passing through villages.

During a heavy rainstorm, the hills emptied their numerous streams into the spring, as it flowed along the valley to an estuary – a large river flowing through villages. Folk watched in awe as the sparkling green water in the river glide through the villages, carrying away small trees and whatever objects lie in its path. No one had dared to venture into a river so wide and deep as it made its way to its destination – a seashore many miles away. The river's vast expanse occupied valuable lands, making parts of the villages inaccessible to the folk.

Days after a heavy rainstorm, the spring gradually regained its normal tranquil calm, thus putting a damper on the children's shrieks and laughter in the valley.

With great enthusiasm, I continued my descent into the valley – tripping and stumbling over unseen withes, thick shrubs and protruding stones. As I descended the rugged hillside, the still silence had set the scene for what awaited my arrival. The still silence, however, didn't deter me from making my descent. There was a compelling force luring me into the valley to see the state of the spring. I was on my final descent, when I suddenly landed, head first into the valley.

I rose to my feet and immediately began to survey the vicinity. To my dismay, the spring where children and grown-ups once swam and had their moments of thrill, lay dry and abandoned. The spring was once the venue where children and grown-ups played in its bubbling streams, and beneath the miniature waterfalls created after heavy torrential rainfalls. I was unable to identify the spring that was once the swimming pool of the village folk. Its streams had dried up, bringing an end to the joyous pleasures it had once brought to the village folk.

The valley was once a place where crystal-clear waters of the spring flowed over rocks and pebbles. The spring, however, lay choked by rocks and the roots of tall trees and shrubs. The valley lay dry and silent – deserted by those who'd once frolicked in its swelling streams.

The valley was once a place of entertainment for the village folk. It was a place of flowing streams and cascading miniature waterfalls. Except for the sounds of creatures of the wild, there hadn't been signs of life of any humans. I immediately perceived a place where time had stood still for the folk who'd once inhabited its space. The place that had once brought great joy and cheerfulness to a village, exists only as a memory. The thrills and laughter of children, once heard in the valley had long subsided. As I stood to ponder the disappearance of the spring, I could hear the sounds and laughter of folk frolicking in its swelling streams. But I awake to the realization that it was just my imagination. The cheerful sounds once heard in the valley, lay beneath rocks, and the roots of tall trees and shrubs. The water once flowing in the spring, had long dried up. The spring had ceased to exist.

I stood in silence in the desolate valley to ponder the vanished spring. In a solitary state of mind, I lamented the demise of another landmark of my village. I had sadly bidden farewell to the abandoned and deserted valley, and commenced my journey up the rugged hillside. While I ascended the hill, the spreading branches of the hillside trees sheltered my path from the crisp afternoon sun.

I had promptly returned from the valley to find Uncle waiting with great enthusiasm. He'd been seated at the dining table, but didn't wish to dine alone. Amidst my tons of apologies, I joined him to enjoy the savory lunch he'd prepared.

The late lunch session had ended, when Uncle rose slowly from around the dining table and returned to his usual chair in the kitchen. He appeared to have been in the mood for an afternoon conversation session. I sat ready to receive whatever new bit of information there was about the village. The sight of the dry spring and a deserted valley had plunged me into a somber mood. But I was certain that a conversation with Uncle would bring some relief. I therefore took my place in the hall, in the comfort of the leather sofa. The stage had been set for an afternoon session of exchanging thoughts and reminiscing on village life, past and present.

The television set stood in one corner of the hall – as if Uncle had been receiving his daily entertainment from whatever appeared on the screen. This didn't appear to have been the case, as he hadn't turned on the television since I arrived at his house. In light of his imported foreign lifestyle, it appeared that Uncle couldn't perceive a home without a television, hence, the large television set placed in his main hall.

Uncle Harry sat poised, in anticipation of an afternoon conversation session. As I had anticipated, he'd been anxiously waiting to know the state of the spring in the valley that had once influenced his life, and the lives of all village folk.

"What did you see in the valley, Jim?" Uncle asked. I pondered whether he felt that he should have accompanied me on the trip to the spring. That was certainly not the kind of adventure he could have handled. Uncle certainly wouldn't have endured the walk down and up the winding hillside path.

"Uncle, the valley is not what it used to be," I said. He sat as one traumatized after hearing sad news.

"I've always wanted to visit the spring since returning home, but I'm unable to walk the rocky hillside path," Uncle said. "I'm afraid of venturing into the valley without having the assurance of a way back up the rough terrain."

"Uncle, there's no direct path to reach the spring. And once in the valley, there's not much to see," I said. Uncle tapped on his forehead, as if to force a recollection of his days of fun in the spring. His action was also a display of grief at the news of the spring's demise.

"Jim, is there no more water in the valley?" Uncle asked. There was a sudden change in his demeanor as he waited in anticipation of a response.

"The spring has practically dried up, Uncle Harry. The valley remains cluttered with rocks, and choked by the roots of tall trees and shrubs." This hadn't been the report Uncle expected to receive. He therefore hung his head forward as one having a moment of silence to give his due respects to a lost landmark.

"Jim, the remaining children of the village no longer have an interest in the spring. A few have the convenience of water flowing inside their homes," Uncle Harry said. "Those who haven't been privileged to have water pipes in their homes, go to alternate locations along the road to fetch water from pipe faucets. Jim, the youth of the village have no reason to go to the spring in the valley with their buckets, like the former children once did," Uncle said with added assurance.

"I wouldn't have known that, Uncle. There's no water in the spring to attract those who would wish to venture into the valley," I reminded Uncle. "The days of fun and laughter in the valley are long gone." Uncle hung his head forward in silence as he waited in anticipation of receiving more sad tales about the spring.

Although rough terrain had impeded my uncle's visit to the spring in the valley, he'd shown much remorse for the silent spring, as well as the abandoned valley.

"The spring was once the pride and joy of the folk in the villages through which it passed," Uncle said. "Since returning home, I've not heard a sound in the valley."

"That's because there's no spring in the valley," I reminded Uncle Harry.

I hung my head in deep despair at another lost landmark of my childhood. The valley that once had a crystal-clear, gently flowing spring – a place of thrill and excitement for the village folk, has been left to solitude. Landmarks and places that once offered entertainment to the folk, have disappeared, leaving a village void of a thriving and lively existence.

Chapter 15

A Look Back

Uncle Harry sat comfortably in his chair – the place where he appeared to find peace of mind and maximum relaxation. He'd been, no doubt, reminiscing on his childhood and adolescent years – playing in the crystal waters of the spring, and enjoying an exhilarating village life. I remained in the hall, still saddened by the dried-up spring in the valley.

I sat poised to exchange pleasant thoughts with Uncle Harry, but had been sadly reminiscing on the things that were no more: the spring in the valley, the home of my childhood, and the many other landmarks that had vanished. Most of all, the folk who'd abandoned the village for life in towns, cities and foreign places. Those were the folk who'd once contributed to the exhilarating existence in the village. Uncle Harry no doubt held deep sentiments of his childhood, and the things that had once contributed to his joyous past.

My conversation with Uncle had taken on momentum, while the village stood bathed in the radiance of the golden afternoon sun. The radiance, however, had suddenly given way to darkness. Swift westerly winds rustled the leaves and swayed the branches of the surrounding trees. Rain-clouds had swiftly formed, expelling whatever sunlight remained. Frequent flashes of lightning, and loud claps of thunder roared in the heavens.

The pattering of raindrops against the window-pane, and on the leaves of the surrounding trees, drowned out the sound of any voice beneath the roof of the house. It had therefore become difficult to continue my conversation with Uncle Harry. Uncle's eyelids had been slowly closing until, as I anticipated, he'd slumped backward into his chair and dozed off. That's the way life used to be during the days of my childhood – the village folk lapsed into a slumber during heavy rainstorms. With no indoor occupation, the entire village remained on a fiesta until the rains let up.

Uncle Harry was overcome by deep slumber while the rain persisted. While he enjoyed his time of relaxation, I had remained partially reclined in the comfort of the sofa. This was a perfect setting to reminisce on life as it used to be during my childhood years.

Folk who'd been caught in a rainstorm while they were away from home, hadn't much time to seek shelter before large raindrops instantaneously hammered the village. The frequent flashes of lightning, loud claps of thunder, and the swift gathering of dark rainclouds, were forewarnings of an impending storm. Folk who'd neglected to heed the warning of the imminent down-pour, didn't stand a chance at escaping large pellets of rain that were heaved from the sky.

When the crescendo of lightning, loud claps of thunder, strong gusty winds and heavy rain began to pound the village, every living creature was forced to seek shelter. Whoever was caught away from home, had no other choice than to seek shelter in the closest neighboring house. Under such circumstances, everyone understood the importance of, "Living peaceably with all men," as neighbors who were in conflict with each other, had not the audacity to seek shelter under each other's roof.

An umbrella was considered an item of luxury most folk couldn't afford. An umbrella, however, didn't provide much protection from the fury of the pounding rain. Folk took cover from the rain by whatever means they had at their disposal: A broad hat which served the dual purpose as a shelter from the heat of the sun, and a protective covering from the rain: A broad leaf which had become a handy protective covering device. Those devices had not provided much shelter during a heavy down-pour, nonetheless.

While heavy rainstorms pounded the village, all activities ground to a halt. All creatures hustled to seek shelter from the fury of the rainstorm.

The raindrops hammering on the window-panes of Uncle's house, had brought back memories of the days of my youth. Unlike Uncle's modern house with roof made of thick concrete, the village houses were covered with metal sheeting, and therefore never evaded the sound of a single object, or matter falling from above. The pattering of raindrops on the metal roof of the houses therefore, turned into a crescendo of harmonious sounds as the heavy raindrops cascaded from the sky.

The hammering of raindrops on the metal roof of the houses had quickly drowned out the voice of anyone wishing to speak. With no indoor pastime for those sheltered beneath the roof, folk were forced into a slumber. The lucky travelers, who'd sought shelter, had also succumbed to the rain-induced slumber. The older folk had often quietly hummed their most melodious tunes, in harmony with the hammering raindrops on the metal roof. The melody of one sheltered beneath the roof, had often turned into harmony, when another voice or two joined the humming session. In the semi-darkness of the big hall of my parent's home, the strangers were overcome by slumber and had therefore succumbed to an irresistible afternoon nap, while they waited out the persistent rainstorm.

As the heavy afternoon showers continued to pound the village, Uncle Harry occasionally turned his head toward the opposite window, as he checked on the status of the rain.

The persistent pounding of raindrops on the metal roof had often ceased intermittently, only to be followed by another downpour. The folk knew the rain had let up, when it ceased from hammering on the metal roof of their houses. At that point, the rain had finally let up, restoring calm to a village whose folk had sought shelter in every nook. The sun had often partially broken through the moisture-thick rain clouds, shedding its beams around the village. As life used to be in my days, the heavy rains ceased, allowing the folk to resume their activities in the rain-soaked village.

Uncle Harry, meanwhile, continued to conduct his vigil of riding out the rainstorm – an old habit he'd resumed since returning home. The persistent showers continued into the late evening. A series of intermittent pattering on the leaves of the surrounding trees, was a signal that the rain had been letting up. Uncle therefore promptly rose from his chair and commenced preparing dinner.

Unlike the days of my youth, after a heavy downpour – while the village folk had to secure dry wood for their wood-burning stove, Uncle had all his cooking needs under one roof. With electric power at his disposal, he had only to press a button, or turn a knob to have his cooking in progress. Uncle didn't have a wood-burning stove, or oil lamps in his modern home. I remember the gruelling task of burning damp logs in order that my parents could kindle a fire to prepare their meals.

The rain had persisted into the late evening hours, forcing me to shelve whatever remaining plans I had in my itinerary for the day. Dusk had slowly crept in, while the night sky gradually divested itself of the moisture and remnants of rain clouds. A crystal-clear, panoramic view of the night sky, exposed innumerable stars in the universe. On the earth, the early dusk had created the setting for turmoil and unrest among the creatures whose sanctuary had been left wet, and in total disarray by the heavy rain showers.

My uncle Harry's frailty had become exposed, when he displayed further signs of fatigue, after his long afternoon rest. Shortly after dinner, he took his leave of absence and retreated to his room, where he retired for the night. It was an "Early-to-bed and early-to-rise" lifestyle, and the rain had further justified Uncle's early departure to bed.

At Uncle's departure, I was quickly reminded of my prior night's sleep deprivation. I had therefore followed suit and retired to bed. This was another opportune moment to reminisce on village life as it used to be during my youth, and to take advantage of a good night's sleep.

As I lay in bed, I waited for some much-needed sleep. My heart, however, had become overwhelmed by memories of my childhood life of joyful pleasures. I could almost hear the screams and laughter of children, darting naked across the neighborhood while the heavy rainstorms pounded the village. My siblings and I had happily joined the joyful children, splashing and wading naked in the puddles formed around the vicinity, and by the side of the pond. While the rain showers persisted, the creek overflowed its banks, causing small fish to be washed onto the grass. The children carried out search and rescue operations to return the little creatures to the creek. The ones that hadn't been rescued, became a quick meal for creatures in the vicinity.

The dusk had long given way to darkness. The night had been teeming with the typical sounds of the village after an evening of pouring rain. I imagined my uncle had no difficulty falling asleep, particularly after his previous night of sleeplessness – while I lay awake in a state of restlessness. Like scenes from an old movie, my past village life began to unveil in the panoramic view of my mind's eye. As I reminisced on my childhood, I could see in my mind's eye, a group of children running along the narrow track leading into the valley. I was among the exuberant children. I could hear the spring taking on momentum; its swollen streams making loud gushes against large rocks, and over pebbles and stones beneath its surface. I was about to take a plunge into the crystal stream, when I realized that I had lapsed into a semi-conscious state between waking and sleeping.

Memories of the state of the village after a heavy shower of rain, remained indelibly in my mind. The early night air had always come alive with the cries and chirps of creatures whose habitat had become disrupted by the heavy rainfall. All creatures were engaged in a scurry as they scrambled to find a dry and safe place to rest for the night. Darkness gradually covered the entire village, thus creating the atmosphere for a night of sound sleep for all creatures. Most creatures rested quietly among the tree branches, and wherever they found a dry and safe sanctuary under the night sky. With the creatures quietly resting, a long night of rest ensued in the rain-drenched village. In the still darkness, a sudden squeak had often rung out. It was the cry of an unsuspecting rodent captured by the beak, or the sharp claws of a hungry night owl.

The feeling of being sheltered and secured indoor, had always brought an early slumber to the folk of the village. The pale glow of the oil lamp resting on a table, was the only light the indoor afforded during the night hours. Although there was a natural fear of the unseen, and shadows that lurk in the darkness, no one in the village has had any apparition.

Eunice, one of my older siblings, had gained the notoriety as the cunning member of the household. Never a day went by that she hadn't created unfavorable excitement of sorts.

It was a typically black night in the month of February. It had been one of those black nights when Grandfather Grovel looked out into the night and had quickly shut the door to close out the blackness – fearing what might have been lurking without.

I had remained with my siblings in the outdoors to pop corn grains beneath the ashes of the dying bonfire. The village was warm and dry, an enticement for my siblings and me to take advantage of an extra hour in the outdoors – an action that wouldn't have gained my parents' endorsement. Eunice had asked to be excused as she said she hadn't felt well. She'd therefore promptly entered the house by way of the front door. I had remained with my other siblings to retrieve the popped corn grains as they emerged from beneath the hot ashes. My other siblings and I had become preoccupied with eating the fluffy popped corn kernels, and had therefore failed to notice that the night had gotten a bit too black.

Larry, my younger sibling, was quite certain that he'd seen a white image beside the cedar tree closest to the house. Rita, my other older sibling, was quite certain that it was a figment of Larry's imagination – he'd just been imagining things as a result of fear and anxiety, being in the outdoors after dusk. But Larry had immediately yelled for help as he remained frozen on the spot.

I peered into the darkness and immediately noticed a tall white object that appeared to have had no legs. I relied on whatever strength remained to lug Larry along as I yelled and darted toward the main door – Rita following on our heels. My siblings and I had made it to the doorsteps where we collapsed. At the sound of loud screams and cries, Father quickly opened the door. He stood at the opened door with that, "I told you so," look on his face.

"What in the name of the Almighty is the matter, children?" Father shouted. He'd remained partially hidden behind the open door, in an effort to shield himself from whatever had threatened his children. In a faint voice, Larry cried out with whatever breath remained;

"There's a ghost, Father! A white ghost." Father immediately pulled his children, one by one into the hall before he promptly shut the door. He waited with great urgency to get in on the ghost story.

"Come on children, tell me. What's the matter?" Father's eyes glared beneath the glow of the lantern suspended from the ceiling of the hall.

"There's a ghost, Father! It's beside the tree," Larry said as he lay trembling on the floor. Although Father had quickly barred the door, I sat with my other siblings, trembling, while seeking the mercy of whoever could have rendered some assistance.

My father had remained perturbed by the ghostly encounter of his offspring, and therefore began his investigation. However, when he looked at his three offspring sprawled on the floor, he immediately asked;

"Where's Eunice?" Father's fears had been compounded by the thought that, if there was a real ghost, it might have taken off with Eunice. He therefore took the lantern from the ceiling of the hall to commence his frantic search for Eunice – peradventure, he might also behold the white ghost that had frightened his children. Father was determined to look danger in the face when he ventured outdoor in his quest to find Eunice. I had remained huddled to my two siblings, fearing Father's plight, and his ominous encounter with the ghost.

While I waited in added fear and trembling, ensuing seconds of silence were immediately followed by swift scurrying in the outdoors. There were sharp words and argumentative conversations uttered in the darkness. Is Father having an encounter with the ghost? I asked myself. Loud mutterings in the darkness had brought more fear and trembling to my already quivering body. The muttering sounds had quickly changed to loud screams when Father shouted;

"Get into the house this minute. You're a menace to the children. Give me that white sheet. Return that chair to the buttery. Now!" Loud cries were heard as Eunice entered the house. She'd promptly made a mad dash to her room.

Mother had been preoccupied with performing her night chores, and was therefore unaware of the scurrying in the big hall, and in the outdoors. She came bursting into the hall to investigate the cause of the commotion after hearing Eunice's loud screams. The children she'd raised, and whose behaviour had been so well perfected, were not as perfect as she'd thought.

"What's the cause of the commotion?" Mother asked. My father quickly held up the white sheet Eunice had taken from the linen closet to be the scary ghost.

"Mabel!" Father said, "Eunice took the wooden chair from the buttery," he stopped for a quick breath. "It was that chair on which she stood in the pitch-black night beneath the cedar tree." He was overcome by a fit of anxiety. "See Mabel," Father took a series of sharp breaths, "Eunice took a white sheet from the house and placed it over her body to appear like a tall, white ghost and frightened the children." Before Father got to the end of his scary ghost details, Mother had administered the rod of correction to Eunice and ordered her to remain in her room. My siblings and I felt that Eunice had finally gotten her long overdue punishment from Mother – a good lashing from the long hide strap suspended behind the door – punishment that should keep her tricks at bay.

Mother emerged from Eunice's room in a fury. At the same time, she'd become sympathetic to Eunice's dilemma.

"There's no end to the tricks that child has played," Mother said. "There ought to be something the matter with her." Meanwhile, Father had been pacing around the hall, still a bit shaken from the ghostly dilemma.

"Eunice has always been getting into mischief," Father said. "I must have a talk with her first thing in the morning. She shouldn't be allowed to continue with her scare tactics that intimidate the other children, and cause such commotion."

Eunice had remained quietly in her room, while occasional audible sobs were heard through the crevices of her door. Whether she'd been sobbing, or just having a fit of laughter, no one knew, since she'd remained alone behind her closed door. There was no telling what new tricks she'd been planning to further intimidate her siblings, and the entire household.

I felt that a million apologies couldn't have saved Eunice from the chastisement awaiting her from my father. Her apologies didn't bring the pardon she may have sought from Mother prior to her administration of the rod of correction. It had been doubtful whether Father would administer the rod of correction to Eunice. He'd never flogged any of his offspring, particularly since the strap was hung behind the door in the hall.

Did Eunice deserve a flogging? Her action was not that of a coward. It was an act of sheer genius, though menacing to her siblings, and the entire household. It takes one of great bravery to orchestrate such a prank. Mother's administration of the rod of correction was the first my siblings and I recalled. No one had ever received the long end of the strap since it was placed behind the door. At one time, my brother Larry was overdue for a severe punishment for his wrong-doing. Mother had just waved the strap in front of his eyes before letting him go free. At that time, my siblings and I saw the strap as having a loud bark, but no bite.

The presence of the strap was a constant reminder that rules should not be broken. However, it had become obvious that the long hide strap hanging behind the door, hadn't been a deterrent to Eunice's constant pranks she habitually pulled around the house. There hadn't been screaming and whaling sounds heard in Eunice's room. As she'd habitually done, Mother may have simply held the strap as another of her warnings of looming punishment, should Eunice dare to have caused another commotion.

My parents had earlier committed themselves to the stringent rule; "Don't spare the rod and spoil the child." However, my siblings and I felt that, Mother had been violating the rule by not taking punitive measures whenever Eunice, or any other of her offspring got out of hand. Despite Mother's violation of the rule, my siblings and I had always performed every assigned duty – fearing the impending consequences.

Although Eunice had been scolded for her act of appearing as a white ghost, I, along with my other siblings, Larry and Rita, remained convinced that we'd seen a real ghost. Throughout my teen years, my siblings and I, inclusive of Eunice, had never sat around the bonfire after dusk.

Despite her tendency to pull pranks that intimidated the household, some of Eunice's actions were mere acts of courage, for which she'd been duly rewarded by my parents.

Eunice was only twelve, when she ventured out into the still of the night, unannounced. When her door was left open on a warm, dry summer night, Rita looked into Eunice's room and found it empty. Eunice wasn't the girl who would have ventured out at 3 a.m., while the night was still and dark. Rita had quickly announced Eunice's absence. The entire household searched every corner and crevice of the house in search of her, until Father noticed that a side door had been left ajar. Fear gripped the hearts of the entire household. There hadn't been a doubt in anyone's mind that Eunice had been kidnapped. Another reason had popped up in Father's mind;

"Has Eunice been up to another of her pranks to intimidate the family?" Father asked. After her white ghost prank, and the consequences that followed, Mother didn't think Eunice would dare to try another of her pranks.

"John," Mother said, "Eunice wouldn't dare to pull another prank at this time of the night. If she does, she'll certainly not be spared a good spanking this time around."

At her tender age of twelve, there hadn't been a thought that Eunice could have eloped. This was a highly unlikely occurrence in Coopers Village, or anywhere else on Cavers Cove. But no one had eliminated the possibility of her being kidnapped.

"But by whom? How? Where? And why?" The questions fell from Mother's lips as she pondered the disappearance of her offspring. By a stroke of luck, Father looked out into the pitch-black night and noticed a pale figure. With tearful eyes, Mother looked out and confirmed that there was in fact, a figure moving slowly toward the side entrance of the house.

My father, being the strong defender and protector of his household, kept guard by the entrance of the side door. While he waited for the imminent, Father yelled out into the still black night;

"Oh! Who're you?" There wasn't a response, but the figure moved closer to the house, and toward the open door where Father stood. There hadn't been a doubt in anyone's mind that another kidnapping was in progress. Mother and her remaining offspring took cover in the buttery. She'd hoped to escape what she perceived as impending devastation of her household. Mother had been quite certain that whoever, or whatever had taken Eunice, was on its way to snatch another of her offspring.

While my remaining siblings and I sat huddled by Mother's side beneath the buttery shelves, Father's voice resounded once more in the still night air;

"Stop! Where are you going?" he called out to the mysterious advancing pale figure, but it kept moving closer to the open door. Father stood at the entrance of the door, bracing himself for the imminent. He'd been in dire straits as he waited to defend his territory from an imminent encounter. Being the brave defender of his household, my father couldn't have retreated from that which he'd perceived as an advancing omen. He felt that he must fend off the attack of whatever loomed in the darkness.

Fear struck Father's heart as the figure moved closer to the house. The strange object had come within a few steps from the side door, when Father's voice resonated in the still black night;

"Is that you, Eunice?" All fears and frenzy had cautiously subsided, when a voice was finally heard in the still black atmosphere.

"Dad, is everything ok?" Eunice asked, as she passed by her panic-stricken father. Upon Eunice's entry into the house, Father quickly barred the door. There hadn't been a speck of fear, or trembling, or any indication of defeat in her demeanor. Reasons continued to filter through Father's mind like speeding bullets, but one particular reason had evaded his thoughts.

"Why are you out at this time of the night, Eunice?" Father asked. His eyes pierced Eunice's lips for any response she might have had for being in the outdoors, and in the dead of night. The entire household needed relief from the panic and fear that had gripped their hearts and wouldn't let go.

"Dad," Eunice said in a frail voice, "Daisy, the big brown cow, had escaped through a wide opening in the fence. She came by my window, and with her ravenous bites, devoured practically all of the corn growing by the side of the house. By my quick reaction, I rushed through the side door and herded her back into the field. I took the rope hanging from the chicken coop and temporarily mend the broken fence so Daisy and the other cows would remain in the field." While Eunice spoke, Father's lips fell a few inches below his nose.

"Eunice, that was a most courageous act," Father said, as he proudly held Eunice's hand and assisted her up the flight of stairs leading into the big hall.

Mother, along with her remaining trembling offspring, upon hearing Eunice's elaborate details, had reluctantly streamed from the buttery – one-by-one, to embrace and pay homage to her for her act of bravery.

Throughout her teen and adolescent years, Eunice had never been a coward. Although the village folk held deep-rooted beliefs and fears of ghostly apparition, and whatever unseen forces that might be wrapped up in the darkness of the night – Eunice had had no fear of the unseen.

While I lay sleepless in the quiet night atmosphere, images from my childhood continued to overwhelmed my mind. I had vivid memory of the emerald green pond in the field, beside the large cedar tree. The pond was a masterpiece of Grandfather Grovel. It had been a strong belief of the folk that a village house-setting should include a pond – situated in the field, and within close proximity to the house. With the help of hired men, Grandfather Grovel had therefore made the pond, which served as a drinking place for his animals, and for its sheer beauty. It was also the belief of my father, who'd taken great pride in maintaining the pond after he'd built his house, adjacent to Grandfather's. I hold lasting memories of summer days when the emerald green water sparkled in the brilliant sunlight. Under the night sky, the pond glittered in the clear moonlight as quiet ripples shivered across its surface. To complement its green setting in the field, my grandfather had planted water lilies around the edge of the pond. All year round, pure white lilies, suspending from long green stems, waved in the calm breeze that gently fanned the surface of the pond.

Frequent heavy rain showers had often triggered a myriad of activities in the pond. The children delightfully gathered to watch fish of various sizes swim gleefully, as if to welcome the abundance of fresh water. The flying creatures enjoyed a quick meal from the unsuspecting fish that lingered at the surface of the pond. In the night atmosphere, the sounds of numerous frogs had often filled the air. A medley of gurgling sounds echoed from within the pond, as if their mating activities were triggered by the presence of fresh water.

As I surveyed the ruins of my home, I was sadly disappointed at the sight of the pond. It remained only as a shallow hole in the ground – identifiable by a single lily plant with a white flower suspending from its long green stem. I perceived the dry pond as another landmark of my childhood that had vanished over time.

The birds in the vicinity of Uncle Harry's house, never failed to chirp and sing their melodies at the slow emergence of the dawn. They'd no doubt sought the admiration, and the presence of Uncle Harry who'd returned to the vicinity after the great exodus that had left the village practically void of human existence. My heart was thrilled as I listened to the sounds of chirping birds – the way they'd chirped during the days of my youth. The birds sang their melodies to welcome the dawn of a new day, when they commenced their day's activities. For me, this was the beginning of another day to explore the place where I once had the pride and joy of belonging; most of all, to further survey the ruins of my home and surrounding places.

My night's sleep was inadequate, but I woke up nonetheless, to welcome the dawn of another day of my visit. I had remained in bed to allow my tired body a few more minutes of rest, and to reminisce on life as it once was during my youth. I also began to focus on my day's activities. My thoughts, however, were interrupted when I heard a faint voice, and a soft knock on my door.

"Jim! Are you awake? Breakfast is ready." It was the voice of Uncle Harry. I didn't wish to shun my uncle's kind hospitality in any way. I therefore promptly got out of bed and commenced my morning routine.

"I'll be out shortly, Uncle," I said. I heard continuous sounds of footsteps in the hall, as if my uncle had been pacing the floor while he waited.

I had completed my usual chore of getting dressed before entering the big hall. Upon entering the dining room, I found Uncle already seated at the table. With his state-of-the-art electrical appliances, his meals were prepared in less time, and with less effort.

"Good morning, Uncle," I greeted him with great enthusiasm and cheerfulness.

"Hello, Jim! Your breakfast is a bit cold," he said. I promptly joined Uncle at the breakfast table, after pleading the universal reason of having slept-in. I had not seen Uncle in such gleeful spirit since arriving at his home. His strength and vitality appeared to have been fully replenished by the long night's restful sleep. Uncle Harry sat at the table in great anticipation of continuing the conversation from where he'd left off the evening prior – a somber discussion about life in the village since he returned home, and memories of the thriving civilization he'd left at the time of his departure – traditions and lifestyles that had been considered lost forever.

At the end of the long breakfast session, Uncle had commenced his usual daily activities. As Uncle's visitor, I had played the role of his handyman, doing minor renovations, and performing tasks his visiting offspring had left unfinished. Most of all, I conducted short tours around the vicinity, taking my uncle to places he couldn't have visited alone. During my most coveted tours, I had sadly observed key places that had once contributed to the joys of my childhood – places that remained as rubble.

Chapter 16

Erwin Skanlon

The days had been swiftly passing, while I visited significant places that were once conducive to my growing-up. Many places had become impassable, as they were reoccupied by the roots of tall trees, stubborn shrubs, and protruding rocks. The exodus of folk from the village allowed the trees and shrubs the freedom to grow and expand beyond their once permissible boundaries. Tall trees and shrubs formed miniature forests in the village, creating obstacles to human thoroughfare.

Since returning home, I had visited Aunt Edith, who'd remained within the confines of her home. I had no doubt that she'd been reminiscing on the days when the entire village, and Brighton Town, were her playgrounds. But in her old age, physical and debilitating conditions had drastically restricted her movements.

My cousin, Erwin's farm duties had kept him within the confines of his father's farm. Aunt Edith counted her blessings to have had an offspring who didn't join the exodus from the village. Erwin performed farm duties and assumed the daily activities in the home, while my aunt remains in her incapacitated state.

In my heart, I remained hopeful that some day I'll reunite with my siblings. When last I saw Eunice and Rita, they'd taken up residence in Brighton Town. At the time of my departure, they'd returned to the village to bid their goodbyes. Given time, I remained confident that

Uncle Harry will obtain news of my siblings' whereabouts. I had been particularly longing to see my brother Larry, who was left to maintain the family home. But he'd subsequently joined the exodus to take up residence elsewhere.

While I remain in my foreign homeland, I didn't forsake my siblings, particularly my brother Larry. My foreign lifestyle had caused me to cast them into the shadows. As for my siblings, Rita and Eunice, there hadn't been exchange of letters, or telegrams that could have maintained a link between us. A telegram arriving in the village, and to my siblings in the town at the spur of the moment, would have denoted the sad news of death. This had been the case during my childhood years. Before a telegram was opened, saddened hearts had often quivered and failed.

There hadn't been a need to stir up fear in the hearts of my siblings by sending them a telegram. Time and patience didn't permit me to sit and write letters about my new life in the U.K. Not to ignore the fact that my siblings' address in the town was unknown. There was the possibility that they'd moved to another town, or to other villages in search of a better livelihood. As for my brother, Larry, it was a futile effort writing a letter to him – knowing that he wouldn't have responded. Based on information obtained by Uncle Harry, Larry had joined the exodus to reside elsewhere. His whereabouts was also unknown.

I had remained confident that my upcoming meeting with Erwin would shed some light on the whereabouts of my siblings, particularly Larry. A living soul will always provide a more accurate tale of events than the history book.

My cousin, Erwin had devoted his time and effort to toiling in the field – working alongside his father to till the soil and raise the animals. I was inclined to believe that, Erwin was enslaved in a village, and on a family farm where he'd been devoted to a life of hard work. But I remember when, as a boy, he'd committed himself to helping his father maintain the farm. Erwin's devotion to farm life brought back memories of my adolescent years toiling alongside my father, at a time when his health had failed him. I remember the rugged terrain, my tottered, muddy boots and rough work clothes.

Throughout my childhood, Erwin had remained my confidant. I had often sat with him, under the radiant moonlight, on my grandfather's bench beneath the Red Top tree.

As a young teen, I had often sat in the outdoors with Erwin – and other times when our siblings were present, to bask in the brilliant moonlight, and the fresh and soothing evening air. I was most grateful for the privilege to be in the outdoor, long after nightfall. The brilliant moonlight, being the only source of light under the night sky, had extended the curfew of the children beyond the time allotted for them to be in the outdoors after dusk. And while I basked in the brilliant glow of the moon, there was an overwhelming silence, not only in the village, but of the quiet moon on its westward journey. No one had ever seen the moon move across the sky, but it was always on time – on its precise due course, and in its precise position as it made its way toward the western horizon. Its immensely brilliant glow cast a shadow behind every creature that ventured out into the night. On a moon-lit night, the village folk basked in the glow of the radiant moon. In the stillness of the night, the full silvery moon casts its glow across the hills and in the deep valleys. Grandfather Grovel, as well as my father, had often enjoyed the moonlight from the comfort of the porch. Father had often said that the village folk enjoyed much brighter light under the glow of the moon, than the electric lighting available to the town folk.

While the village lay asleep, and long after Erwin and I retreated indoor, the moon waxed and waned in the stillness of the dawn. Its glow slowly diminished as the sun began to ascend in the eastern horizon, to brighten up the universe for another day of active village life. Vivid memories of my village, time spent with Erwin and my siblings beneath the brilliant moonlight, remain indelibly in my mind.

While I bathed in the brilliant glow of the moon, Erwin and I had solidified our intents and endeavors as we faced the imminent adult life ahead. We'd endeavored to have the largest estate, and own the most animals. It was my dream, and that of Erwin, to have the most beautiful wives, and as many offspring as time and fortune permitted.

As each year passed, Erwin had remained instrumental in maintaining my hopes and dreams of an ensuing life of good fortune.

No one had gazed into a crystal ball to fore-see that Erwin and I would have gone our separate ways – one away from the village, after having dreams of making a livelihood there.

On that bright, sunny morning in May, I was on my way to meet Erwin, after fifty years of separation. There was no telling what memories the meeting would bring to light – after not seeing him since his adolescent years.

As I walked through the gate to Aunt Edith's house, a radiant glow appeared on Erwin's face. Although he'd been up in years, Erwin had maintained his muscular physique. His head was slightly above my point of view, but I immediately noticed his partially bald head – a drastic change from the last time I saw him, when his head was crowned with an abundance of hair.

I perceived that, a dialogue with Erwin might shed some light on happenings in the village, and on his own well-being. There hadn't been many questions I could have asked my cousin. He'd, for the greater part of his adult life, tended to his father's farm. Erwin's devotion to hard work – tilling the soil and attending to the animals, had taken their toll on his physique. He'd been waiting by a gate leading into the field when I arrived at Aunt Edith's house.

"It's so nice to see you, Cousin Erwin," I said, as I gave him a vigorous handshake and a heart-felt hug.

"Hello, Cousin Jimmy," Erwin said, as tears flowed profusely down his cheeks. "I had often wondered whether you were still on this earth. Uncle Harry said he'd had regular contacts with you while he lived in America. My spirit was revived when Uncle said you were coming home."

Erwin stood with his face toward the ground as the tears streamed down his cheeks. Although Aunt Edith had informed him of my visit, upon my arrival he stood as one dumfounded. I immediately had the feeling of being back home, when I saw Erwin after a long separation.

"Erwin, how has life been after these many years?" I asked. He gazed across the field before hesitantly responding.

"Life has been good, Jimmy. I still have the breath of life," Erwin said, as he tried to hold back the tears flooding his eyes. "As you can see,

I remain in the village to work my father's farm. I had gotten married and raised a family. My offspring have established themselves in the society, but I'm alone again." The tears began to flow over his entire face. After regaining a measure of composure, Erwin continued to speak; "As I was saying, Cousin Jimmy, I raised my family and established them in the society, but my wife of thirty years has passed away." Tears cascaded down his face as he spoke.

"Erwin, accept my condolence on the passing of your wife. I was quite saddened when Aunt Edith informed me that she'd passed away." Erwin stood in silence while the tears continued to flow profusely.

The conversation continued as I gathered whatever facts I could about Erwin's life in general, and about the state of the village – certainly not about his deceased wife, Clarice.

"Erwin, there was a time when it appeared, all the folk had joined an exodus from Coopers Village, but you chose to remain here. Didn't you have an interest in joining the exodus to the towns and places elsewhere?" After my prior conversation with Aunt Edith, I had hoped that my discussion with Erwin would shed new light on the exodus from the village. He repeatedly glanced around the farm, and at Aunt Edith's house on the west side of the place where he stood. One would think that his answers to my questions came from across the field.

"Jimmy, I couldn't have left my parents alone in the village to seek a livelihood elsewhere. Farming and household duties are the only occupational skills I have." Erwin turned his head in every direction before he continued to speak. "There wasn't much I could do in a town without a farm to operate," Erwin said. "I had therefore remained in the village to secure a livelihood. I found me a beautiful wife, Clarice, who gave me three adorable offspring; a son and two daughters." As Erwin spoke, his voice slowly began to fade. At that point, I knew it was time to change the subject matter.

"Erwin, my brother, Larry was left to maintain my parents' farm, but it appears he didn't remain in the village. Do you know the whereabouts of Larry?" Erwin looked across the adjacent hill at my parents' abandoned property.

"Cousin Jimmy, Larry didn't remain in the village. He'd left home, and the farm to nature. Larry sold the animals whenever he needed money to visit Brighton Town. He'd emptied the chicken coop, only months after your departure to the U.K," Erwin said, as he stood poised to provide further details about Larry and my ravaged home.

"Permit me to interject, Cousin Erwin. What had Larry done with the dozens of chickens that were left in the coop?" Erwin turned his face toward the field before he responded.

"Larry killed and ate the chickens, as he said, he needed meat for his daily consumption," Erwin said.

"It's unfortunate that Larry didn't raise the cows, and the chickens for his livelihood, instead of consuming them. But where is Larry?" I asked, as my curiosity took on momentum.

"Larry had handed me the large key to the front door of the house before leaving to take up residence in Brighton Town. Since the day he left, he hasn't returned to the village," Erwin said.

As Erwin spoke, I felt confident that I had begun to obtain vital information that would lead me to finding my brother Larry. If Erwin knew that much about him, more information should be forthcoming, I thought to myself as I continued to press for further details.

"Erwin, do you recall the last time you obtained information about Larry?" I had strongly believed that, that was the moment for which I had been waiting. After a moment of silence and vigorous head-scratching, Erwin continued to speak;

"When last I heard, Larry had been moving around from place-to-place. He was not readily employable, since he had no skills to do the work available in town. He also had not the readiness to obtain further education. Larry had no source of income, or a fixed place of residence. His whereabouts therefore remains unknown," Erwin said.

"Erwin, do you know the whereabouts of Eunice and Rita?" I asked in earnest. Erwin swiftly wiped his face with a dark stained handkerchief he pulled from his pocket. He'd remained poised, as if to take a few breaths before he spoke.

"Cousin Jimmy, when last I heard, both Rita and Eunice were still happily married to their first husband, and were no longer residing in Brighton Town. I'm not aware of their whereabouts. Whether they'd moved back to Brighton Town, or to some other village, their whereabouts is unknown," Erwin said. "I'm aware that my uncle, Harry has been hoping to learn of their whereabouts, however, he has not been successful."

I had become somewhat disappointed, after realizing that Erwin had limited information on the whereabouts of my siblings.

"Erwin, I wish you'd asked Larry to return home to the village. There's the possibility he might know the whereabouts of Eunice and Rita." Erwin stood in silence, while he kept his gaze toward my ravaged home.

"Cousin, when last I saw Larry in Brighton Town, he didn't know the whereabouts of his siblings. I had encouraged him to return home to the village as he didn't look good. I had further suggested that he return to the farm so we could both work in the field and raise the animals. Larry's response was, negative. "Farm life is not for me," he said."

Erwin spoke with such sincerity as he provided the limited information he had on the whereabouts of my siblings. With the tidbits of information obtained from Erwin, I perceived the difficult in locating my siblings.

Before adjourning my meeting with Erwin, I had clearly heard the word, "Key." Erwin had mentioned having the key to my home.

"Erwin," I said in great exhilaration, "did you say Larry had left the key to the front door of my home?" Erwin looked toward the field where his animals had been grazing. A pleasant glow appeared on his face as he turned to speak.

"Yes, Cousin Jimmy. Larry had handed me the key to the front door before he left the village. Pardon me, Cousin Jim." Erwin walked across the rugged yard and entered Aunt Edith's house – which was also the place where he resided. Minutes had elapsed, when he returned with a broad grin on his face.

"This is the key to the front door of your home, Cousin Jimmy. It's still in perfect condition." I wept as Erwin handed me the large brass key.

"Cousin Erwin, it has been my greatest pleasure to receive an item from my lost home. I can never use this key to get back home, but I'll hold it close to my heart and cherish it until death do us part." I clutched the key firmly in the palm of my hand while I continued to weep bitter tears. There was a feeling of great accomplishment as a bright glow appeared on Erwin's face – he'd preserved the key to my lost home over the many years since it was abandoned by my brother, Larry.

While my conversation with Erwin took on momentum, the mid-afternoon sunlight was quickly obscured by thick rainclouds forming in the sky. I promptly adjourned my meeting with Erwin so I could take Uncle Harry home. Uncle was engaged in his conversation with Aunt Edith as they reminisced on their past livelihood in the village.

Chapter 17

The Sports' Park

Saturday was once a typical day when Coopers Village teemed with activities: Folk rallying to fetch a large supply of water from the valley spring, in order that there would be an adequate supply for Sunday: Children sweeping the yard in preparation for the Saturday and Sunday games: Parents on their way from Brighton Town, bringing all the essentials for the household, and treats for the children: The ladies of the households rallying around the coal pot to heat the irons they used to press the family's Sunday garments for church. The day, however, remained silent and void of the usual Saturday activities.

A visit to the sports park, was the next item on my itinerary. The sports park was the place where the most memorable events of my youth had taken place. As my uncle had participated in many local sports prior to his migration, I felt that, taking him on the tour would be one of his greatest delights.

It was Uncle's typical Saturday morning pastime, sitting on his porch to soak up the warmth of the morning sunlight. He also had the opportunity to greet a village folk or two, who occasionally waved a hand as they passed by his house. Brighton Town was off Uncle's list of places to go; unless his visiting children, and friends from the town dropped by to take him on a tour of places of interest.

On that bright and cheerful Saturday morning, I felt it was appropriate to extend an invitation to Uncle Harry. It would certainly be his greatest delight to go on another adventurous tour, while he had the opportunity. I therefore exited onto the porch to inform him of my intent on visiting the sports park.

"Uncle, do you recall the large village playground on the plains, opposite the Stone Church?" I asked. Uncle's cheeks trembled. His eyes twitched behind thick spectacles as they wandered around the porch.

"I remember the field quite well, Jim. I had participated in many local sports during my youth, also during my years as a teacher at the Villa School. It was the field where the boys of the village practiced baseball for the school's sporting events," Uncle said. "As you can imagine, Jim, I haven't had the opportunity to visit the park since returning home." Understandably, my uncle's frailty had made the park out of bounds to his visit. Like everywhere else, he needed assistance to get to the park.

"This is your opportunity, Uncle. I'll take you across the field to visit the park." Uncle was in high spirit as he stood in readiness to take on the challenge. His eyes glittered behind wide spectacles as he sat in the brilliant morning sunlight.

"Jim, I wouldn't pass up on this opportunity. There are many places of interest I would love to visit, but for my inability to get around," he said. Uncle's key interest was to survey the outdoors while retracing his steps during the days of his youth. Without some assistance, he'd remained confined indoor. There were endless possibilities, had my uncle not lost much of his mobility.

As quickly as he'd left the porch and re-entered the house – almost instantaneously, Uncle had firmly laced up his thick outdoor shoes. He was equipped for any rough terrain, even though his aching knees had set restraints on the places he could visit. Uncle promptly reached for his walking cane he'd left on the porch. He stepped in strides toward the main door and walked onto the roadway.

The glow of the mid-morning sun was still inviting to a stroll. Uncle therefore took the opportunity to put his idle muscles and inflamed joints to the test – although they'd impeded his progress. He approached the journey as the adventurous hiker making his way along mountain tracks and through deep valleys.

In anticipation of rough paths and thick shrubs along the way, I had taken the lead. The journey led me off the narrow road and onto the beaten path leading to the sports park. As I traveled along un-trodden paths, each step was impeded by rugged tracks and frequent stumbles. Uncle had been making bold strides along the rugged path, nonetheless.

More than half an hour had elapsed since the journey commenced. My rough estimate was that we'd traveled less than a quarter of a mile. A long winding narrow path had once led to the park. However, it had become more difficult finding the path, which had been overgrown by tall shrubs and protruding rocks. There were fierce insects zapping around, and angry mosquitoes buzzing in defence of their territory.

The journey had finally ended, when I stood at the place that was once a landmark – approximately a quarter mile from Uncle's house.

There hadn't been a clearly defined field that could have facilitated my search for key places. The sports park lay overgrown by tall shrubs and trees – its structures crumbled beneath tons of rubble. With heightened curiosity, I immediately began to scrutinize the vicinity. I felt I was walking on familiar territory, but soon realized that the sports park was unlike the way it once was during my childhood.

With curious eyes, I continued to survey the ruins, but there hadn't been much that was left to my imagination, when the entire park remained overgrown by tall trees, shrubs and protruding rocks. Uncle Harry continued to survey the vicinity for whatever recollections he had of the park where he'd once played school sports. He took a few steps among the thick shrubs while staring speechlessly at particular areas he'd identified.

I knew we'd reached the park when I clearly identified the crumbled concrete batter's plate on the west side of the field. This was the area where the village team competed in baseball tournaments with visiting teams. To find the pitcher's mound, I imagined the distance from which the pitcher sent the ball at high speeds towards the plate. I walked along the imaginary line from the batter's plate to the distance from which the pitcher tossed the ball to the plate, but had no luck finding the pitcher's mound. My attempt at imagining the lay-out of the entire field, and finding the bases, was also unsuccessful. There hadn't been a clearly defined field that could have facilitated my search for key places on the park.

With the tip of his walking cane, Uncle scratched the surface of a concrete block he happened to have stumbled upon. Uncle carefully guarded the area while he waited for my identification of the block. I walked toward the spot where my uncle stood and identified the block, carefully concealed by thick shrubs. It was the concrete mound from which the pitcher threw the ball to the batter's plate.

"Uncle, this is the pitcher's mound," I said gleefully. "It's the place where I had once stood to throw many winning pitches during the village's baseball tournaments."

"Jim, during my time, the folk didn't have such words as, pitcher's mound, in their vocabulary," Uncle Harry said. "The boys had simply placed a small stone where the pitcher stood to throw the ball."

"Uncle, during the village's golden days of sports, after your migration, visitors from other distant villages met to compete in baseball and many other competitive sports, hence, the terms, "Pitcher's Mound," and "Batter's Plate," which were introduced into the village. It wasn't like your time when only local residents played simple games on this ground." Uncle listened attentively to my details.

"Jim, there weren't enough professionals in Coopers Village to compete in the game of baseball. I can imagine the visiting teams winning the tournaments," Uncle said.

"Uncle Harry, there were village folk who'd learned the techniques of playing the game. They'd also practiced regularly to perfect their skills. As a member of the baseball team during that time, I had made several pitches from this very mound. My team had also won many trophies," I assured Uncle. "There were many trophies won by athletes of Coopers Village. These trophies were put on display in the sports building." Uncle appeared puzzled at my mention of a sports building.

"Where are the sports building and its trophies, Jim?" Uncle asked. He began to turn in every direction to see a building, or a structure in the vicinity.

A short distance from the east side of what was once the sports park, blocks of concrete lay strewn below the place where the building had once stood. I could clearly see another landmark lying partially buried beneath the earth. I stepped closer to the crumbled concrete foundation of what was once the sports building.

"Uncle, the concrete blocks strewn around this area are evidence that a building had once stood here. The whereabouts of the valued gold, silver and bronze trophies the building had once housed remain anyone's guess," I said.

As evident on Uncle's face, there was the question of why the building was no longer standing. This had also been that which I pondered in my mind.

"Uncle, this crumbled sports building was built after your departure from the village. It's the building where the village fairs and dances were once held." Uncle stood wide-eyed at the thought that a structure was built after he'd left the village. More appalling was the dance facility which it accommodated.

"I'm flabbergasted by this news, Jim. This field was once a simple place where the local residents met for a game of baseball. I can't imagine the extent to which it had been restructured to accommodate competitive sports and dance events." Uncle stood with his ears literally perked up as he waited to hear more tales about the sports park. His keen eyes continued to survey the vicinity, but there hadn't been much left to his imagination when he'd left the village for such a long time. My short briefings had hopefully, bridged the imaginary gap from where Uncle had left off at the time of his departure from the village.

Although he'd listened intently, my uncle's interest was only to be in the outdoors; an activity he normally wouldn't engage himself in without assistance. I continued to fill him in on past events, nonetheless.

The sun was swiftly advancing toward the mid-sky, casting a warm glow across the field.

I continued to survey the vicinity for whatever relic there were. Uncle had been showing signs of fatigue, thus putting a damper on my endeavors. I assisted him onto a comfortable seat on a fallen tree trunk. From that vantage point, he listened with heightened curiosity to my tales of the park, and structures that had been erected, but were no longer standing.

The entire field was once surrounded by pruned hedges and neatly groomed grass. It was once the duty of hired men to maintain the ground and have it ready for upcoming events. The village had often buzzed with excitement as the sports fans waited to see whether their team would win the trophy, or whether it would be awarded to the visiting team.

While Uncle Harry enjoyed the outdoors, I continued to provide more elaborate details about life as it had once been on the sports park.

"Uncle, left of the place where you're seated was the area set aside for village dances – under the stars." My tales of events had further sparked Uncle's curiosity. He therefore shuffled himself to be more comfortable on the fallen log.

"Jim, are you saying that there were real outdoor dances in Coopers Village?" My account of events in the village had certainly brought back memories of Uncle's days throwing garden parties. As a young teacher in the community, Uncle had often held garden parties where he entertained his friends and associates.

"Yes, Uncle. There were real dances held in the village. The young as well as the old folk came out to amuse themselves." Uncle's ears had remained perked up. "It had become a tradition when, every sporting event ended with a village fair, followed by a dance. The dance continued until the crack of dawn." Uncle made himself more comfortable on the log as he became engrossed in my tales of past village events.

"Jim, I wouldn't have thought there was a venue in the village for sports and public dance events. Public dancing contravenes the moral standards of the community. In my time, there were wedding dances held in the garden. Social parties were held in homes and backyards, and only for invited guests. The folk wouldn't have endorsed public parties and dances. It was a taboo for the young folk to be out dancing in a public place, particularly after dark." In my heart I felt that Uncle had spoken.

"That was during your time, Uncle Harry. Back then, the youth were prohibited from engaging in public events, particularly social dances." Uncle turned his head to gaze at the crumbled sports building. "Uncle, there was an age of transition in the villages shortly after your departure. Village folk interacted socially, at weddings as well as public dance events. You wouldn't imagine the fun-filled days enjoyed by the folk of the village." I continued to brief Uncle Harry on the changes after his departure. He soon realized that there were structural and social changes during his absence from the village, and from his homeland. He'd therefore become quite keen on hearing more details.

"Did all the activities take place on this small field?" Uncle asked.

"Uncle, you wouldn't imagine what years of abandonment can do to a place, and its structures. Over time, thick shrubs, protruding rocks and tall trees have reduced this field to a mere half its original size." Uncle's eyes surveyed the vicinity. "To prepare the field for the sports and dance events, men of the village toiled long hours to bring it to a considerable size. After their work was done, there was adequate space for all of the scheduled events." I continued to fill Uncle in on the exciting events held in the village during his absence.

"Jim, there appeared to have been many exciting events that had taken place on this park. I've certainly missed out on all the good times," Uncle said, as he continued to pay his undivided attention to every detail.

"Most entertaining was the village fair, which had further fostered a spirit of togetherness among the folk," I said, as I further briefed Uncle Harry.

Uncle wouldn't imagine the fun and excitement the fair had brought into the village, and to the folk who'd lacked certain means of entertainment. At the village fairs, there'd always been a merry-go-round for children and adults alike. Strong men of the village built a rotatable structure, using solid logs they cut in the forest. The structure was equipped with strong sisal ropes that provided seating for six riders. The men took turns to manually spin the merry-go-round while the music played. Children had the opportunity to enjoy riding on the merry-go-round, made in their own neighborhood: Not to ignore the thrill-seeking adults who couldn't resist going for a spin.

Uncle had remained joyously amused by my tales of events, particularly about the village fair and dance.

"Sounds like real entertainment, Jim. It seems like the village teemed with lively pleasures during my absence," Uncle said. "Coopers Village could certainly benefit from similar events these days."

"You're absolutely right, Uncle. Similar events would certainly bring the few remaining village folk together. In the past, the fair had offered fun for all, and had contributed to a thriving and social community."

Uncle was unaware that the village folk saw the sporting events as an entrepreneurial opportunity to find a captive market for goods they produced locally. Their products were available for sale to folk of many villages as they gathered for the sports and dance events. The ladies of the villages set up stands around the sports compound. Prior to the commencement of the sports activities, they unloaded their hampers, displaying well prepared lunches, home-made tarts, cakes and candies for sale. The men also brought their products from the fields to be sold to the visiting guests. The sports venture had brought into the village, much needed cash to purchase goods and some services in the town – goods the village folk couldn't have produced.

The details of events had profoundly captured Uncle's attention while he rested on the log.

"Uncle, during your time, no one had the knowledge of making simple things like ribbon candies and ice cream." Uncle scratched his head as he listened to more details of changes in the quiet village he'd left behind at the time of his departure.

I had vivid memory of Chavis, the only ice cream maker in Coopers Village. He'd learned the skill by observing the merchants in Brighton Town. Chavis made ice cream by spinning milk, spiced with sugar and vanilla, in a bucket packed with ice cubes. The ice cream was served in brown sugar cones he purchased in the town. It was a tongue-licking moment when the children were served cones stacked with a mound of ivory-colored ice cream. Many adults didn't mind being children for the occasion. They'd licked those mounds of ice cream quicker than the children.

Uncle sat comfortably on the fallen log while he anticipated hearing more details about the park. I remained eager to brief him on what had transpired during his absence, and prior to my departure to the U.K. Uncle had been giving the occasional nod, whenever he didn't wish to speak.

"Uncle, you've missed those golden days of lifestyle changes among the folk, and the past thrills in Coopers Village. This park was not just for sports and dances. It was once the place where young gentlemen, and fine ladies met their soul mate." At this point, Uncle's eyes began to sparkle as he routinely shuffled himself to be more comfortable on the log. "The hopeful ladies took their position in the cool shade beneath the surrounding trees. From that angle, they observed the traits of the men as they were actively engaged in the sports. At the end of the sports competition, the ladies selected the gentlemen they'd targeted."

Uncle Harry repositioned himself on the log while he waited for more details.

"And while the after-sports dance progressed, the ladies discovered whether they'd made the right choice. They'd either gained acceptance, or were sadly shunned by the young men to whom they'd been so fatally attracted. That's the way life used to be during those joyful days, Uncle."

"This is so beautiful, Jim. I can imagine the village coming alive during those exciting events." Uncle had become fascinated by tales of love and marriage – as life had been during his absence.

As life had been prior to joining the exodus, sporting events in the village brought hope to anxious parents who'd wished to someday, give their daughters and sons away in marriage. The parents of the village were hopeful that their good parenting, and immaculate grooming would be displayed in the appearance, as well as in the character of their fine daughters, and their well-groomed sons.

During the sporting events, the young men of the host village, and men from the visiting teams, had made every effort to impress the parents, who'd stood poised to determine whether they qualified to take the hand of their daughters in marriage. Hopeful young ladies and gentlemen had therefore made desperate efforts to put their proper upbringing on full display.

At the end of a sports-filled day, the venue for the dance was prepared by the host village. Beautiful ladies and fine young gentlemen stepped out into the evening atmosphere, charged with love and great anticipation of meeting their soul mate.

It was the moment of decision as the young hopefuls waited to discover whether they'd met their soul mate.

Just after the sun made its way over the horizon, evening shadows slowly shrouded the village. The young ladies stepped out into the evening air, flaunting their flare for fashion – displaying elegant garments meticulously designed for the occasion. Elegantly designed dresses were often made from taffeta fabric, satin and bridal net, heavily doused with thick starch to expand the circumference of the skirt. There was a competitive spirit among the ladies as they eyed their rivals to see whose crinoline skirt displayed the widest circumference: Not to overlook their ultimate motive – to show off slender waist and beautiful long legs, in their attempt at attracting and winning over the young men. The ladies' long slender legs on display were considered acceptable. An exposure of the chest, however, was a taboo among the village folk.

In preparation for the dance, the young men of the host village, and those from the visiting team, were also clad in their best attire. Ladies of adorable beauty and elegance, waited for the moment, when they would put their good etiquette and dance techniques on display. It was the time for the ladies to display their beauty and charm in the presence of the young man they'd selected. It was also an opportunity for the young men to put their good upbringing on display in order to impress the scrutinizing ladies.

At the appearance of dusk, children were duly dismissed from the fair, while the older teens had their curfew. Adults and permitted youths of all neighboring villages, danced from dusk to dawn. There were single and paired dances of whatever dance was in, or out of style. The ladies relied on their skilful partners to control their dance movements so they wouldn't dance into the paths of other dancers. Most importantly, while they danced, the young ladies got a closer look, and the much sought-after touch from their fine young partner.

The dance continued until the crack of dawn, at which time, the dancing couples reluctantly bid goodbye. For some lucky couples, their goodbye was short-lived as their courtship solidified in marriage. The sports and dances had kept wedding bells ringing in the villages.

My details of village fairs and related events brought back memories of the good times Uncle Harry had before his departure. He'd remained comfortably seated on the wooden log, eager to hear more details of the dances, and particularly the young lovers. He'd become absorbed in the intriguing details about the sports park.

"Uncle, the music and dance events during your time were simple," I said, in my attempt at igniting memories of his own good times.

"Jim, I remember my own wedding event, held in my front yard venue. The guests danced gleefully under the night sky. I have vivid memory of other social events held at that venue. As the dance progressed, it was a matter of being careful not to step on your partner's toes during the waltz, and not to fast-dance into someone else's path." A bright glow appeared on Uncle's face as he recalled his most memorable days, prior to his departure to America.

During his young adult life, Uncle Harry was a fine dancer at weddings and other private events. And like his father, Uncle had skillfully entertained the folk with his elegant waltz and swift steps to the rhythm of the music.

"As you might recall, Uncle, village wedding dances, and private parties, were the only entertainment events during your time." He nodded in agreement.

"I remember those exciting days, Jim. Music was provided by older musicians who'd learned the skill of playing on different musical instruments. My neighbor, Waynan, performed well on the drums." Uncle continually changed position on the log as he reflected on his past days of music and fine entertainment.

"Uncle, you remember the days when Uncle Dalton played skillfully on his Rumba Box – providing the bass for the other musical instruments." I jogged Uncle's memory of the music of his time. "I have vivid memory of the wooden box, equipped with pieces of metal of different lengths and widths. Each piece of metal, attached to the front of the box, made a different bass sound to complement the other musical instruments." Uncle's eyes twitched beneath his spectacles as he took in the fresh mid-morning breeze.

"I remember quite well, Jim. Dalton's Rumba Box was finger-licking and spicy, when he had all his fingers picking the metal chords," Uncle said, as he fanned the mosquitos that repeatedly buzzed across his face.

During Uncle's time, village musicians played simple rhythms and sang simple songs they'd learned by listening to the radio, or songs they'd composed locally. Nonetheless, their rhythms kept all feet dancing, and the folk entertained during private events.

Time, and the village's deep-rooted values had changed drastically. In my adolescent years, music was much more than a musician playing his instrument and singing simple songs. Music had become more complex, incredibly louder, and more entertaining to the young. Folk danced more freely, with and without a partner, so that there was less likelihood of one dancer stepping on another's toes.

A drastic change came to my home when Uncle Dalton brought a large box from Brighton Town and handed it to my father. The sight of the box ignited the curiosity of everyone in the household. I, along with my siblings remained curious to find out what Uncle Dalton had brought in the box. Although the family hadn't been accustomed to getting things in wrapped packages at Christmas time, the entire household believed that Uncle Dalton had brought a surprise for the family.

My uncle had sparked everyone's curiosity when he finally opened the box to reveal a square-shaped wooden box. He subsequently retrieved a peculiar arm which he attached to the top of the wooden box. Uncle Dalton had further retrieved another instrument which he'd carefully snapped onto the side of the box. He'd finally removed from the box, a flat black object resembling a plate. My uncle carefully set the black object on top of the box. Everyone waited in suspense while the object remained on top of the box. My siblings and I felt that Uncle Dalton was about to play tricks to boost the Family's Christmas spirit. Uncle finally made a few vigorous turns of the handle he'd attached to the side of the box. He'd finally set the peculiar arm on top of the black plate. The air suddenly became charged with the sound of a male's voice singing, accompanied by loud music – much louder than the radio that had always played music in my home.

It was a life-changing event in the MacLeary household. Before the last song, accompanied by pleasant music was heard from the box, the entire household had been dancing in whichever way they could. Grandfather Grovel took Grandmother Eavie by the hand as they commenced shaking their legs in whichever way they could go.

Despite the household's joyous response to the strange music box, Father had been curiously observing the proceeding with a measure of skepticism. He said that the music sounded fine, but what of the music inside a box that wasn't a radio? How could it be? I pondered whether my uncle Dalton was a magician – one of the men who perform mind-boggling tricks.

My father remained curious about the music box and had finally decided to question Uncle Dalton about it.

"Dalton! What kind of box is this?" Father asked. My uncle's face was aglow with a radiant smile before he'd finally revealed the mystery surrounding the box.

"John, this is called a Gramophone," Uncle Dalton said. "It works by winding this handle, like I just did. To get sounds from the box, you simply place this arm with the needle on top of the black plate. The black plate is called a "Disk." The folk in town also call it a "Record."" Everyone had curiously surrounded Uncle Dalton as he elaborately demonstrated the workings of the box. "There're songs coded into the lines on this Disk. You can hear sounds only when the needle is placed on the spinning disk."

My uncle had done his best, demonstrating the workings of the music box, while everyone observed with eager curiosity.

"This seems like magic to me, Dalton," my father said. But there wasn't anything magical about the box. It was simple technology Uncle Dalton had brought to Coopers Village.

Therein lay the mystery of the box Uncle Dalton gave to my father. Regardless of its mysteries, the gramophone had kept the family entertained for a long time; even while the radio played its classical music. As my uncle had brought a single disk, the household played the same set of music repeatedly during the evening's entertainment session.

Uncle Dalton's gramophone was perceived as an introduction of the Sound System, and the new technology to Coopers Village. The Sound System was the larger and amplified version of the Gramophone. The introduction of the Sound System and its amplified music was an invitation to those within its listening range to get together for a dance session.

My details of music and dance, and a transition from old village entertainment to amplified music, had kept Uncle Harry's attention at bay. He didn't waste much time absorbing the details of what had transpired during his long absence – amplified music in a box, a change in lifestyle, the mass exodus from the village, and the decadence of a once thriving civilization.

"Uncle Harry, I can imagine that you've not attended a dance since coming back home." His face glowed with a radiant smile.

"I haven't heard local music, or seen such events since coming home," he said. "There hasn't been much going on in the village, Jim." As Uncle spoke, I sensed the yearning in his heart for those pleasurable days he once knew.

"Uncle, you wouldn't see the old-time, slow-stepping and turning-to-the-beat, as it once was in your days. Nor would you see the old men chumming their guitars and playing the Rumba Box. Shortly after your departure, music saw a transition from the old to a modern version," I said as I tapped into his memory of the old times. Uncle wouldn't have noticed the changes in music, when everything else in the village had also changed.

"Whenever I listen to my stereo, and the complexity of its music, I thought of the days when simple music was played by the local musicians in the community," he said. Uncle Harry's thoughts were ignited as he reminisced on the music of his time.

"The simple music, once played by devoted men with simple instruments, is a thing of the past, Uncle. The old-time music created by men of the village, playing the guitar, the Rumba Box, and beating a single drum during private events, had been replaced by the Sound

System. Besides, what was once a three, or four-hour wedding dance session, had become an, all night dancing-under-the-stars event – but to the new Sound System – the name given to the modern music."

"From where did the village musicians obtain the Sound Systems, and the devices to operate them?" Uncle asked, as his eyes continued to tremble behind his spectacles.

"Uncle, it was quite simple. Professional and technical musicians in the town, were hired to spin Disks containing music the village folk had often heard over the radio. The sound system delivered the amplified music that set the feet of the young and the old alike, dancing in the open night air, and right on this sports park. To enable the systems to operate, technicians brought batteries and other electricity generators into a village that had no electric wires."

Uncle Harry had become fascinated by the news of developments in Coopers Village and elsewhere, after his departure from the village.

"This sounds like music to my ears, Jim," Uncle said, as he made himself more comfortable on the log.

I had become ecstatic relating my recollection of activities on the sports park, and the changes in Coopers Village. Uncle most likely held deep-rooted sentiments of his own pleasures during his youth. His face had become noticeably aglow as he paid undivided attention to every detail.

My uncle had remained seated, but with his face wedged between his knees. I had intended to further explore the park, but he'd remained in a rather precarious position. Despite his obvious signs of fatigue and displayed hunger, Uncle had been waiting to hear more details about the events once held on the sports park.

"Uncle Harry, I wish you were here during that era of joyful pleasures. If you were here, the loss of this sports park, the crumbled building, and its missing trophies would have stirred your emotions in a more profound way. In that era, everyone in the village was quite content with a life of hard work, play and family reunion – and the new musical entertainment. The folk's activities had always involved sports, village fairs, dance events and meeting soul mates – in this very sports park that lay crumbled beneath your feet." My further comments and gestures were met with a broad grin, but utter silence.

With a heavy heart, I continued to survey the sports park. Each relic brought back memories of life, and the pleasurable events that were once held there. I stood and gazed at the tall trees whose roots had reclaimed the entire sports ground.

My uncle had remained bent forward on the log. He didn't appear to be enjoying what had begun as a pleasurable adventure. It was obviously time to take him back to the comfort of his home. I therefore lent a hand as I guided him along the rugged path leading from the park. Uncle began to show further signs of fatigue which hampered his progress.

"Are you ok, Uncle?" I had become concerned whether he was able to walk the quarter mile journey back home.

"I'm ok, Jim," he said. To prove his travel-worthiness, Uncle had been trying to maintain his slow pace along the rough path. "Are we almost home, Jim?" he asked. I immediately perceived that fatigue had been taking hold of him.

"We're just about home, Uncle," I said, as a gesture of encouragement. The adventurous tour of the sports park had compensated for Uncle's frequent stumbles along the route. After a bout with staggering, stumbling and slipping, I had returned Uncle Harry to the comfort of his home.

Uncle instantaneously returned to his place of attachment – his chair opposite the window in the kitchen. All displayed signs of fatigue had been outweighed by his sense of fulfilment. My uncle had ventured out to explore another landmark he couldn't have visited without some form of assistance.

The day had been far spent, when I arrived back at Uncle's house. There hadn't been much that I could have accomplished during the course of the Saturday afternoon. The thought of being in the village on a Saturday evening brought back intriguing memories of the way life had once been under the crisp evening sun.

The laughter of playing children was once heard across the village – as far as the ears could have heard. However, only the sound of leaves on the surrounding trees could be heard as they were rustled by the gentle evening breeze. It was a somber moment as I sat in Uncle's home to reminisce on life as it used to be in the village.

The sun had made its descent over the western horizon. It was another quiet Saturday making its way into history. After his long afternoon adventure, my uncle was in no shape to venture out into the evening air. His evening meal of lamb chops, mashed potato and vegetables had plunged him into a sluggish state. Besides, there wasn't much that anyone could see around the village once the dusk made its quick appearance.

In a state of solitude, I sat in the big hall, hoping to gather whatever new information I could from Uncle Harry. He'd sat silently in his usual chair, until a low, faint voice was heard. My uncle began to hum a song. He'd been very much reminded of the next day's event. I had become joyously amused by Uncle's faint trembling voice as he hummed the song.

"That's a beautiful song, Uncle Harry. I've heard that song before, but I cannot recall the words." Uncle turned slightly in his chair, his face revealing a cheerful smile;

"Jim, don't you know, "Onward Christian Soldiers?" This is one of the most favourite songs in the Stone Church on the Hill," Uncle said, as a bright glow appeared on his face.

"I do recall the song, but not the words. Uncle, it's good that you're able to carry the tune."

"Tomorrow is Church, and this will be the opening song. You're welcome to join me in church tomorrow, Jim," Uncle said.

After my many years of absence from the village, it would certainly be my delight to accompany Uncle Harry to the village church.

"Uncle, it's good to know that you still attend the Stone Church. I'll be delighted to accompany you to church," I said, as Uncle's ears literally perked up. "My interest also lies in seeing the state the church has been in after more than fifty years. I have lasting memories of the church and its lively events during my youth."

"You're welcome to the church, Jim," he said, as his face glowed with a cheerful smile.

I had attempted to obtain details about the present state of the Stone Church and its congregation. However, Uncle's voice gradually faded to a whisper. In an instant, he'd fallen backward in his chair. It had become obvious that he was out for the night. Uncle rose slowly from his chair and commenced making feeble steps across the hall, while clutching his walking cane in his right hand.

"Good night, Jim." Uncle's faint voice was barely audible as he entered his room – quietly closing the door behind him. I was careful not to interrupt his regimented rule of retiring early to bed. It would be difficult for him to get back into his regular routine after my departure. Most of all, Uncle had to rise early for church the next morning.

Chapter 18

The Stone Church

At Uncle Harry's departure to bed, it was now my exploring mind and I remaining in the hall, under the quiet Saturday evening dusk. There was nothing of interest on the television set resting on a table in one corner of the hall. Besides, looking at the television pictures didn't tickle my fancy. My interest lay in the outdoors – to survey the ruins of my lost home, and a village that lay in ruin.

Like Uncle Harry, I took advantage of the opportunity to retire for the night. I was fully aware that Uncle's early rising would have deprived me of an hour or two of sleep. Besides, the following day would be Sunday, the day he attends church – not to forget that I was also scheduled to attend church.

The night had been slowly advancing, while I lay sleepless. My mind had been processing a myriad of thoughts about life as it used to be during my childhood years.

Uncle Harry's mention of Church, had brought back lasting memories of Sunday activities in the village prior to joining the exodus.

Sunday was the day when all work ceased and village activities ground to a halt. It had always been a typically quiet day, when the folk observed the day of rest from their vigorous activities. Understandably, the animals had to be attended to – Sunday or not, this activity was an exception.

The Stone Church stood on the side of a hill, a short distance from Uncle Harry's house, and not much farther from my home. The church was constructed decades prior, when Coopers Village was first settled by its peasants. It was constructed using rough-cut stones, so that its walls blended with the rugged hillside terrain – making its structure part and parcel of the hill on which it stood. Ironically, it was named, the Stone Church on the Hill. Regardless of each village folk's religious belief, everyone attended the Stone Church on the Hill – the only church in the vicinity.

On Sundays, the loudest noise in the community had always been the peal of the church bell, suspending from its belfry adjacent to the church building. Each loud peal was a call for the folk to make preparation to attend the house of worship. The pealing bell served as a reminder to the folk that the church service was soon to commence.

The peal of the bell could be heard from across the miles – its sound echoing across the hilltops, into the deep valleys, and into every nook where the folk could be found.

The bell had also pealed across the miles to announce the passing of a loved one in the community. The saying, "News travels like wild fire," was a term frequently heard among the folk. Before the bell tolled to announce the passing of a village folk, the news had already spread by word of mouth across the plains and upon the hilltops wherever folk were found. Nonetheless, the bell served its purpose of announcing the passing of a loved one in a village household.

In preparation for Sunday, folk prepared their Sunday outfit on Saturday – to ensure that they were ready to look their best on Sunday. The devoted ladies heated the old-fashioned iron over their coal pots, or on top of their wood-burning stove. With the moderately heated iron, they'd carefully pressed the creases from the men's handwashed suits. The ladies subsequently pressed theirs, as well as their children's garments.

It was considered a taboo to wash or iron clothes, or perform any task that would be against the Day of Rest Rule. This was an act of disrespect to the creator, and a violation of the Day-of-Rest Rule: "There should be no unnecessary work done on Sundays." Folk had therefore respected the rule, to avoid the consequences on the day of reckoning.

It had become a tradition whereby, on Sunday morning, each household ate a big breakfast. Whatever was on the menu, it was regarded as a big breakfast. This special full meal, the folk felt, would prevent their stomach from running on empty during the long church sermon.

To ensure that the village folk got to the church on time, there were three separate peals of the bell. The first peal reminded the folk that it was Sunday morning, the time to rise from their sleep and make preparations to proceed to the place of worship.

The second peal of the bell alerted the folk to the fact that, the church service would commence an hour thereafter. Folk who'd been privileged to own a winding clock, wound their clocks to sound its alarm when it was time for the household to rise from their sleep. The folk who hadn't been privileged to afford the luxury of owning a clock, counted the number of times the village cocks commenced their sequential crowing – from dawn to sunrise. This was the night clock that kept some folk aware of the time to rise and make preparations to attend the church service.

At the peal of the bell, folk rallied to be on time. While they made their way to the church sanctuary, the third peal of the bell echoed across the plains, in the deep valleys and on the hilltops – alerting the folk to the fact that the service was about to commence. Footsteps could be heard as anxious folk hustled along the network of narrow paths leading to the main unpaved gravel road. Under the warm glow of the early morning sun, the sound of footsteps, like marching soldiers, led a procession along a network of winding paths leading to the church. The older and much slower folk got a head-start, as they often needed extra travel time for the journey. Although they'd taken the lead to commence the journey, the older folk were soon overtaken by the youngsters. The older folk were therefore left to slowly bring up the rear.

Some folk who arrived a bit too early, felt their posterior couldn't withstand the hard surface of the solid wooden benches for the duration of the church service – and then some. They'd therefore waited at the two entrances of the church sanctuary. At the commencement of the service, they'd quickly made their way into the sanctuary.

In anticipation of the commencement of the church service, everyone sat in the pews in an atmosphere of deep breaths and low whispers: The house of God demanded honour and respect, and they'd been duly given. In my village, church attendance was perceived as a most sacred occasion.

While the folk waited for the commencement of the service, the atmosphere in the sanctuary had been constantly stirred by homemade paper fans and handkerchiefs, as folk cooled their steaming brow. Some older folk fanned their brow with a broad leaf they'd collected along the way. There were squared handkerchiefs of varying sizes and colors, paper fans, and broad leaves swishing across the congregation, as tired folk dried perspiration pouring down their face. The long walk under the warm glow of the sun had taken its toll on every brow.

To show respects for the solemn moment, the folk had made every effort to be on time before the service commenced.

The sequential crowing of the cocks, and the clanging church bell, however, had often gone unheeded, or had been simply ignored by Miss Grace, a resident of the village. Just a short distance from the church, a small stone house rested on a hill adjacent to the sports park. It was the home of Miss Grace, a rather quaint lady in her mid sixties. No one knew what activities had kept her occupied at home on Sunday mornings. Just as the closing song was being sung, she habitually came rushing into the church sanctuary. There was nothing the village folk could have done to get Miss Grace to church on time. It was often said by those who knew of her tardiness that, she would likely be late for Heaven – showing up after the gate has been locked.

At the commencement of the church service, the voices of men and women in the choir, echoed with great buoyancy above the hilltops and across the miles. The remaining members of the congregation blended their voices in one accord with the choir, as praises rang out from the sanctuary. Folk who didn't enjoy the privilege of owning a hymn book, clutched a corner of the one held by the folk on either side. Voices blended in unison as hymns of praise echoed across the village under an often, radiant Sunday morning sky.

The preacher, Reverend Gordon Edmund, robed in his long swaying white gown lined with gold, walked onto the pulpit to commence his usual Sunday rhetoric. He was a man of average built, and tall in stature. The reverend set his gaze to focus toward the pews – as if certain words were directed at a targeted section of his audience. His glaring eyes occasionally focused in one section of the sanctuary, as if he'd been deliberately casting a guilty spell on certain persons who'd done a sinful act worthy of repentance.

It was time for the folk to give their offerings as an expression of appreciation for the prior week of plenty. The reverend continually reminded all members of the congregation of their blessings. They were encouraged to give thanks for the good soil that caused their crops to flourish, and the rich grass that maintained healthy animals. Most of all, the congregation was encouraged to give thanks for their every meal, and for the children given to them by the creator.

My grandfather, Grovel, had never ceased from walking around his field, giving thanks and, singing praises as he herded his animals each morning to greener pastures. My father, John had followed suit, singing praises each time his animals brought forth a new life – his milking cows and goats, and his coop of chickens whose eggs had continually hatched new chicks.

Reverend Edmund further reminded the congregation of the small seeds that miraculously produced a bountiful crop. He encouraged parents to train their young men to till the soil and raise the animals. The young men, he said, were the future planters and reapers when the days of toil of their parents ended.

The reverend reminded the congregation that, Sunday was the day when they should rest and take time to reflect on the week ahead. He further encouraged his congregation to pray for each other, and to live together in harmony, in order to perpetuate peace, thus making the village a better place. As a result, folk who had conflicts with each other, had quickly reconciled their differences. Arguments stirred up between neighbors, were quickly ended and continued peace ensued.

Sunday sermon was not the only occasion on which the village folk congregated in the Stone Church. Folk brought into the church sanctuary, the first products they'd gathered from the farm. My grandfather, Grovel, had often brought into the church sanctuary, large baskets stacked with the first foods he reaped in his field. My father, John, had also followed in my grandfather's footsteps; bringing the first crops he'd reaped in his field. It had been a tradition when the folk, including Grandfather Grovel, and my father, brought the first pick of their crops to church on the day of Thanksgiving. It was their act of giving thanks to the creator for a bountiful crop. The folk gave thanks to the creator for their household of joyful children, and for a life of cheerfulness beneath brilliant sunshine, refreshing rain showers, and quiet nights of restful sleep, beneath a sky beaming with bright twinkling stars.

My siblings and I were appalled when, on Thanksgiving Day, Father had taken large chickens from the coop, and brought them to the church sanctuary.

In the spirit of giving, no one had ever brought cows, goats, or a horse as a gift at Thanksgiving. To the humble folk, large sacrifices would have been too burdensome, when they had very little. A freewill offering of a cow, or a horse, implied giving until it hurts. No one in the village welcomed such severe and self-inflicting pains. The church sanctuary was often stacked with foods and the largest of the fruits grown in the village, also large chickens – sacrifices the folk could afford.

During the annual Thanksgiving sermon, Reverend Edmund encouraged the congregation to bring their harvested products into the church sanctuary, in obeisance to the requirement of their creator. Thanksgiving was an annual tradition which continued, even at the time of my departure from Coopers Village.

Another bitter-sweet occasion when the folk congregated in the Stone Church sanctuary, was to honour and pay their respects to the crucifixion. On that sacred occasion, the Reverend held up the cross to the congregation as a reminder of the death and resurrection of their redeemer.

It had long past midnight. Sleep had failed to linger in my mind that had been tormented by the loss of the place where I once had a joyful existence. While I lay sleepless, my mind remained preoccupied with thoughts of many memorable events of my childhood, particularly in the Stone Church.

It was a general perception among the folk, that the church was a place of refuge, and a sanctuary opened to everyone, and for many occasions. A wedding was no exception.

A wedding was the most authentic and entertaining event of the Stone Church, and among the general village population. The bridegroom and his bride-to-be, had therefore extended an invitation to everyone in the community to attend the wedding ceremony. The Reverend had further encouraged the church congregation to participate in the ceremonies. The congregation had therefore eagerly joined him in extending good wishes and imploring blessings on newly married couples.

With the cordial invitation extended to everyone, curious folk attended the wedding ceremonies. Some folk, particularly young marriage hopefuls, admired the wedding gown of the bride – with hopes of adopting a trendy outfit. The bridegroom's black and white suit no doubt, remained under the close scrutiny of the parents of a young hopeful unwed son. The folk in general, attended weddings to be in the formal wedding atmosphere.

The wedding gown of the bride, her bridesmaids' dresses, as well as the bridegroom's suit, were often made by a seamstress, and a fine tailor in Brighton Town. A crafty seamstress and a tailor in the village were often engaged to design and sew the wedding outfits. The wedding outfits of the bride, and her bridegroom were simple and meticulously designed for the occasion. The word, "Tuxedo," wasn't in the vocabulary of the village folk.

The bridal bouquets were beautifully arranged from freshly cut flowers grown in the garden of the bride's parents, or obtained from a neighbor's garden. I remember my mother's painstaking work, collecting flowers from her garden to arrange beautiful bouquets for the wedding ceremony of a villager's daughter. The sturdy and beautiful flowers were freshly cut and arranged, just in time for the wedding ceremony.

The folk perceived the wedding ceremony as the most exciting and entertaining event in the village. The anxious folk had therefore filed into the church sanctuary, long before the bridegroom and his father arrived. As the bridegroom proudly stood by his father's side, and the elegantly clad bridesmaids took their places in the sanctuary, the stage was set for the most entertaining event of the village. The bridesmaids and maid of honour, were spectacularly displayed, as they brought color, charm and grace to the ceremonious event.

Most entertaining and spectacular was the wedding march. The organist joyfully pulled out all the stops as she played on the antique organ; "Here comes the bride." The bride entered the church sanctuary and commenced her sacred steps. Necks craned and eyes popped wider to take in the most spectacular event of the village. The father of the bride had his beautifully adorned daughter on full display as he proudly guided her every step up the aisle.

Amidst the audience, charged with curiosity, the adorable bride walked gracefully toward the pulpit. Her waiting bridegroom and his father, her maid of honour, and the beautifully adorned bridesmaids joyously acknowledged her arrival.

It was the moment of her life when the bride put her best foot forward. Her face glowed with the most brilliant smile on the most exciting day of her life. That was the moment the bride wished she could have captured, had there been a camera.

On the day Uncle Brayson brought a camera to my home, there were no weddings to capture at that moment. There were cameras in the town, but the village folk held on to tradition – their belief in a sacred marriage ceremony without fanfare. There was also that general feeling that photography was for the town folk, and the glamorous film stars appearing in magazines. Spectacular events, and precious moments to cherish, had therefore gone uncaptured by village folk.

Reverend Edmund conducted the wedding ceremony with poise and grace, as he duly performed the act of bonding the bride and the bridegroom in holy matrimony. It was his appointed duty to join in holy matrimony, the man and the woman who were expected to spend the rest of their lives together in love. The reverend therefore admonished each couple to love each other and dwell in peace: To nurture the children they bear. Most of all, he encouraged the couple to be the mirror through which their offspring look and learn to love, so that they may continue to perpetuate love and peace in the households of the village.

At the end of each marriage ceremony, Reverend Edmund dutifully introduced the newly married couple while they were at the height of their ecstatic moment. The cheering audience rose to welcome the newlyweds. Amidst prolonged rounds of applause, the couple exited the sanctuary; followed closely by the maid of honour, and the colorfully adorned bridesmaids. As the procession exited the sanctuary, the cheering audience acknowledged another married couple being added to their society.

To get in on the spectacle, curious on-lookers, including those who hadn't made it to the church ceremony, lined the path leading to the newlyweds' home. Like a scene out of the movie show, anxious folk pressed in to get a glimpse of the newlyweds at the peak of their most exhilarating moment. The bride, adorned in her elaborate bridal dress – complemented by her beautiful bouquet, walked gracefully by the side of her adorable bridegroom as he proudly displayed his black and white attire. A wedding had always brought live entertainment to a village, and to its folk who lacked excitement in their daily lives.

The village seamstress, as well as the tailor, anxiously waited to see their fine creation on full display. It was a most exciting and sacred moment, as onlookers waited to see the bride walk by the side of her bridegroom after the marriage ceremony. The words, "Stretch limousine," were not a part of the village folk's vocabulary. The only automobile in the community was often hired to transport the newlyweds to the reception venue. This had often been the case when the journey from the church to the reception venue was beyond walking distance.

The word, "Honeymoon," was also not in the vocabulary of the village folk. The newlyweds therefore spent their after-wedding night, at the village home where they planned to live for the rest of their lives.

A humble and genuine wedding had become a village tradition spanning across generations prior to, and during my childhood years in Coopers Village. The technological revolution in the village had no doubt brought an end to traditional weddings, as it has done to the village and its infrastructure.

Just as church sermons and exciting wedding ceremonies were key activities in the Stone Church, sorrow had also made its appearance – unexpectedly knocking at the door of the sanctuary. Throughout the year, the church had become a revolving door to joyful and sorrowful events. The joy which ensued after a village wedding had often been interrupted by a funeral. Whether the one who'd passed was a relative, or just a resident of the community, a funeral signalled a call to grieve the loss of a loved one. Everyone in the village had a heart-felt attachment, and an obligation to express grief for the one who'd parted.

At the home of the deceased, folk gathered from the moment the victims took their last breath, to the night of the interment. Sacred songs, sung by the grieving folk, filled the night air – from dusk to dawn, as folk continually congregated at the home of the deceased to pay their respects.

On the final day, just before the interment, folk assembled in the church sanctuary to honour the one who'd passed on. It was a general expectation that everyone assemble in the church sanctuary to say a final farewell, and to bid the deceased a safe journey to the other side.

As life continued in the jubilant village, the door of the Stone Church revolved to welcome the joyous celebration of Christmas. Except for the passing of a loved one, December had always been a month of cheerfulness.

During the festive season, every passing breeze and every chirping bird created the setting for an anticipation of cheerfulness. Adorably bright miniature sunflowers had always made their appearance during the Christmas season – as if to add cheerfulness to the festive season. The sunflowers dancing in the fields, the swaying branches of the trees, and the birds chanting their melodies, jogged the memory of the folk, and aroused their awareness of the arrival of another Christmas season.

Christmas was the season for household celebrations, and joyful gatherings in the Stone Church. As the cheerful season commenced, amateur actors and actresses rehearsed for the annual Christmas concerts. This was a village tradition, and an exciting part of life in a small community where life had been typically low-keyed. Folk put on a series of Christmas concerts in which there were performances, amidst joyful Christmas carols. The amateur cast was made up of teachers, students, and parents representing the older characters in the stories of Christmas.

It had become a tradition when, proud parents gathered in the Stone Church to see their children perform roles in the Christmas plays. Likewise, children watched the older folk play their roles. Christmas was about gathering in the Stone Church for a season of carolling and concerts. It was a time to hear the Christmas story once more – in songs and through dramatization, as if it had never been told.

It was the season when folk spread the spirit of cheerfulness in their households and throughout the village. The season offered the folk the opportunity to mingle and exchange the pleasantries of the festive occasion. My parents' and grandparents' beautiful and delicious bakes; cookies, puddings and other tasty delights, had always toasted the season of cheers.

Christmas was the season for the reunion of families and friends from near and far. Families had the opportunity to see what changes a year of absence had made to those they hadn't seen since the prior Christmas. The festive season had brought the folk together; giving them an opportunity to show their extended families. After a long period of not seeing or hearing each other's voice, Christmas had always created the setting for folk to exchange laughter and friendly gossips. It was the season for dancing in the barn, caroling in the village church, and along the network of winding paths throughout the village. A reunion of families and friends had always offered young adults, and often older adolescents, the opportunity to eye potential soul mates – under the watchful eye of hopeful parents.

Grandfather and Grandmother Goodwin habitually traveled across the miles during the Christmas season to visit their offspring – my mother Mabel, Uncle Harry, prior to his migration, and my aunt Edith. Mother had always been delighted to see her parents, who'd traveled from their distant estate to pay their special Christmas visit.

My grandparents had always looked forward to the Christmas season when they were delighted to see their adorable grandchildren, whom they'd showered with unwrapped gifts and sweet treats.

For the Christmas reunion and celebration, the children were adorably dressed and put on display before relatives and friends. Parents proudly showed off their beautiful daughters, and handsome sons. Those who didn't have little Cuties to show to relatives, took the opportunity to show off their spouse. The males showed off their newly married beautiful wives, while the females proudly showed their handsome husbands.

My parents didn't hesitate to put their adorable children on display for the visiting families and friends to see them. Christmas was the only time my siblings and I had gotten new clothes and shoes. My younger siblings had gladly settled for the hand-me-downs, while the older ones proudly showed off their brand-new outfits. As children, hand-me-downs were accepted as a way of life – no hard feelings.

On Christmas eve, the shades on the oil lamps and lanterns were thoroughly cleaned of black soot. The lamps were returned to the vanity in each room, and on the table in the large hall. At the appearance of dusk, a candle was carried throughout the house to ignite a flame on each lamp. Thick flames flickered and trembled behind sparkling clean shades displaying "Home Sweet Home" around their mid-section. The bright flame trembling behind the shade of the lamps, and lanterns welcomed the arrival of Christmas day.

On the days leading up to Christmas eve, at the commencement of each dawn, carollers walked throughout the village, spreading the good tidings of Christmas. It was always a delight to listen as adults and youth sang Christmas carols during the early dawn. It was like waking up in the stillness of the night to hear the singing of a heavenly choir. The folk were thrilled to be solaced by beautiful harmonious Christmas carols in the quiet dawn. As the dawn approached, no one had dared to sleep and miss the cheerful voices carolling the good tidings of the birth of a king.

It was in this atmosphere the village folk celebrated throughout the Christmas season. Folk didn't have mistletoes hung over the doors. Nor were there decorated Christmas trees with beautifully wrapped presents stacked beneath their branches. The Christmas season of fun and good cheers had once been celebrated in a way, only the village folk knew how.

This was the epitome of a simple village life in a place where the sun ruled by day and the flickering flame of the oil lamps, and the brilliant glow of the moon ruled by night.

As I lay sleepless and reminisced on the Christmas of old, my heart was overwhelmed with grief at the thought that, I'll never again hear Christmas carols sung in that atmosphere. Nor will I hear the Christmas story told the way it had once been told through dramatization in the village school, and by amateur actors and actresses in the Stone Church. I'll forever reminisce on the joyous exchange of cheers among the folk during the festive season.

I had remained wide awake, and in a state of restlessness, while entertaining memories of the joyful pleasures of my childhood. My heart, however, bore the pangs and pains of my lost home. The night had been far spent when I realized that sleep had still lurked in the distance. The repeated crowing of a single cock across the way reminded me that I hadn't fallen asleep, although it was time to get out of bed.

When the first chirp of a lone songbird was heard close to the window of my room, I had to face the grim reality that I had stayed awake throughout the night.

As I had anticipated, a familiar knock, followed by a faint voice, was heard at my door.

"Jim! It's Sunday. Will you join me for breakfast?" The thought of waking up from a sleep I didn't have, was rather excruciating, but I was careful not to shun Uncle's generous hospitality.

I also knew that Uncle's knock was a reminder that I was scheduled to accompany him to church.

It had been difficult forcing my tired body out of bed, but Uncle's persistence had paid off. He'd made another soft tap on my door as a reminder that I hadn't responded to his first. After scrambling out of bed, I made my way toward the bathroom. All efforts to wash sleep from my eyes had not been successful. Nonetheless, I had checked my saggy face in the mirror of the hardwood dresser, positioned beside my bed, before slowly throwing on my robe. I had been making slow strides toward the door of my room when I heard a much louder knock at my door.

"Jim! Are you awake?" It was another of my uncle's efforts to ensure that I had been up for breakfast. It seemed my presence in Uncle's home had rendered him unable to dine alone. Understandably, he had a responsibility to be hospitable to his guest.

"I'll be right out, Uncle!" Like one in a drunken stupor, I walked slowly into the hall, trying desperately to conceal the fact that I had stayed awake throughout the night.

Upon entering the dining room, I found Uncle Harry seated at the breakfast table. I took my usual place around the table as he promptly began to serve coffee.

"Jim, you were usually up bright and early. Your breakfast has gotten cold." I had no choice but to reveal my night of turmoil and sleeplessness.

"Uncle, I'm not too alert today. I had spent the night reminiscing on the state of the village. My heart has been saddened by the loss of my childhood home, and my siblings I haven't been able to locate. I therefore didn't get much sleep."

"Jim, why don't you catch up on some sleep after breakfast?" My uncle's suggestion was like music to my ears. Before the last piece of toast left my mouth, I was already retired to bed, where I waited for that much sought-after sleep to appear.

I had waited to decline Uncle's invitation to church, but his kind suggestion couldn't have come sooner. He certainly wouldn't have been happy to introduce his foreign visitor, having the appearance of a derelict deprived of sleep.

It appeared that I had slept for hours when I was awakened by the screeching hinges of the front door. It was Uncle Harry who'd just returned from church. I had taken the most soothing and refreshing lukewarm shower after getting out of bed. After changing into my Sunday outfit, I promptly entered the hall, feeling refreshed and re-energized.

Upon entering the hall, I found Uncle seated in his usual chair. My thoughts were renewed after the early morning nap. I was therefore in the mood for another conversation session with him. Uncle Harry also seemed refreshed after returning from his church service. He'd therefore sat, poised for whatever would have come his way.

"How was the church service today, Uncle?" He shuffled and repositioned himself on the chair while maintaining that usual bright glow on his face.

"Church was the same as always, Jim. The benches have outnumbered the saints. The reverend often expresses his disapproval of preaching his sermon to the Woods Family," Uncle said.

I was appalled by Uncle's statement that a reverend would have denied God's holy words to a certain family seated in the pews. I also perceived that the Woods Family had been denied entry into the church sanctuary.

"Uncle, who are the Woods Family, and why has the reverend denied preaching his sermon to them?" Uncle stared at the wall opposite his chair as he displayed a silly grin.

"Jim, the Woods Family is made up of the long empty wooden benches in the sanctuary," Uncle said, as he made a loud giggle. "The reverend does not like to preach his sermon to empty pews having neither ears, eyes nor voice," he reiterated.

"I wouldn't have thought that, Uncle," I said, as I admired the brightest and most cheerful glow on his face.

"Jim, if the village had its many residents as it used to, there wouldn't be an empty seat in the sanctuary. The church is not what it used to be, Jim."

Like the reverend, Uncle Harry expressed dissatisfaction with attendance at the Stone Church.

"It's quite understandable, Uncle. The humble saints lying in their graves, wouldn't imagine the poor state the church has been in since they passed on." Uncle remained silent, as if to reflect on those who'd passed.

"Reverend Edmund passed away with the saints who'd once given life and cheerfulness to the church. The young Reverend Grimsby cannot maintain a church with the few folk in the pews," Uncle said. "Jim, the church is in a state of utter despair. The few village folk, loyalists of the church, cannot make up a functioning congregation." As I perceived, my uncle himself was in a state of despair. He was once an active member of a thriving congregation prior to his departure to America.

"I fully understand the plight of the church, Uncle Harry. If the church stands practically empty, in all likelihood, the village school is also sparsely populated." I jogged Uncle's memory of the Coopers Villa School and his days as a fine teacher. "Uncle, there may not be many children remaining in the school. Sunday school in the Stone Church was once overwhelmed with children, who were also the children of Coopers Villa School." My comment had no doubt, aroused Uncle's awareness of the fact that, the school he once taught, may have been in a similar predicament as the church.

"Jim, as you mentioned Coopers Villa School, it had once played an important role in my childhood and young adult life. It was my greatest honor, being a teacher at the village school. My heart has been yearning to know the state of the school house, and to see the children in attendance, but I'm not able to walk the distance up that rugged hillside to revisit the school. I often see a youth or two, walking along the road. Whether they're children on their way to school, or visitors from Brighton Town, I'm unable to tell." A sudden change appeared in Uncle's demeanor as he mentioned the children of Coopers Villa School. "Whereas in my time, children were adorned in school uniform, the children who might have been on their way to school, are clad in their casual wear," Uncle said. "The children of the modern times do not appear to be clothed in school uniform." Deep within his heart, Uncle had been reminiscing on the days of his youth, particularly his school days. He'd returned from his foreign homeland to find a once thriving village buried beneath rubble.

"Uncle Harry, before I return home, I intend to pay a visit to my childhood school. I'll be delighted to take you on the tour." A moment of silence had quickly ensued, followed by screeching sounds from my uncle's chair.

"I'll be quite happy to once more set my feet in my former school – whether or not the building is still standing," Uncle said. There was a sense of urgency as he rose to his feet and had promptly reached for his walking cane.

"Uncle, you've already walked the distance to the Stone Church and back. I'll visit the school in the morning, when you'll be fully rested." Uncle slowly settled back on his chair with that usual disappointing demeanor.

Chapter 19

Beth Fawsythe

My conversation with Uncle continued in the pleasant Sunday afternoon atmosphere. The sun had been slowly making its way toward the western horizon, bringing an end to another brilliant, but quiet Sunday. It was once the kind of dry and sunny Sunday evening, when the village came alive with sounds of playing children. The village, however, lay silent under a radiant evening sky. The cheerful sounds of playing children, bleating animals, chirping birds, and the bubbling waters of the spring in the valley had long dissipated.

The afternoon conversation came to an abrupt end when a knock was heard at the front door. Uncle Harry's face glowed with a radiant smile as he reached for his walking cane and promptly proceeded toward the door. Uncle opened the door to reveal a tall, sturdy figure standing on the steps.

Uncle's radiant smile had quickly emanated toward the elegant elderly woman standing in front of the open door. She stood adorned in a blouse of pure white, and a skirt of variegated colors, extending slightly below her knees. The woman held what appeared to be a package covered with fine linen. Uncle Harry cordially invited her inside. The woman promptly shook her brown sandals from her feet and left them on the "Welcome mat" beside the door. She made brisk steps toward the dining table on which she carefully placed the large package. As she rested the package on the table, Uncle beckoned her to the center of the hall.

"Beth, please meet my nephew, Jim. He's my foreign visitor," Uncle said, as he politely stepped aside. "Jim, meet Beth, my best friend and neighbor." As I extended my greeting, the woman gave the most cheerful smile.

"I'm delighted to meet you, Beth," I said, as I gave her a firm handshake. She stood in the hall with that bashful look on her face.

"It's my pleasure, Jim!" she said. "Harry had told me of your visit." Beth had the most pleasant smile that could ever be found on the face of a female her age. While she stood in the center of the hall, Beth repeatedly fixed strands of silver-grey hair falling over her forehead. From my own estimate, she appeared to have been in her mid-seventies – seventy-six to be more precise.

Beth promptly excused herself and proceeded to uncover the package she'd carefully placed on the dining table. Meanwhile, my uncle had commenced pacing the floor while he provided further information about his guest.

"Jim, Beth hails from South Valley Village, a short distance from here. She too had joined the exodus to America many years prior, but has returned home to resume residency in her home village." Uncle's face continued to glow from excitement at Beth's appearance.

Meanwhile, Beth had uncovered the package to reveal a dinner tray, stacked with the most aromatic foods. The air was immediately charged with the aroma of freshly cooked steak, corn, potatoes and broccoli. She'd quickly spread the table with the finest linens she carried beneath the tray. Beth commenced placing the plates and the cutlery in their respective positions. She took fine crystal stem glasses from Uncle's dark cabinet, which stood in one corner of the dining room. The table was finally set to commence the dinner session.

"Harry," Beth called, "Come to the table please." Uncle walked briskly toward the table where he took his usual position. Beth pulled out a chair and sat around the table, opposite Uncle. She sat poised to serve the meal she'd brought while she waited for Uncle to extend his cordial invitation to his guest.

"Come and join us for dinner, Jim!" Uncle said.

"Jim, please come to the table," Beth said, as she seconded the invitation. I readily accepted the invitation and took my designated place around the table.

Uncle Harry opened a bottle of the finest red wine he took from a small rack resting on the table. He carefully poured a serving in each of the crystal stem glasses Beth had placed at each setting.

In the bright Sunday afternoon atmosphere, an evening of wining and dining ensued, amidst a time of exchanging news and views. That was the order of the quiet Sunday afternoon in Uncle's large dining room. Uncle and his friend, Beth, were engaged in a continuous exchange of tales of their absence from the village – how life had been in their foreign homeland, in comparison to the change in lifestyle upon their return home. Both shared their grief, and the circumstances that had surrounded their loved ones.

The dinner session progressed, amidst heated conversation and interjections to topics of discussion. Uncle wasted no time discussing the plight of folk who'd returned home and those who'd left to places elsewhere.

"Jim, as we've been discussing, Beth is among the folk who returned to their homeland, after spending many years in a foreign country. Some folk soon realized that they could not make a reattachment to the home they'd left behind, when their homes lie in rubble. In their state of despondency, they'd simply turned around and left for their foreign homeland," Uncle said. "While folk have left to seek a livelihood in towns and elsewhere, Beth remained in the village through circumstances beyond her control." Beth nodded her approval of Uncle discussing certain issues on her behalf. Her thoughts, however, had become overwhelmed when she began to speak.

"John and I had been making plans to settle in Brighton Town, but his ailing condition had kept us confined to the village," Beth said – continuing where Uncle Harry had left off. "After he passed away, I no longer have a reason to seek a livelihood in the town. I have no known relatives there." There was a sudden change in Beth's demeanor as she mentioned her husband, John.

"Beth! Having no relations in the town, you couldn't have made it alone there," I insinuated. Beth nodded in agreement.

"Before leaving South Valley for America, I had enjoyed every moment of village life," she said. "Upon my return home, I still enjoy village living. I wouldn't give up life in my quiet village for a livelihood in the town. It was John who felt that town life would be better than starting life over in the village, where everything remains in ruin." She spoke as one desperately trying to hold back an overpowering sob. I fully understood Beth's reason for remaining in her home village.

While Beth and Uncle Harry spoke, I heard tales of their lives in the village before leaving for their foreign homeland, and their experience upon returning home. Neither Beth nor Uncle could reattach themselves to the life of joyful pleasures they'd left behind.

Folk who'd joined the exodus from their homeland, in search of a new way of life in foreign lands, had subsequently returned to attempt a reattachment to the village life they'd once lived. Some folk who attempted to resume life in the villages they'd once abandoned, had made a futile effort to reattach themselves to the place where life was once fulfilling and genuine. This was true of Uncle Harry and his friend, Beth, who'd exchanged tales of the difficulties encountered, and the challenges they faced, attempting to readjust to their village lifestyle.

The social bond that had once defined family and village life had been severed. Former village folk, such as Uncle Harry and his friend, Beth, who endeavored to return to the village life they'd once known, found themselves thrown into their lion's den of despair and impossibilities.

Uncle Harry had left the village for more than sixty years to seek a livelihood in a foreign land. He'd finally answered the call to return to the place of his birth. Upon returning home, however, my uncle realized that the sounds and laughter had faded. Time had passed, taking the people of his time in its grasp. Uncle could no longer reconnect socially and emotionally to his past associates – those he'd left behind in his homeland. Nor could he reattach to the lifestyle he'd once lived. His new home, and his lifestyle, reflected that which he imported from his foreign homeland.

Beth expressed her deep regrets for having joined the exodus from the place of her birth – her place of joyful pleasures, to reside in America. Upon her return home, more than thirty years later, she'd found her home uninhabitable in its present state. And like Uncle Harry, Beth rebuilt her home on its original foundation. Upon returning to her homeland, she'd also imported her foreign lifestyle.

The dinner session progressed, amidst discussions of losses, displacement, and regrets which, on occasion, led to heartbreaks and tears. Beth further expressed remorse as she shared her lasting memory of the vibrancy of her South Valley Village she'd left behind. Upon her return home, she'd found the village abandoned and its infrastructure dilapidated.

"Harry, the days of fun and happiness the village had once offered are long gone," Beth said, as the conversation took on momentum. "As residents of South Valley, my parents did their utmost best to ensure that my brother and I receive our education from Coopers Villa School. It was the best and only school that served the surrounding villages." Uncle listened intensely as Beth spoke.

"I'll sip to that, Beth," Uncle said. "Coopers Villa School was the finest, and had the highest level of education offered in a village-school setting." Uncle took another sip from his glass, then half empty, as he attested to Beth's statement about the quality education once offered in the villa school. "Our village school had offered the best education to its youth," Uncle further stated. Not to forget that he was also a fine teacher at the school.

"I can attest to that fact, Uncle," I interjected. "During my time, the village children received quality education that enabled them to manage their parents' estate once they graduated from Coopers Villa. After their village education, privileged youths moved on to Brighton Town where they pursued higher education and became professionals."

"If I may interject," Beth said, "Despite the excellent education, and farming skills acquired by the young men, shortly after we were married, John and I had joined the exodus in pursuit of a better life in a foreign land. There were opportunities for us to make it as noble peasants in the village, but John and I had happily joined the exodus.

As a new American resident, John was devoted to a life of hard work. But he'd adopted the fast-paced lifestyle – over-indulgence in his newly developed habits that had brought his life to an abrupt end. John went much too soon." Beth was overcome by grief as the tears flowed down her cheeks. Uncle Harry watched helplessly as Beth struggled to regain a measure of composure.

I commenced asking questions, I hoped, would have changed the course of the conversation, and the eerie atmosphere.

"Beth, why did you decide to return home, after being away for thirty years?" I asked. I waited while she wiped the tears flowing down her cheeks.

"Jim, after spending thirty years in America, John and I encountered difficulties adjusting to a foreign lifestyle," Beth said. "John and I did the best we could to adjust in a fast-paced society. At first, it seemed we'd succeeded, but life was nothing like the one we'd once lived in our homeland. We'd finally decided to return home, but it was much too late," Beth said as she continued to sob profusely. My question had no doubt fanned the flames of her already ravaged emotion.

"You and John had therefore returned home to have a fresh start," I said, as Beth repeatedly wiped away new tears flooding her eyes.

"Jim, John was much too ill to adjust back to the village lifestyle we'd once lived. Although he was fully aware of the impossibilities of resuming a livelihood in the village, John answered the call to return home," Beth said with a tremor in her voice. "I wish John was still here, but I know he's gone and will never return to this life." Beth grieved, not only for her lost husband, but due to her inability to reattach to a village that had lost its century-old traditional way of life.

Both my uncle and his friend, Beth, had faced the dilemma of attempting to resume life in a village environment that had drastically changed. With the passing of their spouse, life had become even more difficult.

While the dinner session progressed, I could see new tears flowing from the eyes of both Uncle and Beth. The conversation had stirred up unpleasant feelings that had drastically changed the atmosphere of what began as a pleasant moment around the dinner table.

The conversation continued as the dinner session progressed, but on a more pleasant note. Beth expressed her concerns about the state of the village, particularly the exodus of the youth who should have remained to till the soil and raise the animals. They were the ones who should have maintained the infrastructure of the village after the elders moved up in years.

Like my uncle Harry, Beth had also found refuge in the Stone Church. The church served as a place of attachment for the folk who hadn't joined the exodus. It remained as the only place of refuge for those who'd returned and found no home to which they could make a reattachment. The Stone Church, the only firm structure remaining in the village, was the place where the folk sat to reflect on the state of the ruined infrastructure, their lost home, and the lives of those they'd left behind – those whom time had taken in its grasp, and whom migration had taken away to places elsewhere.

The dinner session ended after Uncle and Beth had shared their grief, and no doubt, revealed their moments of solitude. Beth looked repeatedly at her wristwatch, a signal that she'd been preparing to return home. The evening had been quickly advancing as she cleared the table. In preparation for departure, she'd collected her empty utensils. Uncle Harry began to pace the floor as he watched Beth preparing to leave. I wouldn't let her leave without expressing my delight in savoring her appetizing meal.

"Beth, your dinner was delectably delicious," I said, as she rallied in the dining room. "Thanks to you too, Uncle Harry for a delicious meal." My uncle and Beth glanced at each other with gratitude.

"It has been our pleasure, Jim!" Both responded in unison. Exchanges of gratitude had quickly cleared the air and expelled unpleasant feelings aroused during the dinner session.

"I'm glad you've both enjoyed my cooking," Beth said. "It was my pleasure to have served you, Harry. My pleasure to you as well, Jim." She carefully slipped her feet into the pair of sandals resting on the "Welcome mat," while holding firmly to the dinner tray stacked with empty utensils.

"It's been my pleasure meeting you, Beth. Have a pleasant evening," I said, as she stood ready to make her departure.

"It's been my pleasure, Jim. I wish you a pleasant stay with Harry." She made quick strides toward the exit door.

Uncle Harry made slow strides across the hall, in pursuit of his departing visitor. He politely opened the front door for Beth to make her exit. It was a kind act of deep-rooted respect displayed by a fine gentleman. With his hand still holding onto the door knob, Uncle reluctantly permitted Beth to make her exit.

"Beth, it was very kind of you to have prepared such a delicious meal for me and my guest," Uncle said. "Be careful when walking along the narrow roadway." Uncle Harry stood at the open door as Beth made her departure. His demeanor had quickly changed, as if he would have accompanied Beth, but for the impediment in his feet. "I'll call you on my cellphone," Uncle said, as he and Beth exchanged an amiable smile before she stepped onto the roadway. A sudden change in Uncle's demeanor suggested that Beth's departure had left him heartbroken.

I watched as Beth walked along the quiet road, holding firmly to her tray. The golden evening sun had cast its glow around the vicinity, when she gradually disappeared around the bend.

At Beth's departure, I had promptly returned to my usual place on the sofa, where I had hoped to resume my conversation with Uncle Harry about the state of a once vibrant village. Uncle had taken his usual position on his chair in the kitchen. It wasn't long before darkness had slowly shrouded the village. I was fully aware that Uncle hadn't been the one to sit beneath the night sky, or engage in night-time activities – whether or not there were such activities in the village. The television set stood dark and silent in one corner of the hall – as if it was just another piece of furnishing. Uncle's cellphone had remained suspended by a chain around his neck. It seemed he didn't use the device during the daytime hours.

The night grew progressively darker. Uncle began to show gradual signs of fatigue. I had anticipated another night of thoughtful conversation, but it was to the contrary. Sleep was the order of the night for him, when his eyes began to close. Uncle glanced repeatedly at the clock hanging on the opposite wall. When it appeared that sleep had taken hold of him, in a faint voice, Uncle began to spark up a conversation.

"Jim, tomorrow will be the day we visit the old school house," he said, as he readjusted himself in his chair.

"Yes, Uncle! I'm certainly looking forward to visiting the school of my childhood. In order to be fully rested for the tour, it will be wise to retreat early to bed." There were obvious signs of aches and pains as Uncle attempted to leave his chair. After a few unsuccessful attempts, he finally rose to his feet and commenced making slow strides across the hall. He'd done a short session of stretching and moving his joints, until it appeared, he'd gotten some much-needed relief.

"Good night, Jim," Uncle said. He'd carefully opened the door to his room while holding firmly to his walking cane.

"Good night, Uncle! I'll see you in the morning." The door closed quietly behind him as he retreated to bed.

Chapter 20

Coopers Villa School

Beth had returned home after an evening of fine dining on the appetizing meal she'd served. Uncle Harry had retreated to his room for a night of rest, and to shake off the effects of his fine wine – a complementary to his appetizing meal. I had remained in the big hall, where I spent a few moments to reflect on the state of my dilapidated village.

I continued to ponder the grim reality that a village, once teemed with life and cheerfulness, had remained silent, particularly on a sunny Sunday afternoon. Coopers Village had once bustled with the activities of folk going about their livelihood. The joyful sounds and laughter of playing children, once heard in the near and far distances had long dissipated.

While I sat in the quiet hall to reminisce on my lost home and the still silence of my once lively village, the night had been slowly advancing. The buzzing and scurrying sounds of night creatures reminded me that, as they scurried to find a place to rest, I too must recline for the night. I therefore switched off the chandelier and retreated to my room. With nothing else to occupy my time, I had retired to bed much earlier than usual. Besides, I'd had my bout with sleeplessness the night prior, and had therefore pledged to make up for the lost sleep.

As the night progressed, however, my mind had become inundated with intriguing memories of school days. Coopers Villa School was the place where I had spent the most memorable days of my childhood. Those days had left indelibly on my mind, lasting memories of fun and an education to last a lifetime. My favourite teacher, Miss Gentles, who was also my mentor, had instilled in me the desire to learn more. Her comely and friendly smile could not have been ignored by those who met her.

Miss Gentles had given me the assurance that I would become a teacher after graduating from Coopers Villa School, and after obtaining higher education. As time passed, I had moved to higher grades, but continued to be mentored by her. As I moved to higher grades, her influence had catapulted me to the top of my classes. At the time I graduated from the village school, and subsequently migrated to the U.K, I had proven Miss Gentles' prediction inaccurate – I didn't become the excellent teacher she'd predicted.

As I reminisced on my joyful days of village life, I had vivid memory of my most unforgettable days at the villa school. I reflected on my most pleasurable days with my close friends. At the end of my school tenure, I had sadly separated from my friends, particularly those who'd also graduated – many moving to Brighton Town where they pursued higher education.

Graduation at Coopers Villa School was no fanfare. The word, "Prom," was not a part of the vocabulary of the village folk. It was considered a taboo for a young girl to dance close to a boy in a public place, or even in a private setting. Parents of the village felt that a young boy had no business hugging a teenaged girl, unless they were married. A Prom therefore, didn't gain acceptance among the village folk, even if they had the means to purchase Prom outfits.

Graduation was observed at the end of each school year, for those who'd attained the age at which they had to leave the villa school. During the graduation session, there was a simple roll-call of the youth who'd outgrown the school, and wouldn't be returning at the beginning of the new school-year. Those were the youth who had to face their future, operating the farm – unless providence had favoured their cause and they were privileged to pursue higher education in the town, and elsewhere. The girls were equipped with the skills of home economics so that they could manage their households, as well as assume management of farm operations, alongside their husband.

The night had been swiftly advancing, but I was kept awake as memories of school days continued to inundate my mind. My imagination had been put to the task of tracing the path to the school building. I had vivid recollection of the gravel road leading to the school house – the gravel road being the estuary of a network of winding tracks throughout the village.

As I recalled, the building was a rectangular structure, having entrances along its northernmost section. Its solid wooden structure rested on a high concrete foundation, which served as a protective platform during heavy rainstorms, and possible flooding. I clearly recalled the days when the rain continually pounded the metal roof of the building while the children remained locked inside.

I shouldn't have difficulty finding the building as it stood by the side of a hill, a short distance from the Stone Church. Uncle will find the school blindfolded, whether or not a building remains at the spot. Besides being the prominent teacher of Coopers Villa, it was also the school of Uncle's childhood.

Although he was once a favourite teacher at the villa school, the children of the village, and those who might be in the school, wouldn't recognize Uncle Harry. His days as a teacher at the school ended when he migrated more than sixty years prior. Folk who knew my uncle during his school years had either moved on with time, or they'd joined the exodus to the towns, or elsewhere. Other folk might be confined to their childhood home, not aware of Uncle's return home.

As I made plans to visit the school house, my intention was to bring back the many memories of the place where I had spent my childhood years. Uncle's intention was to no doubt, bring back memories of his days as a student, and the excellent students he'd mentored while a fine teacher at the school.

I had been reminiscing on the days of my childhood, and my memorable days at Coopers Villa School, when sleep gradually took hold of me. Not long thereafter, however, I was awakened by a loud tap at my door. I knew Uncle had reasons more than one, for being up at that early hour of the morning. It was the day when I would take him to visit his old school house. I therefore promptly got out of bed and rallied to join him for breakfast. I wouldn't miss another opportunity to tap into his reservoir of knowledge about village life, past and present. My uncle also wouldn't miss the opportunity to visit his old school. That event had remained on his mind since the day prior.

As it was his custom, Uncle prepared an appetizing breakfast. The usual session of news and views had taken on momentum around the breakfast table. The short breakfast session ended promptly as Uncle looked forward to the early-morning adventure.

Another day of exploration was on my itinerary – my planned visit to my old school house. And like the trip to the sports park, Uncle Harry had promptly dressed for the expedition to visit his old school. It was a slow and strenuous walk under the early morning sun, but for such an occasion, he wasn't complaining. Uncle Harry had no difficulty finding the way to the school house, as the road also led to the Stone Church.

As I approached the hillside where the Stone Church stood, Uncle stopped abruptly.

"Jim, this is the path leading to the church. The next path off this main road leads to the school house," he said, as he hesitantly passed the entrance to the church. I knew my uncle couldn't have missed the way to the school, as it was also the way to the church. The narrow road had brought back memories of the network of winding paths taken by some children on their way to the school house.

The journey along the winding road had become progressively difficult for Uncle. Nonetheless, he continued as one whose eyes were set on the prize.

The next narrow track led to the school building which stood in plain sight – but practically off the beaten track. As I had imagined, the building still stood on its foundation, but in a dilapidated state. Whether it was illusory, or a reality, the building appeared strikingly smaller than it had been during my school days.

I looked toward the north side of the building where the principal's residence once stood. To my dismay, the building that was once the principal's prestigious residence, stood as an abandoned and dilapidated structure. I had no doubt that the vehicle parked on the west side of the school belonged to the principal. Upon close scrutiny of the exterior of the vehicle, I concluded that it was the one that routinely passed by Uncle Harry's house.

The principal of the village school was like a shepherd tending to his sheep. It was therefore a requirement, in my time, as well as during Uncle's time, that the principal's residence be within close proximity to the school house. As my eyes surveyed the vicinity, there wasn't another structure close to the school – one that could be identified as a new principal's residence.

With curious eyes, I commenced my close scrutiny of the building and its surrounding to reacquaint with the place I had not seen for many years. I had been closely scrutinizing the vicinity when I suddenly had the hunch that Uncle and I were trespassing on school premises and could be charged with the same. I had therefore made every effort to avoid being seen by the occupants who might be inside.

"Uncle, we must make our presence discrete," I said. "No one will know who we are until we provide an elaborate explanation." Despite my caveat, Uncle's curiosity had left him with an eagerness to scrutinize the vicinity.

As I closely scrutinized the building, its structure appeared quite uncharacteristic of the way it used to be during my time. Its wooden structure was in a state of disrepair. The concrete foundation could have done with much needed resurfacing. Likewise, the metal roof appeared rusted and corrugated. I imagined the drips and puddles caused by a leaking metal roof during heavy rainstorms.

The exterior of a building often reflects the state of its interior. I therefore walked cautiously toward a door leading to the entrance of the building – Uncle following suit. As I approached the door, there were audible sounds heard on the inside, but no one was seen on the outside. With cautious expectation, I approached the main entrance of the school to catch a glimpse inside. I had remained still, when a door at the far end swung open. A group of children rushed out into a wide area covered by neatly groomed grass. For the time of day, I could only conclude that it was the first recess of the day.

My thoughts immediately reflected on my days at the school, when a recess period permitted socialization and mingling. It was a time to run and play short games, amidst shouts of many children engaged in a short period of excitement. I immediately reminisced on the days when the atmosphere was charged with the yells and shouts of children playing in the once overcrowded playground. The boys tossed Tops on smooth surfaces they'd cleared in a corner of the playground. While the Tops spun smoothly on the ground, curious children became spectators as they waited to see whose Top spun the longest.

With the limited recess period at the children's disposal, time was of the essence for their fun and games. While the boys were engaged in their games, the girls occupied themselves with girls' sports. The older girls were often so absorbed in the game of hopscotch, that it took more than one peal of the bell to get them away from the game. All children had quickly played their series of games until the clanging bell brought an end to their excitement.

I discretely observed the children in the play area and concluded that the school's population had drastically declined.

Curiosity had further compelled me to discreetly scrutinize the place where I was once a student, also where Uncle was once a student and a fine teacher. I commenced my steps up the short staircase leading to the main section of the school, Uncle following closely. As I led Uncle up the short staircase, I was mindful of his vulnerability to stumbles and falls, and had therefore guided his every step.

Immediately on the left side of the interior of the building, an office came into view. It was the principal's office, where children were sent to be punished for their bad behavior. A female who appeared to be in her mid-thirties, and small in stature, sat around a table in the office. She sat facing an open window where the children in the play area were within her direct view. The female periodically shuffled herself in the chair to maintain a closer scrutiny of the playing children. Whether there were teachers in the classrooms, I couldn't have determined from my point of view. Uncle Harry had carefully scrutinized the interior, as much as his eyes could have caught and his mind perceived.

At the sight of the female, I quickly retreated down the staircase.

"Uncle, let's leave the premises before we're charged with trespassing, and putting children's lives in danger," I said, as I led Uncle down the short staircase, and through the exit door.

I had walked discreetly along the entire length of the building to survey its exterior – Uncle Harry following closely. I took quick glances into its interior, through rows of open wooden windows. A quick scrutiny of the empty classrooms confirmed my suspicion that the school's population had drastically declined. The children who were playing on the outside appeared to have been the only ones in attendance at the school. This was a far cry from the five hundred or more children the school had accommodated during my time, also during Uncle's time, when he was a student, and subsequently, a teacher at the school.

"Where are the children, Uncle Harry?" I asked, in a low voice. Moments had elapsed before he responded;

"Where do you think they might be, Jim? Don't forget the continuous flight of folk to the towns and distant cities – many to foreign countries," Uncle said, as he followed closely. "That exodus had taken many children away from the village." Uncle jolted my memory as I looked back to the days when I had joined the exodus to the U.K. It was the beginning of a period when parents escaped the village in pursuit of a different lifestyle. As they fled to towns and cities, many to foreign countries, they'd taken their children along.

"I should have thought of this, Uncle. It was a foregone conclusion that the exodus from the villages had taken many children to towns and cities. This had a great impact on the village school, as well as the Stone Church." Uncle stood in silence, no doubt, to reminisce on the time he and Harriet had migrated from the village, taking their children with them.

The school yard was left in silence as the children retreated indoor. It appeared that the playing children were incognizant of the presence of strangers surveying their territory. With the absence of the children, I continued my scrutiny of the school's exterior without further concerns that Uncle and I might become a menace to the children, and to others inside.

I had remained on the quiet school grounds to scrutinize the vicinity for whatever my memory could have brought into view. However, I had concluded that a second attempt at entering the building was unwarranted – Unless I was prepared to introduce myself as a former student, and Uncle Harry as a former teacher of the school.

I felt that I was an uninvited guest, and a trespasser at a place where I was a stranger to the occupants inside. Had the female seated in the office, noticed my presence, she might have challenged me to question my motive for scrutinizing the premises – the same would apply to Uncle Harry. To be lurking around the school while a sole occupant sat inside an office, and while children played outside, appeared to be just cause for alarm.

"Uncle, let's leave immediately," I said. "There's no reason to prolong our loitering, unless we're prepared to fully identify ourselves to the occupants inside." I walked discretely onto the road-way. Uncle Harry followed suit. From that vantage point, I stood to further inspect the vicinity.

As I inspected my old school house, I felt like a stranger at the school I attended throughout my childhood. Not knowing anyone, and not being known by anyone, I had become a stranger to the place. Uncle Harry had become a stranger in the school he'd taught during his young adult life.

There was a time when Uncle Harry's presence on the premises of Coopers Villa School, had been cordially welcomed. My uncle was once the young teacher to whom everyone looked for guidance and support. The days when everyone, and everything in the school reached out to him, were long gone.

As I surveyed the exterior of the school, and its vicinity, I realized that an important part of my childhood history lay in front of me. I further realized how important a role Coopers Villa School had played in my life.

I had remained haunted by the feeling that Uncle and I were uninvited visitors, who were invading the premises. While I viewed the school building from afar, Uncle's demeanor suggested that his thoughts were elsewhere. He stood and gazed steadfastly toward the school house, as one in a daze. As Uncle gazed at the old school building, I clearly understood his dilemma. Coopers Villa was the place where he obtained his childhood education. Uncle had pursued a higher level of education, and subsequently became a teacher. As a school teacher, he'd mentored and developed the young students. His excellent teaching and mentoring had produced the many fine young adults of the village.

Coopers Villa School was the place where, as a distinguished teacher, Uncle had once gained the respect of, not only the students, but the parents of the village. Uncle Harry appeared heavy-hearted to see a place to which he too could no longer make a reattachment, and he had a reason to be that way. He'd no doubt, loathed the place where he once had a reputable existence, but to which he couldn't return with a feeling of belonging. The village school was the place where Uncle was once a prodigy. However, the years had passed, leaving him on the outside without recognition. Time had gradually taken the era, and the folk who would have given their due honour to him.

I perceived Coopers Villa School as a landmark, in memory of those who'd once attained their level of learning, and those who'd once served as honorable teachers.

I had completed my tour of the exterior of my childhood school, and the place where Uncle had earned his honor and reputation as a fine teacher. I therefore walked along the narrow track, and onto the road leading toward Uncle's house – my uncle following suit.

Just around the corner from the school, I saw the Stone Church – still standing against the bushy hillside. The building stood nestled in a miniature forest. The structure was barely visible from the road below, for the tall trees and thick shrubs obscuring its full view. Uncle didn't hesitate to stop and silently take a closer look at its exterior.

"I'm delighted to see the Stone Church still intact, Uncle Harry. Its appearance hasn't changed much since the days of my youth," I said, as

Uncle continued to look steadfastly at the church building – the place to which he had a firm attachment.

"Jim, this church stands as a memorial to those who'd once sat in its sanctuary. It brings back memories of the days of my youth, and my days as a young adult, when I had taught Sunday school," Uncle said. "Jim, the church is a place of refuge for me, and others who returned to find no place to call home, and no one to whom they can readily reacquaint."

For a moment, Uncle stood in silence at the gate leading to the church. It appeared he'd remained to lament the loss of those who'd once made up the large congregation – many being his friends and associates. I could imagine that his silence was to give due respects to the church folk who'd passed on, and those who'd been swept away during the wave of exodus from the village. While Uncle stood motionless in front of the gate, I felt I had touched a tender chord of his already ravaged emotion, and had therefore prompted him to move on.

I walked along the road leading back to Uncle Harry's house. The journey continued a short distance along the road, and ended at Uncle's house around the noon hour.

Chapter 21

A night to reflect

Upon arriving back at uncle's house, he'd returned promptly to his place of attachment – his chair in the kitchen. I sat in the big hall and was immediately overcome by grief at the loss of my home, and my childhood school to which I could no longer make a reattachment. These are places that were once conducive to my growing up. I also grieved the loss of my parents, and my grandparents who'd created such a wonderland of pleasures during my childhood.

Uncle Harry had subsequently commenced preparing lunch to replenish his empty stomach – after visiting his old school house. I sat in the hall to reflect on my memorable and joyful days at my school. To Uncle Harry, the tour had given him an opportunity to revisit the school, where he was once a distinguished young teacher. Uncle had left the school premises, grieving at its dilapidated structure. He'd left with the knowledge that he could no longer enter the school with the same cordial welcome, when the folk he once knew, and those who knew him were no longer there. I could imagine the yearning in his heart to re-establish his presence at the school, but the passing years had taken with them, all prospects of achieving that goal.

At the end of the short lunch session, Uncle Harry retreated to his chair, the place where he appeared to find comfort in times of deep distress. I had returned to the big hall, where I resumed my position on the leather sofa.

The days had come and left much too quickly. The next day being Tuesday, I would be returning to my foreign homeland. Having no other item on my itinerary, I felt that a short stroll in the immediate vicinity would be in my best interest. I had the assurance that Uncle had been taking his much-needed rest from the long walk to his old school house. He therefore wouldn't be in a position to go on another tour. I therefore excused myself and retreated to the outdoors.

The sun was quietly making its way over the western horizon, when I stepped back onto the roadway. I proceeded to stroll along the narrow road to refresh my memory of things and places I once knew. My short stroll had taken me in the opposite direction of Uncle's and Aunt Edith's house. The quiet road wound its way through the village – among thick shrubs and trees of varying sizes. As I walked along the road, it was like taking a stroll through a miniature forest.

Things and places I once knew, had quickly come into view. I took another look at the creek which lay stagnant along the road. The spring whose flowing streams had once added to the serene atmosphere along the valley, was no longer heard. The chirping birds continually frolicked among the branches of the surrounding trees. Their melodious chirps were the only sounds heard in a place that had been practically abandoned by humankind. The sounds of the chirping birds harmonized with the soft breeze that rustled the leaves of the surrounding trees. The harmonious sounds had quickly brought back memories, and the feeling of being back in my home village.

I continued my stroll along the narrow road, when I came upon an old dilapidated house. I quickly recalled that the house was that of Franklin Finneas and his wife, Katharia. The house was once the pride and joy of the couple and their three offspring.

The house stood close to the roadway. However, tall trees and thick shrubs obscured its view from folk who may have passed along the road. Its shades of pure white and grey had once contributed to its beauty and elegance, however, those attributes had long faded. The structure stood stained by green mold and water marks. The rusted metal roof was a tell-tale of the condition of its interior. There wasn't a doubt that the leaky metal roof channelled water into the interior of the house during rain showers.

I observed the many surrounding trees – their branches overhanging the dilapidated structure. The trees with their overhanging branches, continually blocked the sunlight, leaving the house vulnerable to mold and cracks.

The structure was a far cry from the once elegant home Mr. Finneas had built for his family. Like the offspring of other households, his offspring may have moved away to establish their own territory. I immediately perceived that the village folk didn't entertain thoughts of maintaining the home they'd left behind after the exodus. The infrastructure of the place they'd once called home, remained vulnerable to dilapidation and ruin. The elderly folk of the original homes – those who were left behind after the exodus, remain in solitary existence, and in their dilapidated homes. This was true of Aunt Edith, and the old man, Franklin Finneas, who'd been living out their days in their dilapidated homes.

As I continued my stroll along the quiet road, the house gradually came into full view. I immediately recalled the narrow porch where Mr. Finneas and his wife once sat to take in the soothing breeze, and greet travelers walking along the road. I immediately observed an elderly gentleman seated on the porch of the ravaged house, and quickly identified him as Franklin Finneas.

As I stood beside the gate of the house, I felt compelled to have a conversation with the lone man seated on the porch. I therefore stepped toward the entrance of the gate, where I stood to extend my greeting.

"Hello, Mr. Finneas," I said, as I followed the age-old tradition of giving due respects to the seniors of the community. The old man was quickly stirred by an unexpected sound of unknown origin. My unfamiliar accent had likely gotten in the way.

"Hello! Good day," he said in a rather faint voice. The old man had made several attempts to rise before he finally stood to his feet. "Who are you?" he asked, as he made slow steps forward – finally holding firmly to a post at the entrance of the porch.

"My name is, Jim MacLeary," I said. He turned his better ear toward the gate. "The folk once called me, Jimmy. As a child, I had often played with your children." There wasn't a doubt in my mind that Mr. Finneas had had no recollection of my time interacting with his offspring. He'd sparked up a conversation, nonetheless.

"And who did you say you are," he asked, as he held firmly to the post.

"I'm the nephew of Harry Goodwin."

"Harry Goodwin? I habitually stop by Harry's house for a chat," Mr. Finneas said, as he anticipated a prolonged conversation session.

"Mr. Finneas, do you live alone?" I asked, hoping for an answer that would have soothed my grieving heart.

"My children have left the village for life in the town, and in America. My wife has since passed on," he said, after a short pause. There was a period of silence which had left no doubt in my mind that he'd been shedding tears of sadness.

The old man's feet may've signalled that he'd exceeded his standing time, when he slowly scrambled back to his chair on the porch. I watched his frail body moving toward his chair and perceived the hard knocks each passing day can delve to those in its path. I was, however, grateful for the bits of information Mr. Finneas was eager to divulge.

Dusk had been swiftly shrouding the village. I therefore excused myself and commenced the short journey back to Uncle's house.

As Mr. Finneas remained seated on the porch, he'd been no doubt, reminiscing on his most unforgettable days of a joyful village life – a beautiful wife and three adorable offspring, his large field teeming with livestock – representing his wealth and good fortune. The elderly gentleman may have been reminiscent of the days of his youth, when the passing of time had no significance to his most exhilarating existence.

In his old age, he sat to reminisce on his yesteryears – his joyful days toiling in the field, and his time spent making numerous visits to Brighton Town. He'd once basked in the neon lights of a modern town that had always satisfied his insatiable appetite for an escape from his village environment. He'd been watching helplessly as the rapid passing of time takes its toll on his livelihood. As each day passed, he waited in hope to be allotted another day. From his place of attachment on the quiet porch, the old gentleman spends his time counting the days, weeks, months and years, as they quickly pass him by. And like my uncle Harry, and Aunt Edith, he'd been no doubt looking forward to the day when time will take him along in its firm grasp.

Like Uncle Harry, and my aunt Edith, the old man positioned himself at a place where he had a direct view of the road, and no doubt, the resting place of his wife, Katharia. He may have been waiting in hope to someday, finally catching up with his past love.

I had returned from my short stroll to find Uncle partially reclined in his chair. He didn't appear to be in the mood for a conversation. That day being the last of my visit, I fully understood his melancholy mood. I had filled a gap in my uncle's state of loneliness for many days, but had been making preparation to return to my foreign homeland. This would have given him a reason to be in his pensive mood. Amidst sighs and frequent yawning, he'd finally built up the courage to speak.

"Jim," Uncle said in a rather faint voice, "tomorrow will be the end of your visit. I was just beginning to enjoy your presence here." As if he'd lapsed back into his state of emotional turmoil, Uncle reverted to silence.

"Yes, Uncle Harry. I'll be leaving in the early morning. I do appreciate your kind hospitality." Uncle made a loud sigh while he remained reclined in his chair.

"Jim, your visit was a happy welcome, but I'll certainly be saying a sad goodbye," Uncle said, as he slumped forward in his chair. "I've placed a chicken in the oven. It will soon be ready." He turned his eyes toward the clock on the wall opposite his chair. I continued to be impressed by my uncle's adopted modern technology that allowed him to relax while his meals were being cooked.

Dusk had settled over the entire village, when I sat at the dinner table with Uncle. I had waited for any gesture of his willingness to further communicate, but he'd maintained his silence throughout the dinner session. I had readily perceived that Uncle wasn't in the mood to eat up an appetite, when he'd slowly nibbled on a chicken breast and left in on his plate. This was very much out of character for my uncle.

He'd always emptied his plate before rising from the table. At the end of the somber dinner session, Uncle Harry had promptly left the table and returned to his chair.

It appeared that Uncle had taken a vow of silence for the night, when a stuttering voice spoke out of the abyss of the still silence.

"I'll miss you, Jim. I'll certainly miss you," Uncle Harry said, as his voice trembled. He threw his head on the back of the chair as one in a state of grief.

"Uncle, I'll miss you more than you'll miss me," I said with added assurance. "But I must return to my foreign homeland. As your children communicate with you from America, I too will continue to communicate, once I return home." While I spoke, Uncle hung his head forward as he listened attentively to my promises.

"Jim, will you really come again to visit me?" Uncle earnestly asked.

"I'll certainly come again, Uncle Harry – and very soon." Uncle sat motionless while he pondered my impending departure.

Darkness had slowly moved in, enveloping the entire village. The moon was nowhere in that part of the hemisphere. The sounds of creatures could be heard as they shuffled to find a sleeping sanctuary under the quiet night sky. Uncle's deep-set eyes sank slowly beneath thick brows – a sign that the time when he would retire for the night had been drawing near. It wasn't my intention to interrupt his moment of relaxation, and the pensive mood into which he'd suddenly lapsed, but I felt that another communication session would better prepare him for my departure.

"Uncle Harry, tomorrow at this time, I'll be back at home in the U.K." As one instantly awakened from a deep sleep, at the sound of my voice, Uncle sat upright in his chair.

"Jim," he said, "I hope you enjoyed your stay here. Before my eyes are closed forever, I hope to see you back for another visit." I knew it would be a matter of time before the tears began to flow over Uncle's bearded face.

"Uncle, as I promise, I'll certainly come again." Uncle sat dazed as one trying to hold back an overpowering sob. Without further ado, he rose slowly from his chair and walked across the hall, holding firmly to his walking cane.

"Good night, Jim. I'll wake you up at dawn." With those words said, the door to his room closed slowly behind him.

The night was still new when Uncle retreated to his room. I remained alone in the big hall to reminisce on my joyful childhood days at home. Except for the sounds of night creatures, not a sound of children, or any other human was heard under the night sky. With the exception of Uncle Harry, Aunt Edith and her son Erwin, the resident of the modern house on the opposite hill, and Mr. Finneas, the village lay quiet and solitary – as if humankind had taken flight.

As Uncle Harry had earlier retreated to bed, I followed suit – entering my room to retire for the night. In consideration of my uncle's early-rising policy, I knew my next day would begin before the dawn. Also, in anticipation of my early departure, I packed my luggage prior to reclining for the night. My passport and other travel documents had been securely placed into my attaché case. I had selected the travel outfit that was most appropriate for my journey back home. After checking to ensure that everything had been placed intact, I retired early to bed.

After the exhausting tour of my old school house, I had expected to immediately fall asleep. My sleep, however, had been constantly interrupted by thoughts and sighs as I reminisced on the exhilarating village life I once knew, and my home to which I could no more, make a reattachment.

As the night advanced, the moon had made its way up from the eastern horizon. The brilliant moonlight beamed through a fissure of my window, thus contributing to my time of sleeplessness. To entertain my moments of restlessness, I began to piece together, fragments of memories of the days of my youth, and my home village that ceased to exist in its original state.

I continued to focus on my village tours where every scene had brought back unpleasant memories, and added grief. My home was the place where I had the pleasure of growing up under the protective wings of my parents. I, along with my siblings, had a most pleasant childhood existence in an environment conducive to a joyful upbringing.

I held lasting memory of my childhood days in the home that remains in ruin. My siblings, close friends, and acquaintances I had left behind have simply vanished, leaving no one who could provide tales of their whereabouts. For what mattered, they too may have moved on with time, or they may have joined the exodus in their quest to find a better life elsewhere.

My best friend, Tim Kleaver, came into my thoughts. He was another of my confidants with whom I grew up. Tim and I had boldly faced the realities and challenges of growing up – having bright hopes and dreams as we looked forward to entering the world of adulthood. As Tim advanced toward adolescence, he was a tall, quiet and sharp-witted young fellow. He could have made up a brand-new tall-tale at the blink of an eye. Like my brother Larry, Tim's passion for the outdoors had prompted him to learn the skill of making catapults. Discarded horse saddles and old leather shoes had never gone to waste. They had promptly shown up in Tim's skillfully crafted catapults.

On hot summer days, when it was bird season, Tim and I were equipped with home-made catapults. It was once my greatest pleasure, exploring the nearby woods with Tim – hunting for birds and investigating any strange creatures that emerged from the deep woods.

As an adolescent, Tim was a chip off the old block. He liked farming activities, and had therefore tended to the animals, and operated the farm alongside his father. During the exodus of village folk to towns and foreign destinations, Tim didn't have a mind to explore the world beyond the village he knew. He'd therefore remained on the farm to do that which he liked best.

On the day I joined the exodus, I said goodbye to Tim and saw him disappear in the distance behind me, as Mr. Renwick's automobile drove away from the village. I didn't imagine that, that would have been my last time seeing Tim.

As I surveyed key landmarks, I saw the place where Tim's house had once stood. The sight of the relics of his ruined house brought back memories of my childhood. On the east side of Tim's house, I saw the spot where his grandfather was laid to rest. I further identified another older built-up structure, which I presumed belonged to his grandmother. There were three remaining structures, two of which ought to have been the resting place of Tim's parents. My conversation with Erwin had revealed that, Tim was laid to rest a few years prior to my visit. I had therefore concluded that the last freshly built structure was Tim's resting place. I looked solemnly across the hill at the resting place of Tim and his family. In my mind's eye, I perceived the rise and fall of another family I had left behind.

As the night progressed, I had remained in a state of unrest. My heart was overwhelmed at the thought of returning home to find my home in a state of dilapidation and abandonment.

I felt alone in an abandoned village that had once brought joy and thrill to all living creatures. The bits of information I had obtained from Uncle Harry, Aunt Edith, and Erwin, didn't provide adequate details about the past peasants – their progress; success or failure.

I had returned home with hopes of reattaching to those I had left behind, and to the joyous pleasures of life in my village. Upon arriving back home, however, I've been broadsided by the sad reality that, I have no feeling of attachment, or a sense of belonging to the place that was once my childhood home. If I had found my siblings, past friends and associates whom I had left behind, in their sight, I would be regarded as a stranger and a foreigner.

The village peasants had once lived in harmony with the environment – carrying on with their traditional way of doing things. In the present state of Coopers Village, and everywhere else, the few folk remaining, have been technologically deprived – not having the means to survive in a technological society. Aunt Edith still prepares her meals over an open fire in a wood-burning stove. Mr. Finneas, no doubt, maintained his traditional lifestyle – lighting his oil lamps and preparing meals over a wood-burning stove. In contrast, Uncle Harry, his friend Beth, and the new residents of the village, live a structured lifestyle – acquiring the technological equipment that facilitate their new village lifestyle.

Summer had always been a time when the village folk bask in the ambience of the season of cheerfulness – brilliant sunshine, rain showers, gently blowing breeze that swayed the branches of the trees, the gently flowing spring in the valley that created joyfulness and laughter among the village folk. Each new day was once greeted by the sounds of happiness – the joyful sounds of children's laughter, the village bustling with sounds of cheerful folk going about their usual chores. The men went about their daily duties, whistling joyful tunes that made their hearts merry. Folk happily strolled along the wayside – along paths lined with adorable wild flowers; each path lit by brilliant rays of sunlight.

Voices of happy children had once been heard as they played in the wide grassy fields. Children sought pleasure, chasing the brightly colored butterflies that flew around the fields, sucking the sweet nectar from every brilliant flower. Brightly colored flowers and the branches of surrounding trees, waved at the behest of the gentle summer breeze – bringing a sense of cheerfulness to the folk of the village. Birds in their beautiful plumage, frolicked among the swaying tree branches. They basked in the season of abundance of seeds and all pickings the season had provided.

While I lay restless, I reminisced on the days of continuous rainfalls, when children played in puddles, freshly formed around the village. The village creek had once been the center of attraction for hardy children, who waded in the creek while they attempted to catch the tiny fish gathering for a treat of bread crumbs. Sadly, the creek lay choked by modern discards and froth.

The spring in the valley had once been the venue, where children and grown-ups played in its bubbling streams, and in the waterfalls created after heavy torrential rainfalls. The spring in the valley has long dried up, bringing an end to the joyous pleasures it had once brought to the village folk. Its path has been obstructed by entrepreneurs seeking to create tourist attractions on the crest of the surrounding hill.

The spring has remained locked within the caves at the crest of the hill, where folk from distant places travel to observe its crystal streams, surrounded by mysterious crystalized cave rocks. Meanwhile, the spring's path along the valley has remained clogged by the rubble of avalanche, and the roots of tall trees and shrubs that have returned to reclaim their territory. I observed the network of waterpipes running throughout Uncle Harry's house, and those that travel along the roadway to various outlets. I had readily perceived the spring's flow restricted to a network of waterpipes leading from the crest of the hill and channeling into homes, and village meeting places, where the have-nots gather to collect water in buckets for their daily usage. Meanwhile, the valley has remained silent and deserted by those who'd once found pleasure frolicking in the crystal spring that had once traveled along its path.

As the moon cast its brilliant beams on the painted windows of my room, I reminisced on the days of my childhood, when the folk of the village basked in the silvery moonlight. The moon had once been the light that guided the village folk after the sun disappeared over the western horizon. The sounds of cheerfulness and laughter beneath the spectacular moonlight, however, had long dissipated. The folk who'd once contributed to the sounds of cheers and laughter in the clear moonlight, had taken off to towns and elsewhere during the exodus.

My home village was once the place where folk celebrated the Christmas season by way of family reunion, and cheerful caroling and Christmas plays in the Stone Church. Christmas was once observed through concerts and plays that kept the joyful spirit alive throughout the season. While I lay in bed to reminisce on the Christmas of old, I sadly reflected on the cheerful songs of praise, and the festivities that are no longer heard in the church sanctuary or among the folk of the village.

It was once a village tradition where the young folk anticipated meeting their soul mate, getting married and becoming owners of their vast estates – apportioned to them by their elders. The young folk had once carried on the family tradition of establishing their households of adorable offspring, thus extending the branches of the family tree. The old village traditions, however, ceased with the exodus of the young folk to towns and cities, where they adopted new lifestyles. Meanwhile, the village and its century-old traditions have been left to decadence.

Upon returning to my homeland after many years of absence, I have become sadly overwhelmed by a feeling of displacement, and an awakening to the reality that things have drastically changed. The jubilant sounds, and the hustles and bustles of folk had long dissipated from the village atmosphere. My home village remained void of the once joyful sounds of its inhabitants, who'd fled to seek a livelihood elsewhere. For the older folk who'd not joined the exodus, time had been passing slowly. In its passing, time has targeted each of the remaining old folk, randomly taking them in its firm grasp – leaving a louder silence in a village once exuberant with the sounds of folk in a thriving community.

Uncle Harry, meanwhile, had been caught up in his own state of loss and displacement. He had many unanswered questions about his lost childhood home, and a detachment from those he'd left behind. Upon returning home after many years of absence, Uncle was forced to build his new home on the foundation of his former home. There he remained to continually reminisce on his childhood home to which he can never return with a feeling of belonging.

As I made preparations to once more leave my homeland, I sadly face the reality that, my village exists as a tourist haven, where visitors from distant places have come to ignite their senses, and appease their insatiable appetite for adventure. The excavated cave spring, and the hidden treasures within the cave, have become a "must-see" for curious travelers. To appease their curiosity, visitors have come to see the artifacts and relics that have presented themselves for close scrutiny after the folk abandoned the village.

In a state of sleeplessness, my mind had become inundated with many unanswered questions about my lost home, and those I had left behind. The state of my childhood home – the scattered relics, and an atmosphere of utter silence, aroused a greater awareness of my detachment from the place of my beginning. While my mind remained deluged with the many unanswered questions, I felt that I must leave the ruined village behind and return to my foreign place of attachment.

My thoughts and emotions had been torn between two worlds: The childhood world which I cherished and have held close to my heart, and my foreign place of attachment from which I'll always reminisce on, and lament the loss of my childhood home.

Amidst my grief and painful thoughts, I had suddenly become terribly homesick. It wasn't the kind of homesickness of wanting to return to my foreign homeland. It was the feeling aroused by an ardent desire to reattach my body and soul to the place of my beginning. It was the homesickness of wanting to return to my home as it once was during my childhood and adolescent years. I soon realized, however, that I cannot make a reattachment to the place of my youth – to bask in the enchanting atmosphere, and sense the feeling of being back at home. I began to face the grim reality that, wanting to return to the home of my childhood – to sense the joys and thrills of the life I once knew, to rejoin my happy family, and have a sense of belonging, was an unattainable desire – I can't go back home to the exhilarating life I once knew.

The overwhelming silence in my village wasn't the silence resulting from the few village folk who were left behind after the exodus. It was the silence that remained in a place that had once teemed with life and cheerfulness: A place where the air was once continually toasted with cheerful sounds and laughter of playing children and joyful adults. It's the silence remaining in a place that was once alive with the sounds of chirping birds and a bellowing crystal spring along the valley: It was a place of brilliant sunshine and balmy breeze that caused the branches of the trees, and the beautiful flowers to dance. I once had a pleasurable existence at that cheerful place. I remain overwhelmed by the realization that I can't make a reattachment to that place – to once more adore its beauty, to hear the sounds and cheerfulness, and bask in its most enchanting atmosphere.

Chapter 22

Farewell to Coopers Village

In a state of deep thoughts, and anxious fears, I had remained awake until the still hours of the night. Soon after falling asleep, however, I was promptly awakened by the familiar sound of footsteps in the hall. It was the dawn of the morning when I would say goodbye to Uncle Harry, Aunt Edith, and Erwin. Most of all, it was the day when I would bid a sad farewell to my lost home, and the dilapidated village I would be leaving behind. Uncle Harry was certainly not anticipating that moment when I would bid him goodbye. My mind had remained preoccupied with thoughts about going back to my foreign homeland, also leaving Uncle Harry in his state of solitude.

The golden sun had been slowly rising up from the eastern horizon. I had remained in bed to be entertained by the melodious song of the chirping bird, perched beside my window. But it wasn't long before I heard a familiar knock at my door. It was a reminder from Uncle that I should be getting ready for my departure. I therefore promptly got out of bed and carried out my morning routine. After changing into my departure outfit, I walked cautiously into the hall and was greeted by the usual aroma of freshly made coffee.

Uncle Harry had been seated in his usual chair, in still silence. It was much too early for his morning chores, but he'd prepared breakfast in anticipation of my departure.

"Good morning, Jim!" he said. "Have a seat. Your breakfast is on the table." Uncle promptly lapsed back into his mode of silence, while his eyes kept vigil around the breakfast table. Amidst my moment of anxiety, my appetite had refused to be compensated, but I felt honored that Uncle had prepared breakfast for me, and at such an early hour of the morning. I therefore slowly worked up an appetite.

"Uncle Harry, I appreciate your kind hospitality. It was very kind of you to have prepared breakfast for me, and at this early hour of the morning." I was careful not to rouse his emotions in any negative way. Uncle turned slightly toward the breakfast table as he began to speak;

"I hope you enjoyed your stay here, Jim," he said. "As you've promised, please come again; and soon." Uncle's demeanor had suddenly changed as he maintained his focus toward the breakfast table. He appeared ready for an early morning conversation.

"Uncle, as I promised, before long, I'll certainly come again to pay a visit. I'll also keep my promise to visit Aunt Edith – not to forget Erwin." As I spoke, a fountain of tears began to flow down Uncle's cheeks while he sat motionless in his chair.

As the morning progressed, I exchanged assuring thoughts and encouraging words with Uncle Harry. The conversation session, however, was promptly interrupted when a car drove up alongside the entrance to Uncle's house. It was the vehicle owned by the occupant of the modern house on the hill opposite my uncle's. The day prior, Uncle Harry had hired the vehicle of his closest neighbor. At the sound of the horn, Uncle trudged to the front door. I followed closely to assist in whichever way I could.

A man of average built emerged from the vehicle and stood at the entrance of Uncle's house. At the appearance of Uncle Harry at the opened door, the man gave an emphatic nod. At his gesture, I promptly reached for my luggage resting behind the door. I stepped onto the roadway and promptly placed my luggage in the trunk of the waiting vehicle. I was about to commence the long journey back to my foreign homeland.

It was a sad moment when I embraced Uncle Harry and watched fresh tears flow from his red and swollen eyes. Uncle stood at the open door as one frozen in time. He'd remained in a state of shock as the vehicle rolled along the road.

The vehicle made its way around a bend, putting Uncle and my ravaged home out of view. It made a brief stop, allowing me to say another tearful goodbye to Aunt Edith, and Cousin Erwin.

The vehicle had been traveling at a decent speed along the winding road. With a heavy heart and tearful eyes, I turned and twisted my head in every direction as I inspected the ruins of my village, and the relics strewn around.

On the spur of the moment, I felt that the chauffeur could be a good source of information on past and present events in the village and around Brighton Town. Uncle Harry had mentioned that he spends practically all his days in Brighton Town. I had also hoped that he could give his perspective on the state of things as he perceived them.

The vehicle had just made its way onto the main road leading into the town, a short distance away. I therefore had but a few minutes to gather whatever information I could from the chauffeur.

It wasn't my intent to interrupt his cellphone conversation. I therefore waited for an opportunity to engage him in a brief fact-finding session. An opportunity had finally come during a brief intermission, when the chauffeur waited for another phone call. I quickly snatched the opportunity to spark up a conversation.

"Good morning, Sir," I said. "Pardon my interruption. How long have you been a resident of Coopers Village?" The chauffeur turned his head as one overwhelmed by an unexpected interruption. He immediately rested the cellphone on the seat beside him before responding;

"My apology, Mister. Did you ask how much longer before we reach the town?" It had become obvious that the phone had taken precedence over everything else. His thoughts had rested on the traffic, and on receiving or making another phone call. I therefore repeated my question and waited for the chauffeur's response.

"I recently purchased the property on the hill opposite Harry Goodwin's house," he said. The property was once owned by the Gainers' family, but before the modern house was erected. It was the modern structure from whose windows the television lights beamed. There hadn't been any occupants seen, or heard in the house since I arrived in the village.

"Sir, if I may introduce myself. My name is Jimmy MacLeary. You may call me, Jim," I said, under the assumption that he'd been anticipating further conversation. I could have seen the pupil of his eyes as he routinely checked his rear-view mirror.

"It's been my pleasure meeting you, Jim. My name is Michael Fabor," he said, in a polite manner. The chauffeur kept his eyes focused on the road while his ears remained on alert for his next call from the cellphone he had placed on standby.

"Michael, the house you now own is not the one I once knew. Many things have changed in Coopers Village, and it appears, everywhere else in my homeland." Michael didn't quite understand the "Change terminology." As he admitted, he was a total stranger to the place. His modern house and lifestyle suggested that he'd originated from the town, or from a distant shore.

"I came to Coopers Village from America," Michael said. "My fore-parents had once sojourned in another village on the other side of Brighton Town, but I was born in America."

It was my foregone conclusion that Michael wasn't the candidate from whom to solicit information about the village, or about my homeland. For what mattered, he'd come to reside in a solitary place, incognizant of the fact that he'd been treading on the relics of a past thriving civilization. There wasn't a necessity to spark up further conversation with Michael. I felt that there hadn't been much I could have gleaned from him. Changing topic was therefore the wisest thing to do.

"Michael! I'm delighted to know that you've come to reside in Coopers Village. I'm also delighted to know that you have Harry Goodwin as your neighbor." I waited for his response, while he waited for his next phone call.

"Harry Goodwin is a very fine gentleman," Michael said. "A fine gentleman indeed." While he spoke, the cellphone rang. Michael had promptly excused himself as another phone conversation session commenced.

As I had perceived, Michael's lifestyle in the village was just a replica of the one he'd once lived in America. His imported lifestyle revolved around the television set, frequent cellphone conversations, and making frequent visits to the town, where he conducts his business – whatever was his business occupation in Brighton Town. He'd no doubt, spent his days bathing in the glow of neon lights, and joining in the hustle and bustle of town life. For someone who had no background knowledge of the village, or even the town where he spent most of his time, my brief interview with him had been futile.

It was a much shorter ride back to the town. As I had anticipated, the progress of the vehicle had been hampered by the early-morning congested traffic along the main street. I had adequate time to catch my flight, and had therefore become tolerant of the congested traffic situation.

The vehicle had been inching its way along the busy street leading into the town. My eyes quickly surveyed the street, lined with modern shops, and pedestrians hustling to reach their destination. Whether they were on their way to work, or to shop for new fashions, and whatever new items the town had to offer, there was a constant hustle in the congested town.

The vehicle had gradually escaped the traffic, subsequently pulling up to the entrance of the airport, a short distance from the heart of the congested town. After paying Michael a generous sum for his service, I promptly collected my luggage and proceeded toward the check-in area of the crowded airport. I was about to embark on the long journey back to my foreign homeland.

I had been patiently waiting for the departure of my flight, when my thoughts reflected on Uncle Harry, who was left in tears after the painful separation. Uncle had been no doubt, seated in his chair while he lamented my departure.

The clock suspended on the wall of the departure area, had been slowly ticking toward the time of my boarding announcement. In anticipation of boarding the aircraft, my eyes were glued to the television screen, which continually displayed arrivals and departures of flights at the busy airport.

As I waited to leave the place I had once called home, I felt a deep yearning to return to my foreign homeland – my foreign place of attachment. As time permitted, I would return to pay homage to my village. I'll also keep my promise to visit Uncle Harry, Aunt Edith, and Erwin. It has been my greatest wish that my siblings' whereabouts will be determined, at which time, I'll reconnect with them, and commence paying them frequent visits.

With somber thoughts and a saddened heart, I waited among the anxious crowd. It wasn't long before the long-awaited announcement for boarding was finally made. I blended in with the stream of anxious passengers along a path leading toward the entrance of the aircraft. All passengers were finally aboard, waiting in anticipation of departure. In preparation for take-off, the wide-bodied aircraft had commenced making its way to its final run-way. While the aircraft moved gradually toward its point of take-off, there hadn't been incidents of fear or anxiety among the passengers. I had fully overcome my fears and anxieties on the flight to my homeland, and therefore sat in comfort and relaxation.

The aircraft gradually moved onto the final run-way. Its ignited engines roared, as if there was a sudden invasion of a mighty thunderstorm. Folk charged with anticipation, waited in total silence. Without much fanfare, the aircraft, stacked to capacity with its cargo of anxious folk heading to their various destination, soared into a partly cloudy sky.

I had become overwhelmed by tumultuous grief and deep sighs. As I sat in the comfort of the wide-bodied aircraft, I tried to catch up on sleep I had missed during the prior night of unrest. Sleep, however, had lingered in the distance, while my thoughts remained preoccupied with the loss of my childhood home, my lost siblings, and the dilapidated state of my village.

As I headed back to my foreign homeland, I had become broadsided by the grim reality that my childhood home remains buried beneath the rubble of my village, where life had practically ceased to exist. I reminisced on my childhood home of joyous pleasures, and sadly realize that, it's a place to which I can't go back with the same sense of belonging. I can't go back to reattach to the home and livelihood I once knew. Those who'd once inhabited its space, and who had contributed to its once thriving existence, have long left.

Going back home means, seeing the home I grew up in, looking at the beautiful places that had once offered joyous pleasures. I had hoped to hear the sound of the flowing streams of the spring in the valley, and subsequently take a plunge into its crystal waters. Sadly, the spring that was once a mecca for cheerful pleasures for the children and grown-ups, remains dry, and choked by rocks and the root of tall trees.

Upon returning home, I had expected to see the new children of my village – the new additions to the village households. Going back home entails seeing the new children at play and hearing their cheerful shouts and laughter – just as the children of my time had once played in the open fields, and their voice resonated around the village.

I had hoped to say hello to the folk who were once young, but have become the elderly folk of the village. I had wished to hear tales of the older folk whom time had taken along in its firm grasp.

As I boarded the vehicle for my journey to the airport, it was with great sadness that I bade goodbye to Uncle Harry, Aunt Edith and Erwin; most of all, to my abandoned village that had been left in ruins. I was on my way back to my foreign homeland – the place from which I'll dream continuous dreams of my childhood years at the home I had left behind. I'll forever cherish memories of the things and places that were once conducive to my growing up – at the place of my childhood. It's a somber thought, and a feeling that, I cannot make a reattachment to the place that holds the many sentiments of my childhood and adolescent life. My childhood home remains visible only through a panoramic view, which continually passes across my mind's eye, and plays hide-and-seek with my imagination.

If I could go back in time, I would continually return home – to experience the thrilling moments I had once enjoyed. While I remain in my foreign homeland, my heart will forever yearn to go back home to the place where the thrills of my childhood remain indelibly on my mind. With great sadness I face the reality that, I can't go back home to the place where life was about growing up: about continuous rainfalls and brilliant sunshine: the rushing spring in the valley: school days, and a church that had once teemed with exciting events for the young and the old.

There's a gorge between the time and place of my childhood, and my present life. I realize that I'll never cross that gorge to return to my childhood home – the place I had once loved and cherished. Nonetheless, the lingering memories of my childhood home, and my thoughts of the pleasures I had once enjoyed within its confines, will never fade away. In my mind, the thought of "Back Home," remains only as a thought. The words, "Going Back Home," will resonate only as words that will perpetuate joyful memories of the place and time of my childhood years.

While I reminisce on the wonderful home of my childhood, and the joys and pleasures it had once offered, my heart will forever yearn to go back to that place. With a heavy heart and tearful eyes, I was on my way back to my foreign homeland, the place I tried to make my home. But it's only an annex to the place of my childhood – the place from which I'll reminisce on the home, and the pleasures of my youth.

My somber thoughts and imagination were constantly held captive by memories of my childhood, and my lost home, when the wide-bodied aircraft touched down on the soil of my foreign homeland, under a heavy spring rain.

CPSIA information can be obtained
at www.ICGtesting.com
Printed in the USA
BVHW030030250721
612615BV00006B/131/J